The Purr-fect Suspect

Reader Reviews for *The Purr-fect Suspect*

★ ★ ★ ★ ★

"An absolute joy from start to finish!"
I loved everything about this book—the charming town of Willow Creek, the quirky residents, and of course, Goliath, who might just be my favorite literary cat ever. The mystery kept me guessing with plenty of twists and turns, and I appreciated how the story had heartwarming moments alongside the intrigue. Lily is such a relatable protagonist, and her bond with Goliath really shines. This is the perfect cozy mystery to curl up with on a rainy day. I'll be first in line for the next installment!

★ ★ ★ ★

"A cozy mystery with plenty of charm and clever twists!"
This book was such a fun escape! The town of Willow Creek felt like a place I'd love to visit, and the characters were so vivid and entertaining. Goliath's grumpy-but-brilliant personality was the highlight for me he's like a feline Sherlock Holmes. The mystery was well-paced and kept me hooked, though I did feel like a few clues were a little too easy to spot. Still, the humor, heart, and small-town drama made this a great read. I can't wait to see what Lily and Goliath get up to next!

★ ★ ★ ★ ★

"A must-read for animal lovers and mystery fans!"
This book had everything I wanted in a cozy mystery an engaging plot, relatable characters, and a brilliant cat detective who steals the show. Goliath's dynamic with Lily was hilarious and heartwarming, and the mystery itself was full of unexpected twists. I also loved the way the author brought the small-town setting to life, with its quirky residents and hidden secrets. If you love animals and mysteries, don't miss this one it's pure fun from beginning to end!

★ ★ ★ ★ ★

"The perfect cozy mystery for cat lovers!"
As a cat person, I couldn't resist this book, and it absolutely delivered! Goliath's personality was spot-on, and his clever contributions to the mystery made me smile so much. The pacing was great, with plenty of

twists to keep me hooked, and the setting of Willow Creek was so charming it felt like stepping into a Hallmark movie. This book has everything humor, heart, and an unforgettable feline detective. I'll be recommending it to all my friends!

Authors Book List

Accidental Vows
A Krampus Christmas
Sin Takes A Holiday
Barking Up The Wrong Bakery, Thankgiving
Barking Up The Wrong Bakery, Christmas
Best Served Dead
Bewitching Charms
Christmas at Hollybrook Inn
Christmas on Peppermit Lane
Krampus
Hex and the City
Love in Stitches
Pies and Perps
Spectres and Souffles
Mamma Mia It's Murder
Once Upon A Christmas
The Fatman
The Frosted Felony
The Purr-fect Suspect
The Boogeyman
The Gingerdead Men
Vikings Enchantress
Welcome to Scarecrow Hollow
The Pendleton Witches
The Cabinet of Curiosities
Christmas In Pine Haven
Love in the Stacks
Once Upon A Christmas

Patti Petrone Miller

Copyright ©2024 by Patti Petrone Miller
All rights reserved.
    No part of this publication may be reproduced, distributed, or transmitted in any form or by any means, including photocopying, recording, or other electronic or mechanical methods, without the prior written permission of the publisher, except as permitted by U.S. copyright law.
    The story, all names, characters, and incidents portrayed in this production are fictitious. No identification with actual persons (living or deceased), places, buildings, and products is intended or should be inferred.
    Book Cover by Pixel Squirrel
    https://www.facebook.com/groups/5372834529424957
    Edition 1

The Purr-fect Suspect

For Tessa...my constant companion all the way until the day she met her siblings at the rainbow bridge

Patti Petrone Miller

THE PURR~FECT SUSPECT

The Purr-fect Suspect

Chapter 1

Welcome to Willow Creek

Lily Green's Grooming Salon swirled with fur and noise, a snow globe of canine chaos. She stood at the eye of the storm, clippers in hand, her touch on the fluffy terrier's coat as light as a summer breeze. A piece of fur flew past her nose. She didn't flinch.

"Lily, darling, is he ready?" A woman in pearls and cashmere peeked over the counter, her lips a thin, worried line.

"Five more minutes, Mrs. Baxter," Lily said, not looking up. Her hands spoke for her, slicing through the dog's fur with surgeon-like precision. The terrier looked half-drowned, its beady eyes blinking out from a maelstrom of white fluff.

Mrs. Baxter sighed, a sound of long-suffering resignation, and Lily allowed herself the smallest of smiles.

Above, on a wooden beam that stretched across the ceiling, a pair of green eyes surveyed the scene with feline disdain. Goliath stretched his massive frame, yawned, and flicked his tail. He could predict these moments with the accuracy of a weatherman forecasting rain during a monsoon season: the week before the Holiday Dog Show was always the busiest.

Lily finished the last snip and held a mirror up for the terrier. It barked once, wagging its tail in approval. She set her tools down, wiped her hands on her apron, and gently lifted the dog into her arms.

"He's perfect," Mrs. Baxter said, her earlier tension melting away.

The Purr-fect Suspect

Lily handed the terrier over with a warm smile. "Good luck at the show."

Lily moved to the next station, where a poodle sat with the patience of a king enduring a portrait session. Maximus was no ordinary poodle; he was a champion, his coat a cloud of white perfection. His posture was regal, his nose pointed skyward as if even the air around him was beneath his dignity.

"Alright, Maximus," Lily said, her voice soft yet commanding. She picked up a brush and ran it through his coat with the care of an artist applying the first stroke to a canvas. Each pass of the brush was a ritual, a slow and deliberate act that spoke of years of experience.

Maximus closed his eyes, not in relaxation, but in the serene confidence of an emperor knowing his subjects will do their duty. Lily's hands moved with the precision of a clockmaker, her fingers weaving through the poodle's curls, creating a texture that looked almost too perfect to be real.

The upcoming Holiday Dog Show was the pinnacle of the season, and every dog that passed through Lily's salon carried the hopes and dreams of their owners. But none more so than Maximus. His reputation was on the line, and by extension, so was Lily's. She had groomed him for every major competition, turning his natural beauty into something transcendent.

She set the brush down and picked up a pair of scissors, their silver blades catching the light. With a steady hand, she snipped at the fur around Maximus's paws, creating the illusion that he was floating on a bed of cotton. Each cut was a calculated risk, a high-stakes game where one wrong move could spell disaster.

Lily's mind wandered to the first time she had groomed Maximus. He had been a bundle of nervous energy, fidgeting and whining. Now he was a seasoned pro, as still and silent as a sphinx. She took pride in that transformation, in the trust they had built over the years.

The hum of the salon created a background symphony: the whirr of clippers, the clatter of metal on tile, the occasional bark or whine. It was a comforting noise, the sound of work being done, of lives being improved in small but meaningful ways.

Lily finished with the scissors and stepped back, taking in the full picture. Maximus looked like a statue carved from white marble, every curl in place, his eyes two dark, knowing stones. She was not one to boast, but in this moment, she allowed herself a flicker of pride.

A slow smile spread across her face. She was ready for the show.

High above the fray, Goliath perched on his favorite shelf, a wooden beam that spanned the length of the salon. From this vantage point, the massive tomcat could observe the entire operation, and observe he did, with the air of a grumpy old man watching children play on his lawn.

He shifted his weight, his orange and white fur rippling like a small sea. His tail flicked from side to side, each movement a metronome of discontent. Below him, dogs of all shapes and sizes yapped and barked, their owners chattering away. The noise was a constant din, and Goliath's ears twitched in irritation.

If anyone had asked Goliath—and no one ever did—he would have said that the dogs were the worst part of the salon. But deep down, in the place where a cat's pride resides, he knew he didn't truly hate them. He simply disapproved. And yet, there was something almost respectful in the way he watched them, as if he recognized their temporary importance.

Goliath's eyes narrowed as he took in the scene below. Lily was moving with her usual grace, her hands never idle for more than a moment. He had a soft spot for her, though he would never admit it. She was the only human he tolerated, the only one who understood his need for space and his innate superiority.

A small Pomeranian caught his attention, its fluffy body bouncing like a cotton ball on a string. Goliath's eyes widened ever so slightly, a spark of curiosity breaking through his usual mask of indifference. He stretched his neck, craning to get a better look, then quickly turned away as if the sight had bored him.

Despite his grumpiness, Goliath was a creature of habit, and the chaos of the Holiday Dog Show preparation was as much a tradition for him as it was for Lily. He remembered the early days, when the salon had just opened and Lily had been a one-woman operation. Now she had an assistant, a loyal clientele, and even the occasional intern. The growth didn't surprise him; he had always known she would be successful.

Goliath stretched out his paws and settled back down, his green eyes never leaving the scene below. He flicked his tail once more, a silent proclamation of his enduring disapproval.

The Purr-fect Suspect

Lily stepped back, her hands dropping to her sides. Maximus looked like a statue carved from white marble, every curl in place. A slow smile spread across her face. She was ready for the show.

A tug on her apron brought her back to the present. A small, brown dachshund looked up at her with wide, trembling eyes. Its owner had stepped away to take a phone call, leaving the anxious pup in Lily's care for a moment.

"Hey there, little guy," Lily said, kneeling down. The dachshund's long body quivered like a leaf in a storm. She extended a hand slowly, letting the dog sniff her fingers. "Don't worry, you're in good hands."

The dachshund whimpered, its tiny legs scrabbling on the tile floor. Lily stroked its head gently, her touch as soft as a whisper. "I know it's loud and scary, but you'll be just fine."

Her voice had a calming rhythm, like the ebb and flow of a tide, and the dachshund began to relax, its breathing slowing to a more natural pace. Lily had always had a way with animals, a sixth sense for what they needed. It was this ability that set her apart, that made her not just a groomer, but a caretaker.

She thought back to her first pet, a mutt named Scruffy, who had been just as nervous and high-strung as this dachshund. Scruffy had taught her patience and empathy, lessons that carried her through veterinary school and into her career. Every animal that came through her salon was a reminder of him, and she treated each one with the same love and respect.

The dachshund's owner returned, muttering apologies and thanks. Lily stood and watched as the little dog trotted away with a newfound confidence. She loved seeing that transformation, the way a well-groomed coat and a bit of reassurance could change an animal's entire demeanor.

She turned back to Maximus, who sat as still as ever. The poodle was the pinnacle of her work, a living testament to her skill and dedication. She knew how much was riding on the show, for him and for her. But in this moment, she was confident. They were as ready as they could be.

Lily walked to the back of the salon, where her assistant was folding towels. "How's it going?" she asked, leaning against the counter.

"Busy, but good," the assistant replied. "Can you believe the show is only three days away?"

"I know. It always sneaks up on us, doesn't it?"

Their conversation was light, but the underlying tension was palpable. The Holiday Dog Show was not just another event; it was the Super Bowl of their industry. Winning or even placing could make a career, and the pressure was something they both felt keenly.

"Maximus looks amazing," the assistant said. "He's going to crush it."

Lily nodded. "Let's hope so. Evelyn would have my head if he didn't."

They shared a brief laugh, but both knew there was truth in Lily's words. The owners of champion dogs were a demanding lot, and Evelyn Kensington was the most demanding of them all.

"Don't forget to take Goliath's food down," Lily said as she started to walk away. "You know how he gets."

"Yeah, like a grumpy old man," the assistant muttered, but Lily was already out of earshot.

Above, Goliath stretched his massive frame, his muscles rippling under his fur. He let out a long, exaggerated yawn, showing off his sharp, white teeth. The salon was still in full swing, with dogs coming and going, each leaving with a coat that shone like new.

Goliath stood and arched his back, then stretched his front paws out, his claws extending and scratching at the wooden beam. His movements were slow and deliberate, like a tiger in a zoo enclosure. He flicked his tail and sat back down, his green eyes surveying the scene below with their usual mixture of boredom and contempt.

Despite his aloof demeanor, Goliath was more than just a passive observer. He noticed things: the way Lily's shoulders tensed when she talked about the show, the nervous energy of the dogs, the hurried pace of the staff. He may have been a cat, but he understood the stakes.

Goliath yawned again, then settled back down on his perch. His green eyes flickered with a hint of something more than just disinterest.

The day wore on, and the salon maintained its steady rhythm. Dogs came in looking scruffy and left with coats that gleamed. The staff moved with practiced efficiency, each person knowing their role and executing it with precision. It was a well-oiled machine, and Lily took pride in the smooth operation.

The hum of clippers and the occasional bark created a soundtrack that was almost soothing in its familiarity. Every now and then, a burst of laughter or a shout of recognition would cut through the noise, as regular clients ran into friends and neighbors. The community aspect of the salon was something Lily cherished; it made the long hours and hard work worthwhile.

A sharp ring pierced the air, and the entire salon seemed to pause for a split second. Lily wiped her hands on a towel and walked to the front desk, where the phone sat like an anachronism in a sea of modern grooming equipment.

"Green's Grooming, this is Lily," she said, her tone professional and warm.

"Lily, it's Evelyn." The voice on the other end was crisp, authoritative. "I wanted to confirm Maximus's appointment for the show. We're counting on you, you know."

Lily's grip on the phone tightened. "Of course, Evelyn. Maximus will be in top form. You have nothing to worry about."

"I should hope not. This show is crucial. You understand the stakes."

"I do," Lily said, keeping her voice steady. "We'll make sure he's perfect."

There was a pause, and Lily could almost hear Evelyn calculating her next move. "Very well. Thank you, Lily."

The line went dead, and Lily hung up the phone slowly, staring at it as if willing it to ring again. She took a deep breath and let it out in a sigh. The show was so close she could almost feel the tension in the air.

She turned her gaze to Maximus, who still sat like a statue, every inch of him a testament to her craft. A determined look crossed her face. They had one last shot to make everything perfect.

The anticipation of the Holiday Dog Show loomed large, casting a long shadow over the salon. Every snip of the scissors, every stroke of the brush, carried the weight of what was to come.

Lily walked back to Maximus and ran a hand over his coat, feeling the softness, the absolute precision of each curl. "We've got this," she whispered, more to herself than to the poodle.

Above, Goliath stretched and flicked his tail, his green eyes taking in the scene with their usual inscrutability. The salon returned to its bustling routine, but an undercurrent of tension ran through it, like the first rumblings of a storm.

Lily was in her element, yet the stakes had never felt higher. The show was not just a test for Maximus, but for her as well. Every client, every animal, every competition had led to this moment.

She picked up her tools and began the final touches on Maximus, her hands moving with the same practiced care but with an added urgency. Each cut, each adjustment was a note in a symphony she had been composing for years.

The salon might have been a snow globe of canine chaos, but for Lily, it was also a world of her own making, one where she controlled every detail. As the day wound down and the last clients trickled out, she knew that tomorrow would bring a new flurry of activity, a new set of challenges.

But for now, she was focused on one thing: making sure Maximus was ready to take the stage and shine.

Lily finished the last stroke of the brush and stepped back. Maximus looked every bit the champion he was. She wiped her hands on her apron and took a deep breath, letting the moment sink in.

"We're ready," she said, and this time, she believed it.

Chapter 2

Maximus Goes Missing

Lily's stomach lurched as her eyes locked onto the empty grooming table. A hot wave of panic surged through her chest, squeezing her lungs as she stormed into the salon. Her gaze swept the room in disbelief—grooming shears scattered across the floor, towels tossed like confetti, and Maximus's leash dangling from the counter, gently swaying like a pendulum marking time since he'd vanished.

"Maximus!" Her voice broke, brittle and breathless. She burst into the back room, heart thudding, throat tight, eyes wild. Silence met her, thick and unmoving. She flung open cabinets, kicked aside storage bins, checked under the drying tables, refusing to believe what every empty corner confirmed.

Maximus was gone.

Her hands shook violently as she grabbed her phone. Her fingers were numb, clumsy, slipping against the screen. Twice she failed the unlock code. The third try worked. She dialed Evelyn Kensington with desperate urgency.

"Lily?" Evelyn answered crisply. "Is Maximus rea—"

"He's gone." The words rushed out in a frantic blur. "Evelyn, someone took Maximus. I just went to get supplies and came back to this —everything's a mess—the back door was open and—"

"Calm down," Evelyn cut in, her voice flat and cold. "Tell me exactly what happened."

Lily took a deep breath. "I had to run to the supply store for more of that special shampoo we use on his coat. I was only gone twenty minutes, I swear. When I got back, the salon was ransacked, and Maximus...he's nowhere."

"And you're certain he didn't simply wander off?" Evelyn's voice was measured, too controlled.

"The back door was unlocked from the outside," Lily said, her voice catching. "Someone had to have opened it. Maximus couldn't have done that himself."

Silence filled the line for a long moment. Then Evelyn spoke, each word deliberate. "I'll be there in fifteen minutes. Call the police. Tell them exactly what you've told me."

The line went dead, and Lily stood motionless, the phone still pressed to her ear. Her mind raced through possibilities, each more terrifying than the last. Maximus wasn't just any dog; he was Willow Creek's champion, the pride of the community, and the star of the upcoming Holiday Dog Show. His disappearance would send shockwaves through the town.

Twenty agonizing minutes later, the screech of tires tore through the quiet morning. A sleek black Jaguar rolled to a stop outside. Evelyn Kensington stormed through the door like a thundercloud in heels—wrapped in red wool, sunglasses perched high, her blonde hair swept into a severe knot. Her face was a mask of controlled fury.

"Lily," she snapped, yanking off her shades. "Tell me what happened. Everything."

Before Lily could respond, two police officers stepped into the salon. Officer Reynolds, an older man with salt-and-pepper hair, and Officer Chen, a younger woman with sharp, observant eyes.

"Ms. Green?" Officer Reynolds asked, notepad already in hand. "We need to get your statement."

Lily nodded, swallowing the knot in her throat. "I left him here for his final grooming before the show. Evelyn was supposed to pick him up at noon." She gestured to the ransacked salon. "I was gone for twenty minutes, tops. When I came back, this is what I found."

Officer Chen walked the perimeter of the salon, examining the back door with careful attention. "No signs of forced entry," she noted. "Could someone have had a key?"

"No," Lily said firmly. "Only I have keys."

The Purr-fect Suspect

Evelyn stepped forward, her presence commanding the room. "This wasn't a random break-in. Whoever took Maximus knew exactly what they were doing. This was targeted."

Officer Reynolds looked up from his notepad. "And why would you say that, Mrs. Kensington?"

"Because," Evelyn's voice was ice, "Maximus is worth more than this entire salon. He's a five-time champion, the favorite to win the Holiday Dog Show. There are people who would do anything to see him out of the competition."

Lily's eyes widened at the accusation. "You think someone took him to sabotage the show?"

Evelyn's lips thinned. "I think there are several people in this town with motive. And I expect the police to investigate all of them."

Officer Chen returned from the back door. "We'll need a list of anyone who might have had reason to target your dog, Mrs. Kensington. Competitors, rivals, disgruntled employees."

"I'll have my assistant send it over," Evelyn said tersely.

Lily felt a knot forming in her stomach. The situation was escalating faster than she could process. She thought of Tony Blackwood, Evelyn's longtime rival in the dog show circuit. Of Sylvia Brightwell, the ambitious newcomer whose sleek pet spa was threatening Lily's modest grooming business. Even Margot Devereux, whose elegant Whippet had placed second to Maximus three years running.

"Officer," Lily said, finding her voice. "The Holiday Dog Show is in three days. We need to find him before then."

"We'll do our best, Ms. Green," Officer Reynolds said, his tone noncommittal. "But I can't make any promises."

Evelyn's posture stiffened at his words. "That's not good enough. If Maximus isn't found by the show, there will be consequences. I have friends on the town council who would be very interested to hear about the department's... effort."

Officer Reynolds narrowed his eyes but said nothing.

After the officers had finished gathering evidence and taking statements, they left with the promise to start an immediate investigation. Lily and Evelyn stood alone in the ransacked salon.

"I'm so sorry, Evelyn," Lily said, her voice barely above a whisper. "I never should have left him."

Evelyn didn't meet her eyes. "No, you shouldn't have."

The words hit Lily like a slap. She had known Evelyn for years, had groomed Maximus since he was a puppy. Their relationship had always been professional but warm. Now, there was nothing but cold accusation in Evelyn's voice.

"I'll help in any way I can," Lily offered. "I'll put up flyers, talk to clients, anything."

"What I need," Evelyn said, "is for you to remember anything unusual. Anyone who might have been watching the salon, asking questions about Maximus. The smallest detail could matter."

Lily closed her eyes, trying to think. The past week had been a blur of preparations for the show. Clients coming and going, the usual holiday rush. Nothing stood out except—

"There was someone," she said suddenly. "A man I didn't recognize. He came in yesterday, said he was new in town. He asked a lot of questions about the dog show, seemed especially interested in the champions."

Evelyn's gaze sharpened. "What did he look like?"

"Tall, lean. Dark hair, glasses. Said his name was Harris or Harrison, something like that."

Evelyn pulled out her phone and made a note. "I'll pass that along to the officers." She slipped her sunglasses back on and headed toward the door. "Call me immediately if you hear anything."

"I will," Lily promised. "And Evelyn... we'll find him."

Evelyn paused, her hand on the door. "For your sake, I hope so."

After Evelyn left, Lily stood alone in the silent salon. The emptiness pressed in on her like a physical weight. She moved to the grooming table where Maximus had been and ran her fingers over the smooth surface, remembering his patient dignity, his gentle temperament.

She looked around at the destruction—at the tools of her trade scattered across the floor, at the evidence of invasion. Something about the scene bothered her. The mess seemed... deliberate. Too chaotic. Almost staged.

A sound at the door made her turn, hoping against hope that it was Maximus returning on his own. Instead, she found Goliath, her massive Maine Coon, pushing his way through the cat flap. He surveyed the room with cool green eyes, his tail swishing slowly.

"Oh, Goliath," Lily said, kneeling to scratch behind his ears. "Someone took Maximus."

The Purr-fect Suspect

Goliath meowed softly and butted his head against her hand. Then, in an unusual display of affection, he rubbed against her leg and let out a rumbling purr.

Lily looked into his intelligent eyes and felt a strange sense of resolve. "You're right," she said, as if he'd spoken. "We can't just wait for the police. We need to find him ourselves."

Goliath gazed back at her, unblinking. Then he turned and padded toward the back door, stopping to look back at her expectantly.

"You want to show me something?" Lily asked, her heart quickening.

She followed Goliath to the back door and stepped outside. The winter air was crisp and biting. Fresh snow covered the ground, but there was a clear trail of footprints leading away from the salon—two sets, one human and one canine.

"Goliath, you're brilliant," Lily whispered.

The tracks led down the alley, around the corner, and then stopped abruptly at the street. Tire marks in the snow suggested a waiting vehicle.

Lily pulled out her phone and snapped pictures of the footprints and tire tracks. Then she called Officer Chen.

"I found tracks," she said when the officer answered. "And I don't think this was random at all. I think someone planned this very carefully."

As she spoke, Goliath continued to survey the scene, his nose working the air currents. He seemed to catch a scent, and his body tensed with alertness.

Lily felt a tiny spark of hope ignite in her chest. Maximus was out there somewhere, and with Goliath's help, she would find him—no matter what it took.

Chapter 3

Goliath's Call to Action

Goliath slipped out of Lily's grooming salon like a wisp of smoke, silent and sure. The chill of the night settled into his fur as he stepped into the darkened streets of Willow Creek. Above him, the streetlamps buzzed quietly, casting long shadows that danced on the pavement. He paused on the sidewalk, his sharp green eyes narrowing as he sniffed the air, ears perked like satellite dishes tuning into a frequency only he could hear.

The town was too quiet.

Main Street stretched ahead like a stage waiting for its next act. Goliath moved forward, muscles flowing beneath his thick coat. His paws made no sound on the concrete. He reached the corner of Maple and Pine, where the scents changed—damp stone, burnt coffee, motor oil. But he wasn't looking for those. He was hunting something specific. Something that smelled like metal and deception.

A flash of movement made him stop. A wiry Chihuahua darted from beneath a parked car and scampered across the road, its eyes bulging with panic. Goliath knew him. Spike. Nervous. Loud. Useless—usually. But not tonight.

Spike's frantic yipping echoed as he scuttled to the alley behind the bakery, glanced around wildly, and barked again. Goliath melted into the shadows beside the old flower shop, narrowing his eyes. The little dog was trembling, tail tucked so far under it might've curled up his spine. Something had spooked him. And Spike, coward though he was, had a sixth sense for trouble.

The Purr-fect Suspect

The Chihuahua let out another yap, this one softer, and took a tentative step into the alley. Goliath hesitated. Something about the scene scratched at the edge of instinct. With feline caution, he followed, keeping low to the brick wall, his body blending with the night.

The alley smelled of stale bread and wet cardboard, but Goliath filtered past that, chasing the fading trail he'd picked up back at the salon. His whiskers twitched. Maximus had passed through here. Not tonight. But recently.

Spike paused at the far end of the alley, ears swiveling. He gave a soft whimper, then turned his head sharply. A figure had appeared in the courtyard beyond—tall, with a worn leather jacket and a knit cap pulled low. Goliath didn't need a second look.

Tony Blackwood.

Owner of Blackwood Kennels. Longtime competitor. Perpetual second place.

Tony shifted from foot to foot, eyes darting, mouth tight. He looked like a man waiting for a ghost. Goliath crouched behind a stack of pallets, watching every twitch.

Then she arrived.

Sylvia Brightwell strode into the courtyard like a knife in lipstick. Her red coat caught the glow from a flickering sconce, her platinum hair tied back in a sleek twist. She moved like she expected the world to part for her.

"Tony," she purred, her voice low and syrupy. "Hope you haven't been waiting too long."

Tony stiffened. "Let's just get to it. Why did you call me?"

Sylvia smiled, all gloss and sharpness. "I thought we should align our goals. The Holiday Dog Show is days away. And let's be honest—you and I both want the same thing."

Tony crossed his arms. "You mean to win?"

"I mean to eliminate distractions." Her eyes glittered. "We both know Maximus is the favorite. Always is."

Goliath's ears twitched.

"You're suggesting sabotage?" Tony's voice was low, but the tension in it crackled like kindling.

Sylvia stepped closer. "Nothing illegal. Just a little interference. Something to even the playing field."

Tony's jaw clenched. "If you're responsible for Maximus disappearing—"

"I'm not," she said, too quickly. "But I admire whoever did it."

Tony didn't answer. Goliath, watching from his hiding spot, felt the shift. Tony wasn't convinced. And Sylvia? She was a powder keg in perfume.

"Think about it," she said, stepping away. "This could be your year, Tony. But not if you play nice."

Then she was gone, heels clicking into the night.

Tony lingered. Goliath watched him exhale sharply, then turn and call, "Spike."

The Chihuahua scrambled toward him, tail still tucked. Tony scooped him up and left without looking back.

Goliath emerged from the shadows and sat in the center of the courtyard, fur rippling in the breeze. His tail flicked once, twice. He didn't like any of it. But more than that, he didn't like not knowing.

He sniffed the ground where Tony had stood. No trace of Maximus. But the poodle had been here. Goliath followed the scent to the far side of the courtyard where a discarded ribbon fluttered near a drain. It smelled of lavender shampoo and poodle fur.

He padded away from the alley, winding through the narrow streets behind the town square. Christmas lights blinked above storefronts. A man hosed down the sidewalk in front of the butcher shop. A teenage girl laughed into her phone by the diner.

They had no idea.

The scent trail curled down the alley near the post office. Goliath paused at the corner, sniffed, then pressed on. The scent was older now—hours, not minutes. But it was still there.

He reached the edge of Willow Park and crouched behind a stone bench. The poodle's scent stopped cold at the curb. Goliath looked up, gaze flicking across the street.

There—a dented Volvo parked beneath a lamppost. Empty. Quiet. Ordinary. But the license plate was speckled with the same mud he'd smelled in the alley. Whoever had taken Maximus had used that car.

He crept closer, silent as breath. The car was locked. No signs of a dog inside. But Goliath leapt to the hood and crouched low, scanning the surroundings. From this perch, he could see the entire square.

The pieces were moving. But the picture was still murky.

The Purr-fect Suspect

Goliath slipped off the car and padded back toward the salon. His thoughts moved as fast as his paws. If Tony and Sylvia weren't behind Maximus's disappearance, then who? And why would Maximus go willingly?

He reached the back door of the grooming shop and pushed it open with his head. The salon was quiet now, dimly lit and empty. He leapt onto the counter and then to the high shelf where he kept watch.

He lay down, tail curled neatly, but sleep didn't come. He stared at the dark window, ears alert. Somewhere out there, Maximus was waiting.

And Goliath intended to find him.

Chapter 4

Lily's Unlikely Mentor

Lily paced the length of her grooming salon, arms crossed, eyes repeatedly drawn to the space where Maximus's crate used to sit. That spot had been warm and alive with presence only yesterday. Now it felt hollow, a quiet absence that echoed louder than any bark or whimper.

She picked up a brush, turned it in her hand, then set it down again. Nothing soothed her. Not the scent of lavender shampoo in the air, not the gentle hum of clippers from the back room. Maximus was gone. The salon felt like a stranger.

The bell over the door jingled gently.

Lily turned, expecting a customer she'd forgotten to cancel. Instead, a small, elderly woman entered, tapping her cane in time with each step. Mrs. Whiskers. Her silver hair was pulled back into a tidy knot, her long navy coat brushing the tops of her practical shoes. She moved like someone used to being underestimated—and prepared to use that to her advantage.

"Lily, dear," she said with a warm smile. "How are you holding up?"

The words caught Lily off guard. Everyone else had been frantic or accusing—no one had asked how *she* was.

"I... I'm managing," Lily replied, her voice thinner than she expected. "Barely."

The Purr-fect Suspect

Mrs. Whiskers shuffled closer and placed a gentle hand on Lily's arm. "I heard about Maximus. Such a handsome boy. This town won't be the same without him strutting through the park."

Lily's throat tightened. "He was supposed to be picked up yesterday. I waited. Then Evelyn called. I told her I'd take him home overnight. I never imagined someone would…"

Her voice trailed off. She didn't want to cry again. Not in front of anyone else.

Mrs. Whiskers guided her to the nearest bench with the grace of a woman who had calmed many storms. "Sit, dear. Breathe."

Lily obeyed. For a few seconds, the silence between them felt like balm on a wound.

"The police aren't doing much," Lily finally muttered. "They said they'd follow up, but they looked more annoyed than concerned. Like I was wasting their time."

Mrs. Whiskers gave a wry smile. "That's because they haven't had the pleasure of losing something they truly cared about. Not recently, anyway."

Lily stared at the scuffed floor tiles. "He's more than a dog. He's the heart of the Holiday Show. Evelyn's pride and joy. Everyone's, really. And now…"

"Now he's missing," Mrs. Whiskers finished. "But not forgotten. And certainly not beyond help."

Lily's brows knit. "I don't even know where to begin. I've gone over everything a dozen times. The back door was locked when I left. I was only gone twenty minutes."

"And in that window," Mrs. Whiskers said, "someone took him."

"Yes." Lily pressed her fingers to her temples. "I should have stayed. I should have—"

"No." Mrs. Whiskers's voice cut through with quiet certainty. "You should not blame yourself for someone else's cruelty."

Lily swallowed. "But Evelyn does. She didn't say it directly, but… she doesn't have to. If Maximus isn't found, she'll cancel the show. And I'll lose everything."

Mrs. Whiskers sighed. "Then let's make sure that doesn't happen."

Lily blinked at her. "What do you mean?"

"I mean," the older woman said as she leaned on her cane, "that you need to think like a sleuth."

"A sleuth?" Lily let out a small, dry laugh. "I groom poodles, Mrs. Whiskers. I don't solve crimes."

"You think that's all I ever did?" Mrs. Whiskers's eyes twinkled. "Back in '97, I cracked the case of the missing museum bell."

Lily tilted her head. "I always thought that was an accident. A donation miscount."

"That's what *they* said," Mrs. Whiskers replied smugly. "But I found it in the pastor's garage, being used to call his dog for dinner."

Lily chuckled despite herself.

"And let's not forget the Great Cookie Heist of 2002," Mrs. Whiskers added, ticking events off her fingers. "Or the picnic sabotage during the Founder's Festival. Or the time someone snuck into the library archives to rewrite the town charter."

"Okay, okay," Lily said, smiling faintly. "I get it. You have experience."

"I do. And I can tell when something's fishy. Maximus wasn't snatched by coincidence. Someone wanted him gone—and not for money."

Lily frowned. "But why?"

"Jealousy. Sabotage. Revenge. Willow Creek may look like a snow globe, but trust me—it's got layers."

Lily thought about Sylvia Brightwell's smug expression and overly perfect poodles. About Tony Blackwood and his sour comments. And then there was Charlotte, Evelyn's assistant, who'd been unusually quiet since the disappearance. All possible suspects.

"It could be anyone," she murmured.

Mrs. Whiskers nodded. "Which is why we'll start with what you *do* know. Who had reason to want Maximus out of the picture?"

"I guess... other competitors," Lily said. "Tony. Sylvia. Maybe even someone with a grudge against Evelyn."

"Good," Mrs. Whiskers said. "Now, what's your next move?"

"I was going to wait for the police."

"And how's that working for you?"

Lily gave a helpless shrug.

Mrs. Whiskers leaned in. "Then it's time to stop waiting. Time to ask questions, knock on doors, and watch reactions. People give themselves away, Lily. You just have to know what to look for."

Goliath leapt gracefully onto the counter behind them. He stretched long and slow, then settled down with a lazy flick of his tail.

"Start with him," Mrs. Whiskers said. "That cat knows more than he lets on."

Lily raised a brow. "You think Goliath's going to give us a lead?"

"I think he already has." She pointed to the smear of mud by the back door. "He came in through there last night. From outside. And that muddy paw print isn't from any dog I've seen here."

Lily followed the trail of prints with her eyes. They led across the floor, around the counter, and ended near Maximus's old crate.

Goliath blinked slowly.

"He followed something," Lily said, the realization dawning. "Or *someone*."

"Precisely." Mrs. Whiskers smiled. "Follow him."

Lily considered it. It sounded ridiculous—chasing her grumpy cat through town on a hunch. And yet… Goliath had always had impeccable timing. She remembered the time he growled at Mr. Larson just before the man was caught stealing charity funds. Or when he refused to enter the bakery the day it failed a health inspection.

She stood, smoothing her apron.

"Alright. I'll follow Goliath."

Mrs. Whiskers nodded in approval. "Good girl. And remember—sometimes it's not what people say. It's what they *don't*."

Lily paused, then turned to the older woman. "Why are you helping me?"

Mrs. Whiskers's expression softened. "Because this town needs people who care. And you, Lily Green, care more than most."

Lily felt the weight of the words settle gently into her chest. She hadn't realized how much she needed someone to believe in her.

"I won't let you down," she said.

"You'd better not," Mrs. Whiskers replied, then added with a wink, "Besides, Goliath hates being followed. That alone should make things interesting."

Goliath let out a long, annoyed sigh and closed his eyes.

Lily chuckled. "He'll get over it."

Mrs. Whiskers turned toward the door, her cane tapping softly as she left. Lily stood alone now, watching the door swing shut. For the first time in days, she felt grounded.

She looked at Goliath. "Well, partner. I guess we're detectives now."

Goliath didn't respond, but Lily imagined he was rolling his eyes internally.

She moved to the counter and picked up a small notepad she usually used for scheduling appointments. Now it would hold names. Clues. Observations. She wrote "Tony Blackwood," "Sylvia Brightwell," and "Charlotte" across the top, then added bullet points beneath each.

Motives. Opportunities. Weak alibis.

It was a start.

Outside, the sun had begun to set, casting long shadows through the salon windows. The holiday decorations in the square across the street blinked to life, twinkling merrily, unaware of the undercurrent of tension winding through town.

Lily took a deep breath and opened the front door, letting the brisk air rush in. Goliath jumped down from his perch and slinked past her legs toward the sidewalk, tail high, regal.

She followed.

As they crossed the street together, Lily realized that she wasn't just trying to save a show. She was trying to save something that meant far more—her town's trust, her own confidence, and the creature who had become a symbol of all of it.

She wouldn't stop until Maximus was safe.

And she had a feeling her unlikely mentor—and her even more unlikely feline partner—wouldn't let her quit even if she tried.

Chapter 5

The Investigation Begins

Lily stepped into the bustling pet supply store, her eyes scanning the aisles for familiar faces. The air was thick with the scent of kibble and catnip, and the din of barking dogs and chirping birds created a symphony of animal sounds. She spotted the store owner, Mr. Jenkins, behind the counter and made her way over, waving.

"Lily! How's business?" Mr. Jenkins' face lit up with a broad smile, his graying mustache twitching with enthusiasm.

"Busy, as always," Lily replied. "The Holiday Dog Show always brings in a rush."

Mr. Jenkins leaned in, conspiratorially. "Speaking of the show, have you heard about poor Evelyn Kensington's Maximus?"

Lily feigned surprise. "I heard he's gone missing. That's terrible news."

Mr. Jenkins nodded, his expression somber. "She thinks someone took him. Can you imagine? The show won't be the same without Maximus. That dog is a legend."

Lily picked up a bag of gourmet dog treats and examined the label. "Do they have any leads?"

"Not a one," Mr. Jenkins said. "The whole town is talking. Some folks think it's sabotage."

"Sabotage?" Lily raised an eyebrow, her curiosity piqued.

"You know how competitive it gets," Mr. Jenkins said, shrugging. "Whoever wins this year will have an asterisk next to their name if Maximus isn't in the running. It's a real mess."

Lily placed the treats back on the shelf and smiled at Mr. Jenkins. "I'm sure he'll turn up. Evelyn has a lot of pull in this town."

"I hope you're right," Mr. Jenkins said. "So, what can I get for you today?"

Lily handed him a list. "Just the usual. I'm stocking up for the rush."

As Mr. Jenkins gathered her supplies, Lily's attention was drawn to a heated conversation in the next aisle. Two women stood near a display of dog collars, speaking in urgent, hushed tones.

"...can't believe she had the gall to accuse Margot," one of the women said.

The other woman scoffed. "You know Evelyn. She thinks she owns this town. Margot would never stoop that low."

Lily pretended to browse a rack of leashes, her ears straining to catch every word.

"The argument was epic. Evelyn practically screamed that Margot had 'the most to gain' by Maximus disappearing."

"Sounds like Evelyn is more worried about her own reputation than poor Maximus."

Lily's mind raced as she pieced together the new information. An argument between Evelyn and Margot? That explained the tension she had sensed but couldn't quite put her finger on.

"Here you go, Lily," Mr. Jenkins said, returning with a bulging tote bag. "Good luck with the rush."

"Thanks, Mr. Jenkins," Lily said, taking the bag. "And good luck to Maximus."

She stepped out into the crisp winter air, her breath forming small clouds as she exhaled. The bells on the store's door jingled shut behind her. She walked to her car, her mind whirling with the possibilities. Could Margot Devereux really be involved in Maximus's disappearance? She had always been ambitious, but would she go that far?

Lily loaded the supplies into her car and glanced at the community park across the street. A large Christmas tree stood in the center, adorned with ornaments and tinsel. Dog owners and their pets milled about, a familiar sight in Willow Creek. She locked her car and headed towards the park, hoping to glean more insights.

As she crossed the street, a large Tom cat with black and white fur slipped out from beneath a parked car. Goliath stretched lazily, his green eyes tracking Lily's movements. He padded after her, keeping a cautious distance, his steps silent on the snow-dusted pavement.

Lily reached the park and surveyed the scene. A group of dog owners stood near the tree, engaged in animated discussion. She recognized most of them: long-time participants in the Holiday Dog Show. She made her way over, smiling and waving.

"Hey, everyone! How are the pups doing?"

The group turned to greet her, their faces a mix of warmth and wariness. Lily had groomed most of their dogs at one time or another, and she knew how passionate they were about the show.

"We're hanging in there," said Claire, a petite woman with a Pomeranian perched on her shoulder. "It's all so crazy with Maximus missing."

Lily nodded. "I just heard. It's awful. Do they think he'll be found in time for the show?"

A man with a Labrador spoke up. "Evelyn is convinced he'll be found. She even postponed the show by a week to give the police more time."

"Postponed?" Lily said, feigning surprise. "I hadn't heard that. Makes sense, though. Maximus is basically the mascot."

"That's one way to put it," Claire said, rolling her eyes. "He's won five years straight. Some of us were looking forward to a fair competition for once."

Lily noted the resentment in Claire's voice. "Do you think someone would actually take him just to even the playing field?"

The group fell silent, exchanging uneasy glances. Lily waited, her heart pounding with anticipation.

"It's not like it hasn't happened before," Claire said, breaking the silence. "Remember when Tyson's Beagle went missing the night before the show? He turned up a week later, perfectly fine."

"Are you saying someone here would—" the man with the Labrador began, but Claire cut him off.

"I'm just saying that history has a way of repeating itself. And now Evelyn is pointing fingers at Margot, like she had anything to do with it."

Lily's ears perked at the mention of Margot. "Why would Evelyn suspect Margot?"

"Because Margot is the front-runner this year," Claire said. "Her Whippet is in top form, and with Maximus out of the picture, she has a real shot at winning. At least, that's how Evelyn sees it."

"So Evelyn thinks Margot kidnapped Maximus?" Lily asked, her voice neutral.

"That's the rumor," Claire said. "But who knows? Maybe Evelyn took him herself, just to drum up sympathy and buy more time."

Lily's eyes widened. "You really think Evelyn would do something like that?"

"I think people are capable of all sorts of things when their backs are against the wall," Claire said. "But honestly, I don't know what to think anymore."

The man with the Labrador shook his head. "Speculating isn't going to help anyone. We just need to focus on finding Maximus and let the police sort it out."

Lily glanced around the park. Goliath sat under a bench, his eyes unblinking as he watched the group. She wondered how Evelyn was holding up, and if she truly believed Margot was responsible.

"You're right," Lily said. "The most important thing is that Maximus comes home safe. I'm sure the police will figure it out."

The tension in the group eased slightly. Lily made a mental note of everything she had heard: the postponed show, the suspicions about Margot, the possibility that Evelyn could be playing a deeper game. She thanked the group and started walking back to her car, her thoughts consumed by the mystery.

Goliath slipped from his hiding spot and followed Lily at a distance. The cold didn't bother him; his thick fur provided ample insulation. He moved with the grace of a seasoned hunter, his path weaving through the park's obstacles with fluid precision.

Lily reached her car and unlocked it, then paused. She looked back at the park, her expression thoughtful. Goliath stopped and crouched low, his body tensed as if ready to spring. He studied her intently, noting the lines of worry on her face.

She got into the car and drove off. Goliath watched until she was out of sight, then turned and headed towards the town center. He had work to do.

Lily arrived at her grooming salon and unloaded the supplies. The storefront was decorated with an array of festive ornaments and lights,

The Purr-fect Suspect

giving it a warm, inviting glow. She unlocked the door and stepped inside, the familiar scent of shampoo and wet fur enveloping her.

She set the supplies on the front counter and took off her coat. The salon was quiet, a stark contrast to the chaos outside. Lily liked the quiet. It gave her time to think.

She retrieved a notepad from beneath the counter and flipped it open. At the top of the first page, she had written in large letters: "Who Took Maximus?" Below that was a list of names, each with a question mark next to it. She added a few more lines:

- Claire?
- Margot?
- Evelyn herself?

She tapped the pen against her lips, remembering the various accusations and theories she had heard. Could Claire be right about history repeating itself? Had someone taken Maximus just to keep him out of the competition, with the intention of returning him later? Or was this something more sinister?

Lily's thoughts drifted to Margot Devereux. She had always admired Margot's determination and poise, even if others found her cold and calculating. The argument between Evelyn and Margot must have been explosive. Had Margot cracked under the pressure and done something desperate?

The bell on the salon's door tinkled. Lily looked up to see Goliath slip inside, his large frame almost too big for the cat-sized door she had installed for him. He shook the snow from his paws and surveyed the room with his usual air of disdain.

"Hello, Goliath," Lily said. "Come to warm up?"

Goliath sauntered over to a heating vent and stretched out, his body forming a lazy curve. He closed his eyes, but Lily knew better than to think he was sleeping. Goliath was always observing, always calculating.

"I heard some interesting things today," Lily said, as if the cat could understand her. "It seems like everyone has a motive, and no one has an alibi."

She looked at her notepad again, the list of suspects growing in her mind. Could she really add Margot to the list? She hesitated, then wrote the name at the bottom:

- Margot

Lily sighed and set the notepad down. She walked to the back of the salon, where a small kitchen area provided space for her to make tea and heat up lunches. She filled a kettle and put it on the stove, then returned to the front, leaning against the counter.

"I don't suppose you have any ideas, do you?" she asked Goliath.

The cat opened one eye and flicked his tail, as if to say, "Of course I do."

Lily smiled. "I didn't think so."

The kettle whistled, and Lily went to pour herself a cup of chamomile. She let the steam warm her face, breathing in the soothing aroma. Thoughts of Maximus and the dog show swirled in her head like snowflakes in a globe.

She walked back to the front and sipped her tea, watching Goliath as he basked in the heat from the vent. The cat had been a fixture in her life for the past three years, ever since he started showing up at the salon. At first, Lily thought he was a stray, but soon realized he was just an incredibly independent house cat. His owner, old Mrs. Whiskers, had passed away, and Goliath had taken to roaming the town, claiming various territories as his own.

Despite his grumpy demeanor, Lily had grown fond of the big Tom. She liked to think that he had adopted her, in his own aloof way.

"I suppose I could just ask Margot," Lily said, more to herself than to Goliath. "She comes in tomorrow to get Apollo groomed. Maybe she'll tell me what really happened."

Goliath yawned, showing a formidable set of teeth, then rolled onto his side. His fur rippled with the movement, and he looked like a beached whale in miniature.

Lily finished her tea and set the cup down on the counter. She picked up the notepad again and stared at Margot's name. Could she really believe that Margot would risk everything by taking Maximus? It seemed too obvious, too simple.

The salon's phone rang, and Lily jumped. She walked over to the front desk and checked the caller ID. It read "Kensington."

She hesitated, then picked up the receiver. "Lily's Pet Grooming. How can I help you?"

A familiar, refined voice came through the line. "Lily, it's Evelyn."

Lily's grip on the phone tightened. "Evelyn. How are you holding up?"

The Purr-fect Suspect

"We're surviving," Evelyn said, her tone clipped. "Lily, I need to cancel Fluffy's appointment for tomorrow. Something has come up."

"Of course," Lily said. "I hope everything is okay."

Evelyn paused, and Lily thought she could hear the older woman take a deep breath. "Lily, I hate to ask, but... have you heard anything? Any rumors about Maximus?"

Lily's mind raced. Should she tell Evelyn what she had heard in the store, in the park? Would it help or hurt the situation?

"I've heard that some people think it's sabotage," Lily said, choosing her words carefully. "That someone took him to level the playing field."

"People will say anything," Evelyn said, her voice growing colder. "Lily, if you hear anything concrete, please let me know. Maximus is more than just a dog to me."

"I will," Lily said. "I hope he comes home soon, Evelyn. Really."

"Thank you," Evelyn said, and the line went dead.

Lily set the receiver down slowly, her thoughts a tangled mess. Why had Evelyn called her? Did she suspect something, or was she just desperate for information?

She looked at the notepad in her hand and flipped it closed. None of this added up. The more she learned, the less she understood.

Goliath stretched and stood, his movements slow and deliberate. He walked over to Lily and sat at her feet, looking up at her with his piercing green eyes.

"I'm just trying to help," Lily said, as if defending herself against the cat's silent judgment. "I don't want to see anyone hurt."

Goliath flicked his tail and rose, walking towards the door. He pushed through the cat flap and disappeared into the night.

Lily sighed and locked the door behind him. She turned off the salon's lights and walked to the back, where a small cot served as her makeshift bed. During busy times like these, she often stayed at the salon to catch up on work and be available for last-minute appointments.

She lay down on the cot and stared at the ceiling, her mind replaying the day's events. Theories and suspicions swirled in her head, each one more convoluted than the last. She thought about Evelyn's call, about Margot's ambition, about the dog owners in the park and their various grievances.

Sleep came slowly.

Outside, Goliath made his way through the snow-covered streets of Willow Creek. The town was quiet, its residents hunkered down in their warm homes. He moved with purpose, his steps sure and measured.

He thought of Lily and her growing list of suspects. She was getting closer, but she still didn't see the full picture. Goliath knew that if he waited for the humans to figure it out, Maximus would never be found.

The Tom cat arrived at the gates of Margot Devereux's estate. The tall, wrought-iron bars were topped with decorative spikes, and a thick layer of snow coated the grounds. Goliath stopped and sat, his breath forming small clouds in the cold air.

He surveyed the mansion, its windows dark and uninviting. Margot's Whippet, Apollo, was a frequent visitor to Lily's salon, and Goliath had grown to tolerate the sleek dog. He knew the layout of the estate well enough, thanks to his occasional patrols with Apollo.

Goliath stood and stretched, then slipped through the bars of the gate with ease. His movements were slow and deliberate, each step placed with the care of a bomb technician. He followed a path through the snow, circling around to the back of the mansion.

A small door for the groundskeeper's cottage stood ajar, its wooden frame warped from years of exposure. Goliath poked his head inside and sniffed the air. The scent of tobacco and old leather filled his nostrils, mingling with the sharper tang of cleaning supplies. He entered and shook the snow from his fur, then made his way to a set of stairs that led to the second floor.

At the top of the stairs, a narrow hallway connected to a balcony that overlooked the mansion's main living area. Goliath crept along the hallway, his paws silent on the threadbare carpet. He reached the balcony and peeked over the edge, his eyes scanning the room below.

The living area was expansive, with high ceilings and tall windows that framed the snow-covered landscape outside. A large Christmas tree dominated one corner of the room, its ornaments and lights reflecting off a polished marble floor. The tree looked out of place in the otherwise austere setting, like a child's toy in a museum.

Goliath's eyes narrowed as he spotted Margot. She stood near a fireplace, its flickering flames casting long shadows on the walls. In her hands was a glass of wine, the deep red liquid swirling as she moved. Her face was pensive, her usual mask of confidence and poise giving way to something more vulnerable.

The Purr-fect Suspect

Next to her, lying on a plush dog bed, was Apollo. The Whippet's long, angular body was draped with a festive blanket, and he looked up at Margot with an expression of quiet loyalty.

Goliath watched as Margot took a sip of her wine and stroked Apollo's head. She muttered something under her breath, but Goliath's keen ears couldn't make out the words. He shifted his weight, preparing to move, when a figure entered the room from an adjoining hallway.

It was a man, tall and slender, with salt-and-pepper hair and the gaunt features of a winter wolf. He wore a tailored suit, its dark fabric contrasting sharply with his pale complexion. Goliath recognized him as Margot's lawyer, a man named Sinclair.

"Margot," Sinclair said, his voice cutting through the room like a blade. "We need to talk."

Margot turned to face him, her expression hardening. "Can it wait? I'm in no mood for business."

"This isn't just business," Sinclair said. "It's about the deposition."

Margot sighed and set her wine glass on a nearby table. "What about it?"

Sinclair took a step closer, his movements predatory. "The police have subpoenaed it. They think it's relevant to the investigation."

Goliath's ears perked up. He crouched lower, his eyes unblinking as he took in every detail.

"The investigation?" Margot said, her voice rising. "You mean the farce that Evelyn is orchestrating? What possible relevance could it have?"

Sinclair shrugged, a gesture that seemed almost casual, but Goliath could see the tension in the man's shoulders. "That's for them to decide. Margot, you need to take this seriously. If they find any connection—between you and Maximus's disappearance, it could ruin you."

Margot's lips pressed into a thin line. She walked to the Christmas tree and picked up an ornament, turning it in her hands. "Evelyn is playing a dangerous game. She knows I had nothing to do with it."

"Knowing and proving are different things," Sinclair said. "You need to be prepared."

Margot set the ornament back on the tree with a delicate touch. "What do you suggest?"

Sinclair's eyes glinted with a hard light. "Distance yourself. Postpone the show. Let the heat die down."

Margot shook her head. "If I postpone the show, it will look like an admission of guilt. We go forward as planned."

"Margot—"

"No," she said, cutting him off. "I will not be bullied by Evelyn Kensington or anyone else. The show will go on, and Apollo will win on his merits."

Sinclair sighed, the sound heavy with resignation. "Very well. But remember, I'm here to protect your interests. Sometimes that means making hard choices."

Margot turned her back to Sinclair and looked out one of the tall windows. The snow was falling more heavily now, the flakes dancing in the wind like motes of cotton. "Thank you, Charles. You can go now."

Sinclair hesitated, then nodded. "Call me if you change your mind."

He left the room, his footsteps echoing down the hallway. Margot remained by the window, her silhouette outlined by the glow of the fireplace. Goliath watched her for a moment longer, his mind processing the conversation with the precision of a computer.

He slipped away from the balcony and made his way back to the groundskeeper's cottage. The cold air bit at his nose as he descended the stairs and crept through the open door. Outside, the snow had accumulated enough to muffle his footsteps, creating a soundscape of soft, swirling white.

Goliath paused at the edge of the estate and looked back at the mansion. He had the information he needed, but the path forward was still fraught with uncertainty. Humans were such complicated creatures, driven by emotions and alliances that could shift as quickly as a winter storm.

He turned and made his way back towards the town center, his thoughts on Margot and the upcoming dog show. She was right about one thing: the show would go on, and the winner would take more than just a trophy. They would take the spotlight, the glory, and perhaps even the suspicion that currently rested on Evelyn's shoulders.

Goliath arrived at Lily's grooming salon and sat by the front door, his body a large, snow-covered mass. He considered scratching at the door, but decided against it. Lily needed her rest, and he had no intention of waking her.

The snow had started to fall in thick, heavy flakes, and Goliath shook himself, sending a flurry into the air. He looked down the street, his green eyes cutting through the night, and spotted a figure walking towards him. The person wore a long coat and a fur-lined hat, their hands buried deep in their pockets.

As the figure drew closer, Goliath recognized them and stood, his body tensing with anticipation. The person stopped in front of the salon and looked down at the big Tom cat.

"Goliath," said Claire, her voice soft but not unkind. "We need to talk."

Goliath stared up at her, unblinking. Claire had been a friend of Mrs. Whiskers, and by extension, she had some claim to Goliath's loyalty. But the cat was no fool; he knew that allegiance in the human world was a fickle thing.

Claire shifted her weight from one foot to the other. "I know Lily means well, but she's in over her head with this. You need to convince her to stay out of it."

Goliath flicked his tail, the motion sending a trail through the snow. He could smell the tension on Claire, a mix of fear and determination.

"If she keeps digging, she'll find things that are best left buried," Claire said. "And it won't just be the Kensingtons and the Devereuxs who are hurt. The whole community will suffer."

Goliath's eyes narrowed. He understood now why Claire had been so eager to share her theories earlier. She wasn't just worried about history repeating itself; she was trying to protect something—or someone.

"Lily is a good person," Claire said. "But sometimes, the truth does more harm than lies. Remember that."

With that, she turned and walked away, her footsteps crunching a path through the snow. Goliath watched her until she disappeared around a corner, then sat back down, his mind working through the implications of her words.

He thought of Lily and how she had taken him in, feeding him and giving him a warm place to stay even though she knew he belonged to someone else. She had a habit of helping, of getting involved, and that was what made her so endearing—and so vulnerable.

Goliath stood and stretched, his muscles tight from the cold. He pushed through the cat flap and into the salon, where the warmth struck him like a physical force. He padded to the front counter and leapt up, his claws finding purchase in the wood.

Lily had left her notepad on the counter. Goliath nudged it with his nose, flipping it open. The list of suspects stared back at him, each name a potential culprit, each with their own motive and means.

He knew the humans well enough to predict their next moves. If Lily went to the police with what she had learned, it would only inflame the situation. If she confronted Margot directly, she might receive answers—or she might find herself in deeper trouble.

Goliath considered erasing the list, swiping it with his paw and knocking it to the floor. But he knew that Lily wouldn't give up so easily. She would recreate it from memory, continue to investigate, and put herself at risk.

The big Tom cat jumped down from the counter and walked to the back of the salon, where he could see Lily sleeping on her cot. She looked peaceful, her breathing slow and steady. Goliath thought of Mrs. Whiskers and how she had cared for him, how he had watched over her in her final days.

He had a choice to make.

Silently, he walked back to the front of the salon and sat by the door. He could stay and protect her, guide her through the maze of human conflicts. Or he could take matters into his own paws and solve it quickly, sparing her from the dangers she didn't yet see.

Goliath stood and pushed through the cat flap, back into the cold night. The snow was falling harder now, driven by a biting wind. He looked in the direction of Margot's estate, then towards Claire's house, and finally back to the park where the community's Christmas tree stood tall and proud.

His path was clear.

The snow crunched beneath his paws as he set off, his movements swift and determined. He would find Maximus, and in doing so, he would uncover the truth. Whether the humans could handle that truth was another matter, but Goliath had never been one to shy away from a difficult revelation.

The wind howled through the trees as the Tom cat made his way towards the park. His mind was a flurry of calculations, each step bringing him closer to the answers he sought. The humans thought in terms of weeks and days, but Goliath knew that time was more fluid, more malleable. He had the patience of a creature who lived nine lives, yet the urgency of one who understood the fragility of each moment.

The Purr-fect Suspect

He arrived at the park and circled the perimeter, his eyes scanning for any sign of the missing Poodle. The park was deserted, the late hour and inclement weather keeping even the most dedicated dog walkers at bay. Goliath stopped near the community's Christmas tree and sat, his breath forming small clouds in the air.

The tree was adorned with handmade ornaments and strings of popcorn, its base surrounded by a mound of donated gifts. One of the ornaments caught Goliath's eye; it was shaped like a bone and had the name "Maximus" written on it in glitter. He stared at it for a long moment, his thoughts drifting to the Poodle and the humans who loved him.

A sound broke through the wind, and Goliath's ears perked up. He turned his head slowly, his eyes narrowing as he focused on the source. It was faint, but growing closer: the jingle of bells and the crunch of snow.

A sleigh came into view, its runners gliding over the snowpack with a soft hiss. The driver was an older man, his white beard and red cap giving him the appearance of a down-on-his-luck Santa. Goliath recognized him as the owner of the local feed store.

The sleigh came to a stop near the tree, and the driver dismounted with a groan. He walked to the back of the sleigh and started loading packages into a large sack, his movements slow and deliberate. Goliath stood and stretched, then made his way towards the sleigh, his steps light and unhurried.

The driver noticed Goliath and smiled. "Well, if it isn't old Whiskers. How you doing, fella?"

Goliath flicked his tail and sat, watching as the man continued to load the sack. The driver wiped his brow, despite the cold, and looked down at Goliath.

"Looks like we're in for a real blizzard," he said. "Better get home and hunker down."

The driver finished loading the sack and walked towards the tree, leaving the sleigh unattended. Goliath waited until the man's back was turned, then leapt onto the sleigh's bench. His eyes surveyed the park, taking in the contours and landmarks, each one a potential hiding spot or escape route.

He thought about the conversation he'd overheard at the salon, the one where Lily had voiced her doubts about Margot. Humans were so quick to assign blame, so eager to find a villain. Goliath knew that the true culprit was often the one least suspected.

The driver returned to the sleigh, his hands empty and his cheeks ruddy from the cold. He shooed Goliath off the bench and climbed up, taking the reins in his hands.

"Better get those paws warm, Whiskers," he said, giving the reins a gentle flick. The sleigh started to move, the sound of bells fading into the night.

Goliath watched the sleigh until it was out of sight, then turned his attention back to the Christmas tree. The ornament with Maximus's name swung gently in the wind, its glitter catching the light from a nearby lamppost. Goliath imagined the Poodle hanging from one of the branches, his fluffy white body blending with the snow.

He knew that Maximus wasn't here, but the park held other clues. Goliath walked a slow circuit around the tree, his nose to the ground. The scents were layered and complex, a tapestry of human and canine interactions. He picked out familiar smells: Apollo, Fluffy, even Evelyn's perfume. Each one told a story, a brief snippet of the lives that intersected in this small town.

Halfway through his second pass, Goliath stopped and lifted his head. His eyes locked on a small, snow-covered object near a bench. He walked over and sniffed, his whiskers twitching with anticipation.

It was a collar, the fabric stiff from the cold. Goliath pawed at it, flipping it over to reveal a tag. The name "Maximus" was etched into the metal, along with a phone number and address.

Goliath sat back on his haunches and considered the collar. This was no accident. Someone had left it here, but why? To mislead the humans? To buy time?

The sound of an engine interrupted Goliath's thoughts. He looked towards the park's entrance and saw a police car slowly making its way up the access road. The car stopped, and a figure emerged, silhouetted against the headlights.

Goliath recognized the man as Officer Thompson, one of the town's few policemen. Thompson had a reputation for being fair but somewhat lazy, the kind of officer who preferred to mediate disputes rather than write reports.

Thompson walked into the park, his hands in his pockets and his head down against the wind. Goliath stood and stretched, then casually made his way towards the policeman.

The Purr-fect Suspect

As he closed the distance, Goliath noticed another figure sitting in the back of the police car. The person was hunched over, their features obscured by a heavy coat and knitted cap.

Thompson stopped near the Christmas tree and pulled something from his pocket. It was an ornament, similar to the one with Maximus's name, but this one was unadorned. He took a marker from his jacket and wrote on the ornament, then hung it on the tree with a practiced motion.

Goliath circled behind Thompson, his eyes fixed on the ornament. The policeman stepped back, and Goliath caught a glimpse of the writing: "Rex."

Thompson stood for a moment, his posture rigid, then turned and started walking back to his car. Goliath intercepted him, weaving between the policeman's legs and causing him to stumble.

"Damn cat," Thompson muttered, but he didn't kick or swat at Goliath. Instead, he bent down and scratched the Tom behind his ears. "Thought you were smarter than to be out in this weather."

Goliath purred, a rare concession, and rubbed against Thompson's legs. The policeman straightened and started walking again, and Goliath trotted alongside him.

They reached the police car, and Thompson opened the driver's door. He hesitated, then looked down at Goliath.

"We're doing the best we can, you know," he said, as if the cat had accused him of something. "It's not easy, with so many fingers pointing in different directions."

Thompson got into the car and closed the door. The windows had started to fog, but Goliath could see the policeman talking to the person in the back seat. He strained his ears, trying to catch a snippet of the conversation, but the wind and glass conspired against him.

The engine roared to life, and the car slowly reversed down the access road. Goliath watched until the taillights were specks in the distance, then turned his attention back to the Christmas tree.

He walked to the tree and sat, his eyes studying the ornament with Maximus's name. The wind had calmed, and the park was eerily silent. Goliath's mind worked through the possibilities, each one branching into a new set of questions.

Why leave the collar here? To frame someone? To create a false trail?

He thought of Officer Thompson and the ornament with the name "Rex." Had the policeman lost a dog? Goliath tried to remember if he'd ever seen Thompson with a canine companion, but came up blank.

The collar lay in the snow like a discarded toy. Goliath picked it up in his mouth, the metal tag clinking against his teeth, and started walking. He followed a path that led to the edge of the park, where a row of houses marked the beginning of the town's residential area.

One of the houses belonged to Claire. Goliath slowed as he approached, his steps cautious. The lights in Claire's house were off, but a car he recognized as her daughter's was parked in the driveway.

He stopped and sat, the collar dangling from his mouth. Claire's words echoed in his mind: Sometimes, the truth does more harm than lies.

A light flicked on in the house, and Goliath saw two figures in the kitchen. One was Claire, the other her daughter. They were talking, but their body language suggested more than a casual conversation. Goliath noted the tension in Claire's shoulders, the way her daughter crossed her arms and shifted from foot to foot.

The kitchen light went out, and Goliath stood. He walked to the edge of the driveway and looked back at Claire's house. He thought of the times he'd spent here as a younger cat, accompanying Mrs. Whiskers during her afternoon teas. Those had been simpler days, when loyalties were clear and unchanging.

Goliath turned and headed down the street, his destination set. The collar swung in his mouth, its weight a reminder of the task before him. He moved with the speed of a cat on a mission, his paws leaving a trail of imprints in the fresh snow.

He arrived at Evelyn Kensington's house and stopped. The stately home was illuminated by an array of Christmas lights, their colors casting a festive glow on the surrounding yard. Goliath surveyed the property, his eyes taking in the decorations and the tall wrought-iron fence that enclosed the front lawn.

He thought of Lily and how she would approach this. She would knock on the door, offer the collar, and express her heartfelt concern. She would hope to gain information, to elicit a response that could serve as a clue.

But Goliath was not Lily. He was a creature of action, and he knew that sometimes the direct approach was the most effective.

The Purr-fect Suspect

The big Tom cat walked to the front gate and stood on his hind legs, placing his front paws on the cold metal. He stretched his body and bit down on the collar, hooking it over one of the decorative spikes at the top of the gate. The fabric caught, and the collar dangled like an ornament, the tag spinning in the wind.

Goliath dropped to all fours and stared at the collar for a moment. He imagined how it would look from the front door, how Evelyn or one of her servants would react upon seeing it.

His work done, Goliath turned and started walking back towards the park. The snow had formed drifts along the sidewalks, and he navigated them with the ease of a seasoned traveler. His thoughts were on Margot and Sinclair, on Claire and Thompson, and on the humans' hopelessly entangled lives.

He reached the park and stopped near the community's Christmas tree. The collar had left an imprint in the snow, a perfect outline of its shape and tag. Goliath sat and looked up at the tree, its lights twinkling against the night sky.

The humans saw the world in straight lines, in cause and effect. They believed that if they pulled the right thread, the whole tapestry would unravel and reveal a clear picture. But Goliath knew that life was more like a ball of yarn, with twists and knots that defied simple explanations.

He thought of Maximus and the fear in the Poodle's eyes when the van had taken him. Goliath had followed at a distance, unseen and unheard, knowing that the humans would need every clue if they were to understand the reasons behind this.

The big Tom cat stood and stretched, his muscles rippling under his fur. He started walking towards Lily's salon, his pace unhurried. The snow fell in gentle waves, and the town was as quiet as a held breath.

Goliath knew that the next few days would be critical. The humans would make their moves, driven by their conflicting desires for justice, for victory, for peace. He could only hope that they would see what he had seen, and that they would have the wisdom to act accordingly.

He made his way to the familiar storefront, the sign "Lily's Pet Parlor" swaying gently in the breeze. The windows were fogged, but he could see the soft glow of light seeping through the cracks in the blinds. Goliath paused at the entrance, his fur dusted with snow, and glanced up and down the empty street. Satisfied that no one had followed him, he nudged the cat flap with his nose and slipped inside.

The warmth of the salon enveloped him, a stark contrast to the biting cold outside. It was like sinking into a hot bath after a long, arduous day. The scent of shampoo and wet dog lingered in the air, mingling with the more subtle notes of lavender and vanilla from the candles Lily liked to burn. Goliath shook the snow from his fur, sending a flurry of droplets skittering across the hardwood floor.

He stretched, his claws extending and scraping against the floorboards, then padded over to the nearest grooming table. Hopping up, he surveyed the room with a keen eye. The salon was a cozy space, cluttered with grooming tools, pet toys, and framed photos of Lily with her various four-legged clients. Each picture told a story of its own, a testament to her enduring commitment to the animals of Willow Creek.

In the back of the salon, Lily was hunched over her desk, a pen in one hand and a mug of something steaming in the other. Goliath could see the dark circles under her eyes, the telltale signs of someone burning the candle at both ends. She was making notes on a large pad of paper, her movements slow and deliberate.

Goliath watched her for a moment, his eyes unblinking. He had a grudging respect for Lily. She was the kind of human who put others—animals, in her case—first. Her dedication was unyielding, and in this situation with Maximus, he could see it weighing heavily on her.

She put the pen down and rubbed her eyes, then reached for a small box on the corner of the desk. Goliath recognized it as the ornament kit Lily had used for the community tree. She opened the box and took out an ornament, then closed the box and stared at the ornament in her hands.

Goliath leapt down from the table, landing with a feline grace that barely disturbed the air around him. His steps were soft and measured as he made his way toward Lily, each paw touch as light as a feather on the now-warm floor. The salon's ambient glow cast long, lazy shadows that danced with each flicker of candlelight, creating a serene yet somber atmosphere.

Lily turned the ornament in her hands, her eyes distant and unfocused. Goliath could almost hear her thoughts whirring like an overworked engine, each one a spark of worry or a flash of concern. She was a woman who wore her emotions plainly, and even a cat like Goliath could read the deep lines of stress etching their way into her usually cheerful face.

He stopped a few feet from her, sitting back on his haunches and wrapping his tail around his paws. His green eyes flicked from the ornament in her hands to her tired, drawn features. He wondered what it was like for humans to care so deeply, to let their hearts be tugged in so many directions at once. For all his grumpiness, Goliath had never been burdened with the kind of emotional entanglements that seemed to consume the lives of the people in Willow Creek.

Lily sighed, a long, slow exhalation that deflated her whole body. She set the ornament down on the desk with a tenderness that suggested it was made of the most fragile glass, then picked up her mug and took a sip. The steam kissed her face, momentarily softening the hard edges of her fatigue.

Goliath continued to watch her in silence, his mind ticking through the events of the past few days. He thought about the collar hanging on Evelyn's gate, the tension in Claire's kitchen, the ornament with "Rex" written on it. The humans had created a web of connections, each strand vibrating with the potential to unravel the whole.

Lily looked down at Goliath, her eyes meeting his. In that moment, he could see the plea for understanding, for some kind of reassurance that everything would turn out okay. She was alone in this, but not entirely; Goliath knew that he played a part in her hopes, even if she didn't realize it.

"We're going to need a Christmas miracle, Goliath," she said, her voice soft and wavering. "Who would take him?"

Chapter 6

Roadblocks and Revelations

Lily stood at the mouth of the alley, her silhouette cutting a slim figure against the dim, flickering streetlight. Her hands were shoved deep into the pockets of her green windbreaker. She took a deep breath. "Tony."

The man emerging from the shadows was a hulking mass of muscle and menace. Tony Blackwood's scruffy beard and unkempt hair framed eyes that glinted with something more dangerous than anger. He stopped a few paces from Lily, his shadow stretching long and jagged across the wet pavement. "You shouldn't be here, Green."

The tension in the air crackled like static. Lily held her ground, her voice steady. "Where is Maximus? The police say you were the last person seen with him."

Tony's lips curled into something that might have been a smile if it weren't so predatory. "The police say a lot of things. Like why a pet groomer is sticking her nose into this instead of minding her own business."

"I'm not just a groomer. I'm his friend." Lily took a step closer. "Tony, if you know something—"

The Purr-fect Suspect

He cut her off, his voice a low growl. "This isn't your fight. Walk away while you still can."

She hesitated, just for a heartbeat. "I can't. Tell me he's okay. Tell me you didn't—"

"Enough." Tony's hand shot out, grabbing her by the wrist. He yanked her close, his breath hot and sour on her face. "This is your last warning. Stay out of it."

Lily didn't flinch. "Let go."

For a moment, it seemed he might do something drastic. Then he released her with a shove, sending her stumbling backward. "You're out of your league, Green."

She regained her balance, rubbing her wrist. "I'll take my chances."

Tony shook his head, more in pity than anger. "Fool." He turned and walked away, his heavy boots leaving a trail of water in their wake.

High above on a fire escape, a large Tom cat with black and white fur watched the scene unfold. Goliath's green eyes narrowed as he tracked Tony's movements. When the big man was out of sight, Goliath stood, stretched, and began to descend the metal stairs with the grace of a shadow.

By the time he reached the alley floor, Lily was already walking toward the main street. Goliath padded after her, his steps silent on the wet concrete. He caught up to her at the corner, where she paused and looked back down the alley, her face a mask of worry.

"Goliath," she said, noticing him at last. "Did you see?"

The cat stared up at her, unblinking. Lily sighed. "He didn't deny it. But he didn't admit anything either."

She bent down to scratch Goliath behind the ears. He tolerated it for a moment, then flicked his tail and started to walk away. Lily straightened, watching him go.

"Where are you off to?" she called after him. "I could use your help."

Goliath stopped, turned, and gave her a long, considering look. Then he trotted back to her and rubbed against her leg, making a soft chirping sound in his throat.

Lily allowed herself a small, tired smile. "Okay. Be careful."

With that, Goliath took off into the night, his destination clear in his mind. If Tony was telling the truth—and that was a big if—then the next person to confront was Margot Devereux.

The Devereux mansion loomed like a Gothic castle over the surrounding neighborhood. Tall iron gates and a perimeter of dense hedges gave it an air of impenetrability. Goliath approached from the rear, slipping through a narrow gap in the fencing. The manicured gardens were a maze of topiary and flowerbeds, all dripping with the evening's rain.

Goliath moved with the practiced stealth of a seasoned hunter. He avoided the patches of lawn that would leave his paws muddy, instead sticking to the stone pathways that wound through the estate. He paused occasionally, ears twitching, eyes scanning for the telltale red dots of security cameras.

He found none. The Devereux family had always relied more on human eyes than electronic surveillance, a fact that Goliath counted as a small blessing. He reached the side of the mansion and leaped onto a windowsill, peering into the darkened room beyond. A quick swipe of his paw opened the unlatched window, and he slipped inside with a flick of his tail.

The interior was as ostentatious as ever: crystal chandeliers, marble floors, and walls lined with gaudy, gold-framed art. Goliath's claws clicked softly on the hard surfaces as he made his way through the ground floor, each room more opulent than the last.

He found the study at the end of a long corridor. The door was ajar, and a sliver of light spilled into the hallway. Goliath nosed the door open wider and crept inside.

The study was a shrine to old money. A massive mahogany desk dominated the room, its surface cluttered with papers and a brass desk lamp. Floor-to-ceiling bookshelves groaned under the weight of leather-bound volumes, and a single, overstuffed armchair sat in front of a cold fireplace.

Goliath jumped onto the desk and began to paw through the documents. Most were uninteresting: invoices, invitations, and other ephemera of a socialite's life. He knocked over a small stack of letters, and one caught his eye. It was written on thick, cream-colored stationery and signed with a flourish. He read the first few lines, then the last.

The Purr-fect Suspect

...utterly essential that I win this year. You know how much is riding on it. Whatever it takes, I expect your full cooperation.

Goliath's whiskers twitched. Margot was desperate, but there was nothing here to suggest she had Maximus. He continued to sift through the papers, his movements growing more hurried. Then he heard it: the soft, rhythmic padding of footsteps in the hallway.

He leaped from the desk to the armchair, then to the top of a bookshelf. His claws dug into the wood as he crouched low, eyes fixed on the doorway. The footsteps stopped, and for a moment there was only the sound of his own breathing. Then the doorknob turned slowly, and the door swung open.

Margot Devereux stood in the doorway, backlit by the hall light. She wore a silk dressing gown, her hair cascading over one shoulder. In her hand was a glass of red wine, which she swirled lazily. She took a step into the room and closed the door behind her, plunging the study into a warm, flickering glow.

Goliath held his breath. Margot walked to the desk and took a sip of her wine, then set the glass down and began to tidy the scattered papers. Her movements were unhurried, almost languid. She picked up the letter Goliath had read and paused, a sly smile creeping across her lips.

"Such a troublesome creature," she said to no one in particular. "But useful."

She placed the letter in a drawer and locked it with a small key, then retrieved her wine and turned to leave. Goliath's muscles tensed, ready to spring, but Margot stopped short and looked over her shoulder. Her eyes scanned the room, lingering on the bookshelves. Goliath willed himself invisible.

After a long moment, she shrugged and opened the door. The hallway's light cast her silhouette against the study walls as she walked away, the sound of her footsteps receding into the distance.

Goliath waited until he was sure she was gone, then descended from his perch with a nimble leap. He padded to the door and peeked into the corridor. Empty. He slipped into the hallway and moved quickly, retracing his path through the mansion.

The night air was cool and crisp as he emerged into the garden. He took a moment to savor it, then began to make his way back to the gap in the fence. Halfway there, he heard voices. He ducked behind a rosebush and peered through the foliage.

Two men in dark suits stood near the rear entrance, smoking and talking in low, conspiratorial tones. Goliath's ears perked as he caught fragments of their conversation.

"...can't believe she'd go this far."

"...just a dog. Is it really worth it?"

"...orders. We do what we're told."

Goliath's tail swished with impatience. He considered waiting them out, but time was not on his side. He needed to get back to Lily with what he'd learned, scant as it was.

He circled wide, keeping to the shadows, and found another part of the fence with a small gap at the bottom. He squeezed through, his fur catching on the iron bars, and landed in a muddy alley. He took off at a sprint, the city a blur of lights and sounds around him.

Lily's apartment was modest, a far cry from the luxury of the Devereux estate. She lived above her grooming salon, and Goliath could always smell the lingering scent of wet dog when he visited. He liked it; it was familiar, comforting.

He bounded up the exterior stairwell and perched on the railing of her small balcony. The sliding glass door was closed, but a makeshift cat flap in the bottom allowed him entry. He poked his head through and saw Lily sitting at her kitchen table, a piece of paper in her hands.

She looked up, and Goliath could see the fear in her eyes. "They mean it, you know," she said, holding the note out for him to see. "They'll hurt me."

The note was printed in all capital letters, the kind of thing a child might make using a typewriter in a bad spy movie. BACK OFF OR ELSE. Goliath hopped onto the table and sat, his tail curling around his paws.

Lily set the note down and stared at it, her mind clearly elsewhere. "I don't understand, Goliath. Why would someone go to these lengths? It's just a dog show."

Her words hung in the air like smoke. She knew the answer, of course. Maximus wasn't just any dog. He was the favorite to win, and with that victory came sponsorships, stud fees, and a level of prestige that could set a kennel up for decades. The whole thing was absurd, but in their world, winning really did mean everything.

The Purr-fect Suspect

She reached out to stroke Goliath, but he stood and walked to the edge of the table, out of her reach. He looked back at her, his green eyes piercing. She needed to be strong. He could help her find the truth, but she had to be willing to face it.

"Lily," she said, as if talking to herself. "What am I doing?"

Goliath jumped to the floor and headed toward the sliding door. He stopped at the makeshift cat flap and looked back at her. She met his gaze, and something in her eyes changed. The fear was still there, but now it was tempered with resolve.

"Tell me what you found," she said.

Goliath walked back to her and jumped onto the table. He knocked over a salt shaker, and Lily caught it out of the air. "Margot's in trouble," she said, starting to understand. "But there's no proof she has him."

Lily leaned back in her chair, running a hand through her short, curly hair. "So what do we do? Wait for the police to find him? Hope that Tony or Margot comes clean?"

She was speaking rhetorically, but Goliath knew she needed answers. He let her talk, knowing that she would arrive at the right conclusion if given enough time.

"I could just wash my hands of it," she said. "Focus on the salon. On the other animals." She paused, biting her lower lip. "But if it were you, Goliath..."

She didn't finish the thought. She didn't need to. If it were Goliath missing, she would move heaven and earth to find him. Just as she was trying to do for Maximus now.

Lily stood and walked to the small refrigerator, opening it and staring at the contents as if seeking inspiration. "We're running out of time. The show is in three days. Even if they release him at the last minute, he won't be in any condition to compete."

She closed the fridge and turned back to Goliath. "I don't care if he wins. I just want him back safe."

Goliath believed her. That was the difference. The others—Tony, Margot—they all had something to gain. Lily's only interest was in the well-being of the animals. That's why he had chosen to help her.

She came back to the table and sat, her shoulders slumped. "I don't know, Goliath. Maybe we really are out of our league."

Goliath nudged the threatening note with his paw. Lily picked it up and read it again, then sighed and set it back on the table. "Why am I not more scared?" she wondered aloud. "I should be terrified."

Because you have me, Goliath thought. He knew it wasn't true, but it was a nice thought.

"Lily," she said again, this time with more conviction. "We'll be smart about it. Careful." She reached out and stroked Goliath's back. "But we won't give up."

He began to purr, surprising even himself.

"So," she said, "what's our next move?"

Goliath hopped off the table and walked to the sliding door. He poked his head through the cat flap and looked out at the night. The city was quiet, almost serene. He thought of the men in Margot's garden, of Tony's veiled threats, of the note in Lily's hand.

He pulled his head back in and looked at Lily. She was waiting for him, trusting him. He jumped back onto the table and stared into her eyes, willing her to understand the danger they were in.

But she was right. They couldn't give up.

"We'll need evidence," she said, as if reading his thoughts. "Something concrete that the police can act on."

Lily stood and walked to her bedroom, beckoning Goliath to follow. He trailed behind her, curious. She opened a dresser drawer and pulled out a small box, then sat on the edge of her bed. Goliath jumped up beside her and peered into the box.

It was filled with photographs. Lily started to go through them, one by one. "These are from when I first started the salon. Look how young we all were."

The photos showed a much younger Lily with various pets and their owners. In some, she was holding a pair of scissors or a brush. In others, she was kneeling next to a dog or cat, all of them looking freshly groomed and happy.

"Here," she said, holding one up for Goliath to see. "That's Maximus when he was just a pup. Joanne brought him in for his first bath. He was so scared."

Goliath glanced at the photo. A tiny, trembling Maximus looked out from Lily's arms, his big eyes full of fear and confusion. It was hard to reconcile that image with the confident, statuesque dog he had grown into.

The Purr-fect Suspect

She set the photo aside and continued to leaf through the stack. "I know these people, Goliath. They're like family. That's why it's so hard to believe that Tony—"

She stopped, her hand frozen on a photo. Goliath craned his neck to see. It was a picture of Lily with Tony Blackwood and his dog, Diesel. All three looked content, even happy.

"—that Tony could be involved," she finished softly.

Lily put the stack of photos back in the box and closed it, then stared at it for a long moment. "We need to remember why we're doing this," she said, more to herself than to Goliath. "It's not just for Maximus. It's for all of them."

She placed the box back in the drawer and stood. "Come on. We need a plan."

They returned to the kitchen, and Lily took a notepad and pen from a drawer. She sat at the table and started to write, speaking her thoughts aloud.

"We'll need to watch Margot's place, see who comes and goes. Maybe stake out Tony's as well. We can't confront them again, but we can observe. Gather information."

She scribbled furiously, then paused. "And we need to find out who sent the note. If it's Margot, then that tells us something. If it's Tony, then—" She didn't finish the thought. "—then we know who to be more afraid of."

Lily set the pen down and looked at Goliath. "This is crazy, isn't it? We're playing detective like in some old movie."

Goliath jumped onto her lap, something he almost never did. Lily stroked his fur, and he began to purr again. They sat in silence for a while, each lost in their own thoughts.

"We can do this," she said finally, her voice quiet but firm. "Can't we?"

Goliath didn't answer, but in his heart, he hoped she was right. The stakes were higher than either of them had anticipated, but their resolve was unshaken. They would move forward, together, and uncover the truth one way or another.

Lily stood, gently displacing Goliath to the floor. She stretched, yawned. "We should get some sleep. Tomorrow's going to be a long day."

She walked to her bedroom, and Goliath followed, stopping at the doorway. Lily lay down on her bed, and for a moment it looked like she might drift off immediately. Then she sat up, her face conflicted.

"Goliath," she said, "if it gets too dangerous..."

He waited, wondering what she would ask of him.

"...you should stay out of it. I can't lose you too."

With that, she lay back down and closed her eyes. Goliath watched her for a while, then turned and walked back to the kitchen. He jumped onto the table and looked at the notepad where Lily had written their plan. The words were starting to blur in the darkness.

He thought about Margot's letter, about Tony's grip on Lily's wrist, about the anonymous note threatening her. He thought about Maximus, scared and alone, wondering why no one had come for him.

They were in deep, but there was no turning back now.

Goliath jumped down from the table and made his way to the balcony. The night was still, the city asleep. He had work to do.

Chapter 7

An Unexpected Alliance

Lily pushed open the library door, the soft whoosh of air accompanied by the jingle of a bell. The scent of old paper and lavender polish enveloped her as she stepped into the warmth of Willow Creek's oldest building. Her eyes adjusted to the soft lighting, focusing on the rows of books that stretched toward the high ceiling. Despite the library's size, it felt intimate, cozy even—like stepping into someone's well-loved living room rather than a public space.

At this early hour, the library was nearly empty. A young mother guided two children through the picture book section, and an elderly man dozed in a corner armchair, newspaper spread across his lap. Perfect. The fewer people who overheard her, the better.

Lily made her way to the central desk where Mrs. Whiskers sat enthroned behind an ancient oak counter. Despite her name—which had been bestowed upon her decades ago due to her ever-present cats—there was nothing soft or fuzzy about Eleanor Whiskers. She was all angles and sharp edges, from her silver hair pulled into a severe bun to her wire-rimmed spectacles that magnified her piercing blue eyes. Those eyes tracked Lily's approach with the focus of a hawk spotting a field mouse.

"Mrs. Whiskers," Lily said, keeping her voice low. "Could I have a word?"

The librarian studied her for a moment, her gaze as penetrating as an X-ray. "This wouldn't be about that missing Poodle, would it?"

Lily blinked in surprise. "How did you—"

"When you've been watching this town as long as I have, very little escapes notice," Mrs. Whiskers replied, rising from her chair with unexpected grace for a woman in her seventies. "Come to my office. This isn't a conversation for public consumption."

Lily followed the librarian through a maze of bookshelves to a small office tucked into the back corner of the building. Unlike the meticulously organized library, Mrs. Whiskers' office was a cheerful chaos of papers, books, and curiosities collected over a lifetime. Photos covered one wall—Mrs. Whiskers as a young woman standing in front of famous landmarks, shaking hands with important-looking people, and, surprisingly, receiving what appeared to be some sort of medal.

The old woman caught Lily staring at the pictures. "That was another life," she said dismissively. "Sit."

Lily obediently took a seat in a worn leather chair that seemed to remember the shape of countless visitors before her. Mrs. Whiskers settled behind her desk and fixed Lily with an expectant look.

"Now then. Tell me everything."

And Lily did. She started with Maximus's disappearance from her salon, the ransacked room, the footprints in the snow. She described the police's lukewarm response, Evelyn's barely contained fury, and the subtle threats she'd received from Tony Blackwood when she'd confronted him about his suspicious behavior.

"And then there's Sylvia Brightwell," Lily continued, her voice gaining strength as she spoke. "Suddenly she's everywhere—offering help, asking questions, watching me. It's like she's waiting for something."

"Or making sure you don't discover something," Mrs. Whiskers interjected.

Lily nodded. "Exactly. And the strangest part is Goliath—my cat. He's been acting... different. More alert. Like he's on a mission."

Mrs. Whiskers' eyes gleamed with interest. "The big Maine Coon, black and white? Always looks like he's judging everyone?"

"That's him," Lily said with a small smile.

"Smart cat," Mrs. Whiskers murmured. "Reminds me of Hercule."

"Hercule?"

A shadow passed over the librarian's face, there and gone in an instant. "An old friend. Very observant. Very clever at solving puzzles."

She tapped her fingers on the desk, considering. "You were right to come to me, Lily."

"I don't know what else to do," Lily admitted. "The police think I'm overreacting. Evelyn is threatening to pull her support from the Holiday Dog Show if Maximus isn't found, which would devastate the community. And I keep feeling like I'm being watched."

"You probably are," Mrs. Whiskers said matter-of-factly. "If Maximus was taken deliberately—and I believe he was—then whoever is responsible will want to make sure you don't get too close to the truth."

A chill crept up Lily's spine. "But why take him at all? What's the point?"

Mrs. Whiskers leaned back in her chair, her eyes distant as she pieced things together. "The Holiday Dog Show is in three days. Maximus is the reigning champion five years running. His absence would leave the field open for a new winner."

"So you think it's about the competition?" Lily asked. "That seems... extreme."

"You'd be surprised what people will do for glory," Mrs. Whiskers said dryly. "Or money. The winner of the show receives substantial sponsorships, not to mention breeding fees. For some, that's motivation enough."

"So Tony or Sylvia could be behind it," Lily mused. "Both have dogs entered in the show. Both would benefit from Maximus being out of the picture."

Mrs. Whiskers' mouth twitched in what might have been a suppressed smile. "You have good instincts, Lily. But don't limit your suspects too quickly. The most obvious solution isn't always the correct one."

Lily frowned. "What do you mean?"

Instead of answering directly, Mrs. Whiskers opened a drawer and pulled out a small, leather-bound notebook. "Do you know why people come to the library, Lily?"

The question seemed like a non sequitur, but Lily sensed it was leading somewhere important. "For books, I suppose. Information."

"Precisely. Information." Mrs. Whiskers tapped the notebook with one long finger. "Libraries are repositories of knowledge, yes, but also of secrets. People talk freely here, thinking no one is listening. They research topics they wouldn't want others to know about. They leave behind clues to their true interests, their fears, their plans."

She pushed the notebook across the desk. "This is my record of unusual activities in Willow Creek over the past year. Pay particular attention to the entries from last month."

Lily opened the notebook with careful fingers. Mrs. Whiskers' handwriting was elegant and precise, each entry dated and detailed. She flipped to November's entries and began to read.

Nov 3 - S.B. researching show dog transportation regulations. Requested information on sedatives for animal transport. Claims it's for an article.

Nov 7 - T.B. and S.B. seen arguing behind the café. Mention of "the plan" and "backing out now is not an option."

Nov 12 - M.D. visited, asked for books on dog breeds. Specifically interested in Poodle health issues and vulnerabilities. Said it was for a client.

Nov 18 - E.K. renewed her borrowing privileges. Seemed anxious. Asked if anyone had been inquiring about Maximus. Said she's been receiving anonymous notes.

Nov 21 - S.B. and unknown woman (M.D.?) used the private study room for two hours. Left behind a crumpled paper with what appeared to be a schedule. Maximus's grooming appointment circled.

Lily looked up from the notebook, her mind racing. "M.D.—that must be Margot Devereux, Sylvia's business partner. And E.K. is Evelyn Kensington. You've been tracking them all."

Mrs. Whiskers inclined her head in acknowledgment. "I observe. It's a habit I've never been able to break."

"But these notes... they suggest a conspiracy. A planned kidnapping." Lily's voice dropped to a whisper. "And you think Evelyn knew something was going to happen?"

"I think Evelyn was worried about something happening," Mrs. Whiskers corrected. "Those anonymous notes she mentioned—they were warnings, if I had to guess."

Lily sat back, trying to absorb all the implications. "So we have Tony and Sylvia possibly working together, with Margot involved somehow. But why would someone warn Evelyn? Who else knows about their plan?"

The Purr-fect Suspect

"That," Mrs. Whiskers said, "is where your detective work begins." She reached into another drawer and withdrew a small manila envelope. "I took the liberty of making copies of some documents you might find interesting."

She handed the envelope to Lily, who opened it to find several photocopied pages. The first was a newspaper clipping from five years ago:

CONTROVERSY AT REGIONAL DOG SHOW Claims of Sabotage Mar Competition By James Whitman

Tensions ran high at the Regional Championship as handler Evelyn Kensington accused rival Tony Blackwood of tampering with her Poodle's food before the final judging. Blackwood vehemently denies the allegations, calling them "the desperate tactics of a woman who can't stand losing." The incident comes just weeks after Blackwood left Kensington's employ to start his own competing business.

"They have history," Lily murmured, skimming the article. "Bad history."

"Five years of bad history," Mrs. Whiskers confirmed. "And Sylvia Brightwell entered the picture two years ago, opening her spa directly across from your salon."

"She's always claimed it was coincidence," Lily said. "That she didn't know I was already established here."

Mrs. Whiskers snorted. "In a town this size? Nothing is coincidence."

Lily continued through the documents, finding more articles about dog show controversies, profiles of the key players, and what appeared to be a map of Willow Creek with several locations circled in red ink.

"What are these?" Lily asked, pointing to the circles.

"Places where a dog could be kept hidden," Mrs. Whiskers said. "Isolated. Soundproofed. With access for quick transport if needed."

Lily stared at the older woman in amazement. "You've already investigated this. You knew Maximus would be taken."

Mrs. Whiskers's expression grew solemn. "I suspected something might happen. The signs were all there—the research, the secret meetings, the tension. But I had no proof, only theories." She gestured to the map. "I haven't had time to check all these locations. My knees aren't what they used to be."

"But I could," Lily said, understanding dawning. "Goliath and I could look."

"Indeed." Mrs. Whiskers smiled, and for the first time, Lily saw past the stern librarian to the sharp mind beneath. "You have a connection to these people. A reason to be asking questions. And that cat of yours..." She trailed off, her eyes distant again. "He reminds me so much of Hercule. The same watchfulness, the same intelligence."

"Goliath is special," Lily agreed. "Sometimes I swear he understands everything I say."

"Perhaps he does." Mrs. Whiskers closed the notebook and returned it to her drawer. "Animals often see what we miss, hear what we ignore. They're not clouded by personal bias or social niceties."

She fixed Lily with a penetrating look. "You have good instincts, Lily. Trust them. And trust that cat of yours. Between the two of you, I think you have a real chance of finding Maximus before the show."

Lily gathered the documents, her determination growing. "Thank you, Mrs. Whiskers. This is more than I hoped for."

The librarian waved away her thanks. "I've watched this town for fifty years. Seen the good, the bad, and the downright puzzling. It's about time someone used my observations for something useful."

As Lily rose to leave, a question nagged at her. "Mrs. Whiskers, why do you care so much about this? About Maximus?"

The older woman's face softened slightly. "I care about justice, Lily. Always have. And I don't like seeing bullies get their way—whether they're people or circumstances." She adjusted her glasses with one gnarled finger. "Besides, Maximus always sits nicely when Evelyn brings him for story hour. Never tries to eat the books like that Labrador from Pine Street."

Lily smiled, reading between the lines. Beneath her stern exterior, Mrs. Whiskers had a heart as big as the library she tended.

"I'll let you know what we find," Lily promised.

"I expect you will," Mrs. Whiskers replied. "And Lily? Be careful. People who would steal a dog might do worse if cornered."

The warning followed Lily out of the office, through the library, and into the bright winter morning outside. She blinked in the sudden sunlight, clutching the manila envelope to her chest like a shield.

The Purr-fect Suspect

A movement caught her eye—Goliath, sitting regally on a bench across the street, watching her with unblinking green eyes. He stood as she approached, stretching leisurely as if he had all the time in the world.

"There you are," Lily said. "I've been looking for you all morning."

Goliath gave her an inscrutable look that seemed to say, I've been exactly where I needed to be.

"We have work to do," Lily continued, showing him the envelope. "Mrs. Whiskers has given us some leads. Places where Maximus might be hidden."

The cat's ears perked up, and his tail swished once in what Lily was beginning to recognize as excitement.

"That's right," she said, feeling slightly foolish for talking to him like this, but unable to shake the feeling that he understood every word. "We're going to find him. Together."

Goliath's purr rumbled like distant thunder as he fell into step beside her. The unlikely detective duo made their way down Main Street, their shadows stretching before them like promises of success.

Behind them, watching from the library window, Mrs. Whiskers smiled. Her practiced eye hadn't missed the intelligence in that cat's gaze, nor the determination in Lily's straight shoulders. Together, they just might solve this mystery.

And perhaps, she thought, turning back to her desk, they might uncover a few more of Willow Creek's secrets along the way.

Chapter 8

The Recluse's Secret

The wind whipped down Willow Creek's narrow lanes, tugging at Lily's coat as she made her way toward the end of Sycamore Street. The sun had already dipped below the rooftops, leaving behind a bruised sky streaked with ash-gray clouds. Goliath padded silently at her side, ears twitching at every rustle in the hedges.

This part of town was quieter—older. The sidewalks were uneven here, cracked by years of frost and neglect. Lily tightened her scarf and glanced at the small slip of paper clutched in her glove. *Farnsworth—corner of Sycamore and Wren. Green shutters. Do not knock loudly.*

She spotted the house immediately. It was set farther back from the others, its yard overgrown with ivy and speckled with statues of birds and saints, most of them tilting at odd angles. A pair of green shutters flanked a narrow window that glowed faintly from within.

Lily hesitated. Hilda Farnsworth hadn't been seen in public in months. People in town whispered that she was a recluse, maybe even a hoarder. Some said she used to teach Latin at the high school before she "snapped." Others claimed she ran an underground pet rescue from her basement. No one could agree on what was true.

Still, if the information Lily needed was anywhere, it was here.

Goliath stopped short at the gate, his body tense.

"What is it?" Lily asked under her breath.

He stared at the porch, unmoving.

The Purr-fect Suspect

"Don't start," she said, nudging the gate open. It groaned like something ancient waking from a long sleep.

The narrow stone path to the door was overgrown, the garden wild with rosemary and blackberry vines. A wind chime tinkled mournfully somewhere overhead. Lily stepped carefully up to the door and raised her hand to knock—then stopped herself and knocked gently, three quick taps.

The door opened almost immediately.

Hilda Farnsworth was smaller than Lily expected, thin and sharp-eyed, wrapped in a patchwork cardigan that looked handmade. Her graying hair was braided and pinned atop her head, and her face—lined and unreadable—looked at Lily as if she'd been expecting her for hours.

"You're Lily Green."

It wasn't a question.

"Yes," Lily said. "And you're—"

"I know who I am. Come in."

Hilda stepped aside. Goliath hesitated again, then followed Lily in with wary steps.

The house smelled of peppermint tea and old books. Every surface was cluttered: stacks of newspapers, towers of magazines, baskets overflowing with yarn and thread. Shelves bowed under the weight of encyclopedias and pet-care manuals. A space had been cleared at the kitchen table, where a teapot steamed beside two mismatched mugs.

"You'll want to sit," Hilda said, already pouring. "Milk or lemon?"

"Uh—lemon, thank you."

Hilda plopped a thin slice into Lily's cup and slid it across the table. "You're here about Maximus."

Again, not a question.

Lily blinked. "Yes. How did you—?"

"I saw him walk past this house two nights ago. With someone he trusted."

Lily's hands tightened around the mug. "You... *saw* him?"

"I did."

"Then why didn't you call anyone?"

Hilda's eyes flicked toward Goliath, then back to Lily. "Because calling would have done no good. Not in this town. Not with the people involved."

Lily leaned forward. "Please. I need to know everything."

Hilda studied her for a long moment. Then she stood, shuffled over to a nearby stack of boxes, and returned with an old photo album. She set it between them and opened it to a page near the middle.

The photograph was yellowed with age. In it, a younger Evelyn Kensington stood beside a tall man with dark hair and a familiar smirk—Tony Blackwood.

"That was taken fifteen years ago," Hilda said. "Back when they were... close."

Lily frowned. "I didn't know Evelyn and Tony were—"

"They weren't just close. They were partners. Co-owners of the very first kennel in Willow Creek. It was called Crestwood Companions."

"But Tony owns Blackwood Kennels."

"Now he does. Back then, Evelyn funded everything. Tony handled the training. They were going to turn this town into the next dog-show capital. Until it fell apart."

"What happened?"

Hilda turned the page. A newspaper clipping was taped there—dated from twelve years ago. *Dispute Erupts Over Crestwood Companions. Misused Funds Alleged.*

"Tony accused Evelyn of mismanaging finances. Evelyn accused him of theft. There was no arrest, but the business folded. The town hushed it up. Too messy."

Lily scanned the article, her heart beating faster. "And now they're competing against each other?"

"Not exactly," Hilda said. "Not officially. Evelyn pretends she doesn't care about ribbons or recognition. But make no mistake—she sees Maximus as her redemption."

Lily sat back in her chair, mind racing. "You think Tony took Maximus?"

"I think he wants Evelyn to fall," Hilda said simply. "Taking Maximus might do that."

"But wouldn't that be obvious? Too risky?"

"Not if someone else did the dirty work. Someone with nothing to lose."

"Sylvia Brightwell," Lily whispered.

Hilda's expression remained unreadable. "Newcomer. Flashy. Hungry."

Lily felt dizzy. "Do you know if they've spoken recently? Tony and Sylvia?"

"I've seen them. Near the park. Talking in shadows. Not lovers. Strategists."

Lily rubbed her temples. "This is worse than I thought."

Hilda reached across the table and laid a gnarled hand on Lily's. "You're doing better than anyone else. And the cat knows more than he lets on."

Lily glanced at Goliath, who was sniffing along the baseboard beneath the window.

"He led me here," she said softly.

"Of course he did. Cats always go where the truth lives."

Lily stood. "I need that clipping. And maybe the photo."

Hilda hesitated, then gently pulled the page free from the album and slid it into a plastic sleeve.

"Take it. Just be careful who sees it."

"I will. Thank you."

Hilda nodded, her gaze distant. "Tell Evelyn… nothing. She won't listen. She's too deep in the story she's told herself."

Lily turned to go. Goliath was already at the door, waiting.

"Miss Farnsworth?" she asked, hand on the knob. "Why are you helping me?"

Hilda's mouth twitched. "Because no one helped me. And that makes all the difference."

Outside, the air had turned colder. Lily pulled her coat tight and walked in silence, her boots crunching gravel and frost. Goliath trotted ahead but kept glancing back, making sure she followed.

By the time they reached Main Street, Lily's brain felt like a beehive of questions.

Maximus had been seen. That was huge. But it also meant he was still close—somewhere in town, hidden by someone who knew exactly what they were doing.

Back at the salon, Lily spread the photo and the article across the front counter. The light from the desk lamp cast golden halos over the aging paper. Goliath jumped up beside her and sat, tail wrapped neatly, gaze fixed on the photo.

Tony and Evelyn. Partners once. Rivals now.

Lily's stomach churned.

What had they destroyed together?

She turned toward the notepad she'd started a few days ago. She added a new bullet beneath Tony's name: *Former partnership with Evelyn. Hidden motive?*

Another under Sylvia: *Seen with Tony. Alliance?*

She stared at the words, then crossed the room to the window and looked out at the square. The twinkling lights looked like a celebration waiting to happen—but underneath, the town was hiding something. Several somethings.

She couldn't trust the police to connect the dots. And Evelyn—if she learned about Tony—might explode before the truth was useful.

She had to handle this carefully. Quietly.

And quickly.

The door creaked behind her. She turned.

Goliath sat by the grooming table, his gaze locked on the back door.

"What?" she whispered.

He didn't move.

Lily walked to him, knelt, and followed his gaze. Through the glass, the alley behind the salon lay dark and still.

Then, movement—a flicker of shadow.

Someone was out there.

Chapter 9

The Daring Rescue

Goliath darted through the streets of Willow Creek, a streak of black and white against the gray afternoon sky. His paws struck the pavement with a rhythmic precision, each step a calculated move in a larger plan. He weaved around parked cars and cut through alleys, his green eyes fixed ahead with unerring focus.

Lily Green watched from the window of her pet grooming shop, The Paws Clause, as Goliath sped past. Something about his movement was different today—more urgent, more purposeful. Her stomach tightened with a sense of foreboding. She'd come to know the big Tom cat well over the years, and she trusted his instincts almost as much as her own.

Without a second thought, she grabbed her coat and rushed to the door. "Goliath!" she called, but the cat was already a block away and moving fast. She hesitated for a brief moment, thinking of the schnauzer mix waiting in the back for his turn in the tub, then set off at a run. Her apprentice could handle it. This was more important.

Goliath led her through the town's winding streets, past the familiar landmarks of the small community. The old library, the bake shop, the now-defunct movie theater with its peeling marquee. Each step sent a jolt through Lily's body, her heart pounding not from the exertion but from the growing dread. What had Goliath discovered this time?

The cat took a sharp turn onto Elm Street, and Lily nearly collided with a mailbox as she followed. She was running on pure adrenaline now, her mind a whirl of worst-case scenarios. Had another animal gone missing? Was there an accident? She pushed the thoughts aside, focusing on the immediate task of keeping up with Goliath.

They neared the outskirts of town, where the landscape shifted from suburban comfort to rural expanse. Goliath slowed briefly, and Lily feared he might be losing steam, but then he sprinted across the road and into a field. She stopped at the edge, hands on her knees, sucking in deep breaths. Her eyes tracked the cat as he made a beeline for a dilapidated property in the distance.

The Dooly place.

A chill ran down Lily's spine. The old farmhouse and its surrounding acres had an eerie, abandoned quality, though everyone in town knew that Mr. Gerald Dooly was very much alive. The reclusive ex-professor had become something of a local legend, an enigma wrapped in rumor and speculation. Most recently, he was the subject of quiet accusations concerning the rash of missing pets.

Goliath paused at the edge of the property, his gaze fixed on the large, weather-beaten barn. Lily caught up, her breath forming clouds in the cool air. She looked down at the cat, who met her eyes with an intensity that spoke volumes. This was bad. Very bad.

She pulled out her phone and dialed, her fingers trembling not from the cold but from the weight of what she was about to do. "Willow Creek Police Department," the dispatcher answered.

"This is Lily Green," she said, her voice steadier than she felt. "I'm at the Dooly property. We think—" She glanced at Goliath. "—we think he has the missing animals. You need to send someone. Quickly."

The dispatcher asked a few more questions, and Lily answered with the calm precision of someone used to crises. Yes, she was sure. No, they hadn't seen Dooly yet. Yes, she would wait. She ended the call and slipped the phone back into her coat pocket.

"Come on," she said to Goliath, who had already started toward the barn. They moved slowly, cautiously, their footsteps muffled by the overgrown grass. Lily's mind raced ahead of her, skipping from one horrific possibility to the next. She didn't want to believe that Dooly could be responsible, but the evidence was piling up, and now this...

The barn loomed before them, its red paint long faded to a dull, sun-bleached pink. Lily reached for the door, then pulled back, biting her lower lip. What if Dooly was inside? What if he caught them?

The Purr-fect Suspect

She looked down at Goliath, who stared up with an almost accusatory glare. He wasn't the sort to wait for permission or to cower in fear. He was a doer, and in that moment, Lily envied his straightforward, feline approach to life.

She slid the door open just enough for Goliath to slip through, then peeked inside. The barn was cavernous and dim, its interior a chaotic jumble of old farming equipment and stacked crates. The smell of hay mingled with something more pungent, more alive. Lily's eyes adjusted to the low light, and she spotted Goliath perched on a crate, looking down into what appeared to be a makeshift pen.

She entered quietly, the door creaking on its runners, and walked on tiptoe to where Goliath sat. Her breath caught in her throat as she looked over his shoulder.

Dogs. At least ten of them, all different breeds and sizes, crowded together in the small enclosure. Their eyes were wide with fear, their bodies gaunt and unkempt. One beagle mix had a bandage around its leg; another, a tiny Pomeranian, cowered with the resignation of an animal that had given up hope.

Lily's heart shattered. These were the missing pets, the ones whose flyers had plastered the town for weeks. She recognized each face, and with that recognition came a surge of anger so fierce it took her by surprise.

"We need to get them out," she whispered, more to herself than to Goliath. The cat leapt down and circled the pen, his movements wary but determined. Lily scanned the barn for tools, for anything that might help. Her eyes landed on a set of bolt cutters hanging from a nail, and she rushed to grab them.

The chain around the pen's gate was thick, and Lily's first attempt to cut it failed. She repositioned the cutters and squeezed with all her strength, her jaw clenched, her mind screaming at the injustice of it all. The chain gave way with a metallic snap, and the gate swung open.

The dogs didn't rush out as Lily had expected. They stayed huddled together, too frightened or too weak to move. She knelt and extended a hand, speaking in the soft, soothing tones she used with her most skittish clients. "It's okay. You're safe now."

Goliath circled behind the pen and gave a low, commanding growl. The dogs perked up and looked around, then slowly, hesitantly, began to trickle out of the enclosure. Lily stood and surveyed the barn, wondering where to take them, how to transport so many. Her small car could maybe fit two, and the nearest vet was—

The sound of a door shutting cut through the barn's heavy air. Lily froze, her eyes widening, her body turning to face the source of the noise with the slow inevitability of a rusting weathervane. Goliath slunk into the shadows, his green eyes the only thing visible in the growing gloom.

"Well, well," said a gravelly voice. "What have we here?"

Mr. Gerald Dooly stood at the entrance to the barn, a length of chain draped casually over one shoulder. His scraggly white beard and disheveled hair gave him the look of a deranged shepherd, and his piercing blue eyes surveyed the scene with a mix of curiosity and amusement. He closed the barn door behind him, and Lily's stomach sank as she heard the click of a latch.

"Dooly," she said, the name coming out more as an exhale than a word. Her mind raced, trying to calculate her next move. Stall him. Just stall him until the police get here.

He took a few steps forward, rolling the chain in his hands like a baker working dough. "You know, trespassing is a crime. I could have you arrested."

Lily squared her shoulders. "So is animal theft. And cruelty."

Dooly stopped and tilted his head, as if considering her words. A slow, crooked smile formed on his lips. "Cruelty? Oh, come now. I've only ever had their best interests at heart."

Lily's blood boiled. "Their best interests? Are you serious? Look at them! They're starving, terrified. You've stolen them from their families."

"Stolen?" Dooly let out a short, bark-like laugh. "Rescued is more accurate. Do you really think their so-called families cared for them properly? These creatures were neglected, abandoned. I'm giving them a chance."

His calm, measured tone sent shivers down Lily's spine. He believed what he was saying, or at least he was convincing enough to make her doubt for a split second. She pushed the doubt away, replacing it with the righteous fury of someone who knew the truth.

"You're delusional," she said. "The whole town knows these animals. They have owners who love them and want them back. You can't just take them and—"

"And what?" Dooly interrupted, his voice rising for the first time. "And keep them until they're well? Until they're balanced? Until they can return to their homes without being a burden?" He took a step closer, and Lily fought the urge to retreat. "Do you even understand the concept of stewardship? Of responsibility? These are not toys or accessories. They are living beings with needs, and I am the only one meeting those needs."

The dogs had gathered behind Lily, forming a nervous, shifting mass. She could feel their desperation, their longing for something familiar and safe. She glanced at the barn door, calculating the distance, wondering if she could make a run for it and unlatch it in time. Dooly followed her gaze and shrugged the chain from his shoulder, letting it clatter to the floor.

"Go ahead," he said. "Take them. See how long they last. A week? A month? Until the next holiday when their owners grow tired of them again?"

Lily didn't move. She didn't trust the offer, didn't trust him. But more than that, she didn't trust herself to get the door open and the dogs out before he could intervene. The standoff stretched long and thin, like taffy pulled to its breaking point.

Sirens wailed in the distance, growing closer. Dooly's eyes flickered with something—surprise? Annoyance?—before settling back into their usual, dispassionate stare. "You've really done it now," he said, almost sighing. "I hope you're prepared to take responsibility."

Lily's breathing was shallow, her chest tight. "Responsibility for what?"

"For the truth," Dooly said, turning toward the barn door. "It has a way of weighing heavily on those who seek it."

The sirens were just outside now, accompanied by the crunch of tires on gravel. Dooly unlatched the door and opened it slowly, letting in the harsh glare of police lights. Two officers stepped out of their squad car, hands on their batons, their faces set in grim determination.

Lily walked to the door, keeping a cautious distance from Dooly. The rush of cold air was a shock to her system, a sudden plunge into reality. One of the officers called out, and Dooly raised a hand in a gesture of calm surrender.

"It's all right," he said. "I'm unarmed."

The officers approached, and Lily felt a rush of relief so powerful it nearly brought her to tears. They took Dooly by the arms and began to read him his rights. He didn't resist.

"We've got this, Miss Green," said one of the officers. "You can go."

Lily lingered, watching as they led Dooly to the squad car. He turned his head and caught her eye, his expression unreadable. "They're all microchipped," he said. "You can scan them if you don't believe me."

The officer opened the car door, and Dooly paused, looking back at the barn, at the house, at the land that had been his sanctuary. "I would have returned them," he said, almost to himself. "In time."

The door shut with a heavy, final thud. Lily closed her eyes and took a deep breath, then opened them and looked down. Goliath stood at her feet, his fur bristling from the cold or the tension or both.

"Thank you," she said to him, bending down to stroke his back. He tolerated it for a moment, then flicked his tail and started toward the barn. Lily stood and watched as the police car pulled away, its lights casting erratic, dancing shadows on the surrounding trees.

The dogs. She still had to figure out what to do with the dogs. Her mind was so full she thought it might burst, but she pushed through the overload and started making a mental list. Call the owners. Arrange temporary foster care. Take the injured ones to the vet. She could manage it. She had to.

Lily walked back into the barn, where Goliath was perched on a stack of hay, surveying the scene like a king over his troubled domain. The dogs milled about, slightly more animated now that the immediate threat had passed.

"We'll need to take them in shifts," she said aloud, as if Goliath could offer a better plan. "I don't even have enough crates."

She pulled out her phone and started scrolling through her contacts. Who could she call for help? The animal rescue was understaffed and overworked as it was. Maybe—

The phone rang in her hand, startling her. She fumbled and nearly dropped it, then looked at the screen. It was the police.

"Hello?"

"Lily, this is Officer Stevens. We have a situation."

Her heart sank. "What is it?"

"Your friend Dooly just collapsed. We think it's a heart attack."

Lily put a hand to her forehead, massaging the growing knot of tension. "Is he...?"

"He's alive, but it's touch and go. We're taking him to County General."

Lily didn't know what to say. Despite everything, she hadn't wished harm on Dooly. Anger, yes. Justice, certainly. But not this.

"Okay," she said, her voice small. "Thank you for letting me know."

She ended the call and stared at the phone for a long moment, as if it might offer her an answer to the question she didn't even know how to ask. What now?

"Lily," said a voice from the phone. She started again, confused. Had she left the line open? But no, it was a different voice, a softer, more hesitant voice.

"Lily, it's Claire."

Lily's mind clicked into place. Claire Dooly, Gerald's granddaughter. She worked as a veterinary tech in the next town over. How many times had she come into the shop with her parents' old sheepdog? A dozen? More?

"Claire," Lily said. "I just heard. I'm so sorry."

"I know things have been... tense," Claire said, her words slow and measured. "But he's still my grandfather."

Lily didn't interrupt, didn't argue. She knew what was coming and braced herself for it.

"We won't press charges," Claire said. "But please, just... let the animals come home. He was only trying to help."

Lily's grip tightened on the phone. Could she do it? Could she just let them go, knowing how much pain their families had been in, knowing that Dooly might do it all over again?

The Holiday Dog Show was in two weeks. Where would she find the time to help the owners, to care for the animals, to keep searching for Maximus?

"Please, Lily," Claire said. "You understand, don't you?"

Lily closed her eyes and saw each of the missing animals, not as they were now, but as they had been in the photos: well-fed, happy, loved. Then she saw Goliath, the grumpy old Tom with no one but himself.

"I understand," Lily said, opening her eyes. "I understand the responsibility."

She ended the call before Claire could respond, then put the phone back in her pocket. The weight of it felt like a stone, dragging her down, down, down.

"Lily," said a man's voice. She turned, expecting an apparition, but it was real. Officer Stevens stood in the barn's entrance, his face lit with the glow of a hastily-lit cigarette. "Do you want to press charges?"

Lily thought of Dooly in the hospital, of Claire and her conflicted loyalties, of the dogs behind her and the owners waiting at home. She thought of stewardship, of responsibility, of the truth and its many burdens.

"No," she said at last. "Not yet."

Stevens nodded, took a drag, and flicked the cigarette into the wet grass outside. "It's your call. Let us know."

He left, and Lily walked to the open door, letting the cold seep into her bones. The sky had darkened, and a light drizzle began to fall, each drop a pinprick on her warmed skin.

She had made one decision, but a thousand more loomed. How long could she hold the animals? Would the owners even take them back now? And what about Maximus? Every minute spent here was a minute lost in their search for him.

Lily sighed and turned back to the barn. The dogs had settled into a loose pack, their ranks shifting and fluid. Goliath sat atop his haystack, his eyes half-closed, his posture regal.

"We did the right thing," Lily said, more to convince herself than anyone else. Goliath didn't respond.

She walked to the pen and opened her arms. "Come on," she said to the dogs. "Let's go."

They followed her out into the drizzle, one by one, their steps tentative but growing in confidence. Lily herded them toward her car, then stopped and looked back at the barn. Goliath stood in the doorway, his fur damp and spiky.

"Are you coming?" she called.

The cat hesitated, then trotted out to her, his movements less graceful in the wet grass. He rubbed against her leg, and she bent down to pick him up. He allowed it, settling into her arms with a weary acceptance.

Together, they watched as the dogs started to disperse, each taking a different path. Lily didn't stop them. She hoped that some innate animal instinct would guide them home, that the rain would wash away their fear and that they would be met with open arms and not shut doors.

"We're not done," she said to Goliath. "We still have to find Maximus."

Goliath didn't purr, but he didn't protest, either.

Lily put him down and opened her car door. The drizzle had turned to a steady rain, and she was soaked through, her hair plastered to her forehead. She didn't care.

"We'll check the park again," she said, as if making a plan for the immediate future could push aside the larger, more daunting questions. "Maybe someone has seen him."

Goliath jumped into the passenger seat and curled into a wet ball. Lily slid into the driverseat and closed the door, shutting out the sound of the rain. She started the engine, and the car's heater whirred to life, blowing a cold, damp air that slowly began to clear the fog from the windows. She watched as droplets raced each other down the glass, her mind a swirl of conflicting thoughts and emotions.

The park was empty, its playground and walking trails abandoned to the weather. Lily parked near the dog run and killed the engine, but she didn't move to get out. Instead, she leaned back in her seat and closed her eyes, letting the patter of rain on the car roof lull her into a brief, deceptive calm.

They had searched the park every day since Maximus disappeared, hoping for some sign of him. The big Great Dane had been a fixture here, playing with other dogs and their owners while his own human, Mrs. Kline, walked her slow, arthritic laps around the track. When he vanished, the whole town had rallied, putting up flyers and organizing search parties. That kind of community effort was unthinkable in a larger city, but in Willow Creek, it was just how things were done.

Lily opened her eyes and looked at the passenger seat. Goliath was sleeping, his chest rising and falling in a slow, steady rhythm. She envied him his rest. For her, sleep had been a rare and fragile thing, easily shattered by the sharp edges of worry and guilt.

With a sigh, she reached into the back seat and grabbed an umbrella, then gently opened the car door. The rain had formed small rivers in the parking lot, and she stepped carefully to avoid soaking her shoes. The cold bit at her skin, but she welcomed its clarity, its ability to cut through the fog in her mind.

Opening the umbrella, she walked to the dog run and peered inside. The grass was long and unkempt, a testament to the parks department's stretched resources. No set of gleaming eyes met her gaze, no familiar silhouette stood waiting. She hadn't really expected to find Maximus here, but still, the emptiness gnawed at her.

She turned and looked at the track. Even in the rain, its cinder surface had a dull, percussive quality, like a tambourine struck with a wet towel. She could almost see Mrs. Kline, stoic and determined, plodding along with her cane while Maximus galloped and wrestled. That had been their routine for years, and now it was broken. Lily wondered if Mrs. Kline would ever have the heart to walk the track again, with or without her beloved dog.

A movement caught her eye, and she turned quickly, her heart leaping with a foolish hope. It was a man, tall and thin, walking a Labrador toward the parking lot. He wore a yellow rain slicker, its hood pulled tight around his face, and he carried an umbrella that bobbed with each of his strides. The Labrador was drenched, its coat hanging limp, but it seemed unfazed by the weather, wagging its tail and trotting with a carefree bounce.

"Excuse me!" Lily called, hurrying toward the man. He stopped and turned, and Lily recognized him as Dr. Sloane, the local dentist. She slowed her pace and offered a tentative smile. "Hi, James."

"Hello, Lily," he said, his voice muffled by the hood. "Out in this mess? I thought you'd be at the shop."

Lily glanced back at her car, then turned her attention to the Labrador. It was straining against its leash, eager to get wherever it was going. "Just taking a break from the chaos," she said. "Have you seen Maximus?"

Dr. Sloane shook his head. "Not since he went missing. Poor Kline must be beside herself."

"She is," Lily said. "We're doing everything we can."

Dr. Sloane adjusted his grip on the leash and looked past Lily, as if considering how much longer he was willing to stand in the rain. "You know," he said, "I heard some talk that Dooly had him."

Lily's chest tightened. "Had," she repeated. "Past tense?"

"Just rumors," Dr. Sloane said, shrugging. "But if the other animals are turning up, maybe he's next?"

The Purr-fect Suspect

Lily bit her lip. How much should she say? The town was a small, tightly-knit fabric, and any loose thread of gossip could unravel the whole community. She chose her words carefully. "The police have Dooly in custody. They found all the missing pets, except Maximus."

Dr. Sloane's eyes widened. "So it was him. Jesus. Do the Klines know?"

"Not yet," Lily said. "We're hoping to find Maximus before—"

"Before what?" Dr. Sloane interrupted. "Before you tell them the truth? Come on, Lily. They deserve to know what's going on."

She bristled at his tone. "We don't even know the whole truth yet."

Dr. Sloane pulled back his hood, revealing a head of thinning, rain-soaked hair. "Lily, this isn't some mystery novel where you can withhold the big reveal until the last chapter. These are real people, with real pain."

"I know that!" she said, more loudly than she'd intended. "I know."

The two stood in a charged silence, the rain filling the void with its persistent, droning hum. Lily looked away, focusing on the Labrador. It had sat down and was pawing at a puddle, creating small, chaotic splashes.

"Look," Dr. Sloane said, his voice softening, "we all appreciate what you're doing. But sometimes the kindest thing is just to be honest."

Lily turned back to him, her eyes tired, her posture slumped. "I will tell them. I just need a little more time."

Dr. Sloane nodded, though it seemed more an acknowledgment than an agreement. "Take care, Lily," he said, then gave the Labrador's leash a gentle tug. The dog sprang to its feet, and the two walked toward the parking lot, their figures dissolving into the rain's gray curtain.

Lily stood for a moment longer, soaking in the cold and the wet and the weight of everything. Then she made her way back to the car, collapsing into the driver's seat with a heavy, defeated sigh. Goliath stirred and stretched, his claws extending and retracting on the upholstery.

She didn't start the engine. Instead, she pulled out her phone and stared at it, willing it to give her the answers she needed. Slowly, she navigated to her call history and found the last number she'd dialed. With a deep breath, she pressed the screen and held the phone to her ear.

It rang twice before a familiar, elderly voice answered. "Hello?"

"Mrs. Kline," Lily said. "It's Lily Green."

"Lily, dear. Have you found him?"

Lily's throat tightened. How many times had she called with the same news, the same empty update? Yet every time, Mrs. Kline had answered with hope, with an unyielding faith that this would be the call where Lily told her Maximus was safe and coming home.

"Not yet," Lily said, her voice cracking. "But we have a lead."

"Oh?" said Mrs. Kline. "That's wonderful. Where is he?"

Lily closed her eyes and leaned her head back, letting the phone rest lightly against her ear. "The police think that Gerald Dooly might have taken him. They found a bunch of other missing pets at his farm."

Silence on the other end. Lily imagined Mrs. Kline sitting in her cluttered living room, surrounded by the various knick-knacks and mementos of a long life. In her lap, a photo album, its pages turned to pictures of Maximus as a gangly pup, as a strapping young dog, as the graying companion he was now.

"Why didn't you tell me this sooner?" Mrs. Kline said, her voice thin and hurt.

"I'm telling you now," Lily said. "I just found out. The police have Dooly in custody, but Maximus isn't with them. We're hoping he'll tell us where—"

"Where he will be," Mrs. Kline interrupted. "Not where he is."

Lily sat up, confused. "What do you mean?"

"I mean that Gerald would never hurt an animal. If he took Maximus, it was only to make sure he was well cared for."

Lily couldn't believe what she was hearing. "You think Dooly was justified in taking him? In taking all of them?"

"I think," said Mrs. Kline, "that sometimes people do what they must. Maximus is old now. Perhaps Gerald thought he could ease his final days."

Lily's mouth hung open, speechless. Had the whole town gone mad? First Dooly, now Mrs. Kline, talking as if stealing someone's pet was an act of benevolence.

"Lily," said Mrs. Kline, her tone softening. "We're not upset with you. We know you're doing your best. But maybe it's time to let the professionals handle it."

The words struck Lily like a slap. We're not upset with you. As if she needed their forgiveness, their absolution.

"Of course," Lily said, her voice going cold. "I'll let the police take it from here."

The Purr-fect Suspect

"Lily—" started Mrs. Kline, but Lily had already pulled the phone away from her ear and ended the call. She tossed it onto the dashboard, where it skidded to a stop against the windshield, its screen glowing with the faint, ghostly outline of a raindrop.

She sat in silence, her mind a maelstrom. Had she been wrong to hold back the information? To try to protect everyone, to balance the scales of justice with a cautious hand? The truth had a way of weighing heavily, Dooly had said. She understood that now, understood the crushing load of it.

Goliath uncurled and stretched again, then stood and looked at Lily with his piercing green eyes. She met his gaze and saw in them a reflection of her own weariness, her own doubts.

"We're doing the best we can," she said to him. He stared for a moment longer, then began to groom his wet fur, licking it with slow, deliberate strokes.

Lily started the engine, and the car's heater blew a rush of warm air into the cabin. She watched the rain streak down the windows, then put the car in gear and pulled out of the parking lot.

The drive back to the shop was short, but Lily took it slowly, her thoughts miles ahead of her. When she arrived, she sat in the car for a moment, not wanting to face the chaos that waited inside. The sound of barking and whining penetrated the walls of the small building, a cacophony of need and fear.

She got out of the car, leaving Goliath to sleep, and walked to the shop's entrance. The neon "OPEN" sign buzzed and flickered, its once-bright glow now a tired, desaturated blue. She opened the door, and the noise hit her like a wave.

"Lily!" shouted Kendra, her newest hire. The young woman was in her early twenties, with a punk-rock aesthetic that included a different hair color every week. This week it was lime green. "Thank God you're back. I don't know how much longer I can take this."

Lily walked to the front counter and leaned on it, surveying the scene. Every kennel was full, and the aisles were cluttered with makeshift beds and feeding stations. The animals were in various states of distress, their usual post-grooming calm replaced by a frantic, caged energy.

"I'm so sorry, Kendra," Lily said. "I know this is a lot."

Kendra wiped her hands on a towel, then tossed it onto a pile of laundry. "Are you kidding? This is awesome. It's like we're running a real rescue now."

Lily gave a weak smile. "I just need to figure out where to put them all. The owners should be here soon to—"

"To claim them?" Kendra said, raising an eyebrow. "I thought Dooly had them all microchipped. Isn't that proof enough that—"

"They're not his," Lily said, more sharply than she'd meant. "He took them. The chips don't change that."

Kendra held up her hands in a gesture of surrender. "Hey, I'm just saying what I heard."

Lily rubbed her temples, feeling a headache start to bloom. "I'm going to make some calls. Can you handle things here for a bit longer?"

"Sure," Kendra said, then added, "I hope you're planning to call the owners before the police. Some of them are pretty pissed."

Lily didn't respond. She walked to the back of the shop, where her small office was crammed between the bathing area and the supply room. Closing the door, she sank into her chair and let out a long, exhausted breath.

The first call she made was to the animal hospital, to see if they had any updates on Dooly. The receptionist put her on hold for what felt like an eternity, and Lily's mind wandered to the stack of bills on her desk, to the half-finished groomers' association application, to the framed photo on the wall of her and her mother at the shop's grand opening. The photo was already beginning to fade, the colors leaching out like a sunset in fast-forward.

The receptionist came back on the line and told Lily that Dooly was stable, but sedated. Her relief was tempered by the knowledge that a healthy Dooly was still a problem she had to contend with, but she didn't want his suffering on her conscience.

She thanked the receptionist and ended the call, then stared at the phone in her hand. Who next? The Klines? The police? She thought about what Dr. Sloane had said, about the kindness of honesty. She wasn't sure she believed that, but she knew that withholding the truth any longer would only compound her problems.

With a heavy heart, she dialed the police station. A dispatcher answered, and Lily identified herself.

"One moment," said the dispatcher. "I'll get Officer Stevens."

Lily waited, her fingers tapping a nervous, arrhythmic beat on her desk. She thought about hanging up, about postponing this just a little longer, but before she could act on the impulse, Stevens came on the line.

"Lily," he said. "What can I do for you?"

She took a deep breath. "I just wanted to let you know that I'm not going to press charges."

Stevens was silent for a moment, and Lily imagined him sitting at his cluttered desk, massaging his temples the way she had. "Are you sure?" he said. "Dooly's actions put a lot of people in distress."

"I'm sure," Lily said. "The animals are safe now, and that's what matters. We'll return them to their owners and hope that everyone's learned something from this."

Stevens sighed. "All right. It's your decision. What about Dooly?"

"He'll be fine," Lily said. "He's in good hands."

"Okay," said Stevens. "If you change your mind—"

"I won't," Lily said, cutting him off. "But thank you."

She ended the call and set the phone down on her desk, then leaned back in her chair and closed her eyes. The tension in her shoulders eased, but only a little. She'd made her choice, and now she had to live with it.

A knock on the door jolted her upright. Kendra poked her head in, her multicolored piercings glinting in the dim light. "Lily, there's someone here to see you."

"Who is it?"

Kendra shrugged. "He didn't say, but he looks important."

Lily's mind raced through the possibilities. A reporter? An angry pet owner? Claire Dooly? She stood and followed Kendra to the front of the shop, where a tall man in a tailored suit stood with his hands clasped in front of him. His hair was slicked back, and he had the air of someone who was used to getting what he wanted.

Lily approached with caution. "Can I help you?"

The man extended a hand, and Lily took it, noting the firmness of his grip and the coolness of his skin. "Ms. Green," he said. "My name is Thomas Yates. I represent the Dooly family."

Lily's heart skipped. A lawyer. Of course they would send a lawyer.

"Mr. Yates," she said. "Is Gerald—"

"Mr. Dooly is recovering," Yates said, releasing her hand. "The doctors are optimistic."

Lily nodded, unsure what to say. She waited for Yates to continue, but he stood silent for a moment, studying her with eyes that seemed to calculate and appraise.

"We appreciate your restraint," Yates said finally. "Dropping the charges was the right thing to do."

Lily suppressed a grimace. The right thing. How she hated that phrase, with its smug certitude, its moral high ground. "I'm glad you think so."

Yates produced a business card and handed it to Lily. "If you have any questions or concerns, please don't hesitate to contact me. The Dooly family holds no ill will toward you, Ms. Green. We understand your position."

Lily looked at the card. It was embossed with a gold leaf logo and had a weight to it, like a small, expensive brick. "That's very generous of you."

Yates gave a tight-lipped smile. "We're a generous family."

Lily pocketed the card. "Is there anything else?"

Yates shook his head. "Just remember that we're all trying to do what's best for the animals. That's the most important thing."

"Of course," Lily said.

Yates gave a small bow, then turned and walked out into the rain. Lily watched through the glass door as he made his way to a black sedan, its windows tinted so dark they were almost opaque. He opened the driver's side door and paused, looking back at the shop. Lily thought she could feel his gaze penetrate the building, the walls, even her own skin. He got into the car, and it drove off with a low, growling hum.

"Lily," Kendra said, but Lily was already walking back to her office. She closed the door behind her and sank into her chair, her body collapsing in on itself like a punctured lung.

She took the business card from her pocket and studied it. Yates & Associates, it read, with an address in the city. Below the firm's name was a phone number and the words "Thomas Yates, Esq." She ran her fingers over the embossed lettering, then set the card down on her desk, gently, as if it were made of glass.

Her thoughts drifted to Dooly, to the animals, to Maximus and the Klines. To her mother, who had always known the right thing to do, or at least had convinced Lily that she did. What would Mom have done in this situation? Would she have pressed charges, told the Klines to wait, kept the animals until it was all sorted out? Would she have been as conflicted as Lily felt now, or would she have faced it all with the unshakable certainty that Lily so desperately missed?

Her mother had been a force, a woman who balanced compassion with a fierce sense of justice. Lily wondered if she'd inherited any of that balance, or if she was just floundering, trying to do what she thought her mother would have done. Could she even figure out what the right thing was without her mom's guiding hand?

What would Mom have done in this situation? Would she have pressed charges, told the Klines to wait, kept the animals until it was all sorted out?

Would she have told the Klines the truth about Maximus, knowing how much it would hurt them? Or would she have kept quiet, letting them believe the comforting lie that he was simply missing for a little longer? Lily wasn't even sure which was kinder: the brutal honesty that could crush them or the temporary hope that might sustain them until they were ready to face the reality. Her mother had always been clear about the importance of truth, but had she ever been in a situation this complicated?

Lily remembered how devastated the Klines were when they thought Maximus was lost.

Lily recalled the day the Klines had burst into her shop, tears streaming down their faces, clutching the flier with Maximus's picture on it. They had been absolutely inconsolable, their sorrow a tangible weight in the room. That was just a few days ago, but it felt like an eternity. Their pain had been so raw, so immediate, as if they'd lost a child.

She remembered how their faces had crumpled when she'd told them that Maximus was in Dooly's hands, that he was safe and would be returned. The relief had washed over them like a healing tide, turning their despair into cautious hope.

How could she take that hope away from them now?

Lily hesitated, the phone heavy in her hand, as if it contained all the bad news in the world. How was she supposed to tell them that Maximus was still missing, that the dog show was just days away and they might have to compete without him?

She wasn't even sure she could do it.

Chapter 10

Unveiling the Past

Goliath slid through the shadows of Willow Creek, a black and white ghost against the snow-covered landscape. His eyes, luminous green in the darkness, narrowed as he approached the old storage shed behind Sylvia Brightwell's Pet Spa. This was the third location he'd scouted tonight, each chosen based on the subtle clues he'd gathered over the past two days.

The smell of lavender shampoo and wet fur hung in the air—the unmistakable scent that had lingered on the scrap of white fur he'd found near the salon. He'd known it was Maximus's immediately. What troubled him was the other scent mingled with it: Sylvia's perfume, heavy with jasmine and something chemical.

Goliath's whiskers twitched as he spotted the padlock on the shed door. Unlike most cats, small barriers didn't deter him. His size and intelligence had long since taught him how to navigate human obstacles. He circled the shed, looking for another entry point, and found it: a small ventilation window, partially open despite the cold.

With the nimble grace that belied his massive frame, Goliath leapt onto a stack of empty crates and squeezed through the window. He landed silently on a workbench inside, his eyes adjusting quickly to the gloom.

The shed was larger than it appeared from outside, the interior divided into makeshift rooms by stacked supplies and equipment. A battery-powered space heater hummed in the corner, providing just enough warmth to take the edge off the winter chill. Grooming supplies,

The Purr-fect Suspect

stacked bags of pet food, and what looked like show equipment crowded the shelves.

And there, in a premium travel kennel in the far corner, was Maximus.

The white Poodle's usually immaculate coat was dull and matted in places. He lay curled on a plush blanket, eyes open but vacant, ears pricked at Goliath's entrance. He made no sound, but his tail gave a single, hopeful wag.

Goliath jumped from the workbench and padded silently to the kennel. He and Maximus had never been friends—Goliath found most dogs tediously simple-minded, and Maximus carried himself with a haughty air that even Goliath found pretentious. But seeing the proud champion reduced to this state stirred something protective in the cat's chest.

He examined the kennel's latch, a simple mechanism that would be easy enough for a human to open, but presented a challenge for paws, no matter how dexterous. Goliath worked at it systematically, his claws manipulating the metal parts with careful precision. After several minutes of focused effort, the latch gave way with a soft click.

Maximus blinked, then slowly rose to his feet. He wobbled slightly, as if unsteady, and Goliath caught the scent of sedative in the Poodle's breath. So they'd been drugging him. Keeping him docile. The fur along Goliath's spine bristled with indignation.

The Poodle took a tentative step out of the kennel, then stopped, looking at Goliath with uncertainty. They'd never needed to communicate before, but urgency made for strange alliances.

Goliath meowed softly, then turned toward the window, looking back at Maximus with clear intention. *Follow me.*

The window was too small for Maximus. They would need to exit through the door, which meant dealing with the padlock from the inside. Goliath leapt back onto the workbench and examined the door's construction. The hinges were old and rusted. A weak point.

He returned to Maximus, who was now standing near the door, alert but clearly still affected by whatever they'd given him. Goliath headed to the back of the shed, where a toolbox lay open on the floor. He selected what he needed with his teeth—a screwdriver with a heavy handle—and dragged it back to the door.

Using the tool, he began working at the hinge screws, loosening them bit by bit. It was painstaking work, and twice he had to stop and rest his jaw. All the while, Maximus watched with growing awareness, as if the effort of escape was burning through the sedative in his system.

After what felt like hours, the final screw gave way. The door hung awkwardly on its remaining hinge, creating a gap just wide enough for them to slip through. Goliath went first, making sure the coast was clear, then motioned for Maximus to follow.

The Poodle squeezed through the opening, his white coat catching on the splintered wood. Once outside, he shook himself vigorously, as if trying to shed the last vestiges of his captivity.

They needed to move quickly. Goliath led the way, keeping to the shadows of buildings and hedges, avoiding the main streets where late-night wanderers might spot a champion Poodle and his unlikely feline escort.

Snow began to fall, fat flakes that would soon cover their tracks—a fortunate development. Goliath picked up his pace, Maximus following with increasing steadiness. The effects of the sedative were wearing off, his natural energy returning.

They were halfway back to Lily's salon when disaster struck.

"Hey! Stop right there!"

A flashlight beam cut through the darkness, illuminating them in harsh white light. Tony Blackwood stood at the end of the alley, his face twisted with anger and surprise.

"Maximus? What the—"

Goliath didn't hesitate. He darted toward Tony with a ferocious yowl, claws extended. The man stumbled backwards, more startled than hurt by the cat's attack, but it was enough of a distraction. Maximus bolted past them both, heading straight for the main street.

Goliath pursued, leaving Tony cursing in the alley. He caught up to Maximus at the corner, where the Poodle had stopped, clearly unsure which way to go. Goliath nudged him toward the park—a longer route, but one that would keep them out of sight.

They ran together through the empty expanse of Willow Creek Park, their breath forming small clouds in the cold night air. The snow was falling more heavily now, limiting visibility—another stroke of luck.

At the far end of the park, they paused to catch their breath. Goliath's ears swiveled, picking up the distant sound of a vehicle engine.

The Purr-fect Suspect

Tony must have returned to his car and was now searching the neighborhood.

They needed shelter, somewhere safe to hide until morning. Goliath considered their options. The salon was still too far, and now that Tony had seen them, it would be the first place he'd look. They needed somewhere unexpected.

Hilda Farnsworth's house was just two blocks away. The librarian was an early riser—she'd be up at dawn—and she harbored no love for either Sylvia or Tony. She was their best option.

Goliath led Maximus through a series of backyards and narrow passages, avoiding streetlights and main thoroughfares. The Poodle followed with surprising trust, as if he'd accepted that his fate now rested with this unlikely savior.

When they reached Hilda's small Victorian home, Goliath headed straight for the back porch. He knew from previous explorations that she kept a spare key under a potted fern—a practice he'd always considered foolish, but now welcomed.

The key was where he expected, and though manipulating it with his teeth and paws was challenging, Goliath managed to insert it into the lock and turn it. The door swung open with a soft creak.

Inside, the house was warm and smelled of books and bergamot tea. A dim night light in the kitchen provided just enough illumination for them to navigate. Goliath led Maximus to the small utility room, where a stack of clean towels made for a decent bed.

Maximus hesitated at the threshold, glancing back at the door with obvious concern.

Goliath understood. The Poodle was thinking of Lily, of his owner, of the safety of familiar places. He was wondering if they should have braved the elements and continued to the salon.

But Goliath knew better. Tony was out there, and possibly Sylvia too. They needed to wait for daylight, for safety in numbers and public eyes. He nudged Maximus toward the towels, and after a moment's hesitation, the Poodle relented, curling up in exhaustion.

Goliath settled beside him, keeping vigil. He would not sleep—not with danger so close. Instead, he pondered the next phase of their escape, planning each step with careful precision.

Dawn was still hours away when a sound from the kitchen alerted him. Soft footsteps, a muffled cough. Hilda was awake.

Goliath left Maximus sleeping and padded to the kitchen. Hilda stood at the stove, heating water for her morning tea. She turned as Goliath entered, one eyebrow raised in mild surprise.

"Well," she said, adjusting her glasses. "Look who's decided to visit."

Goliath meowed and walked back toward the utility room, stopping to glance over his shoulder. Hilda understood immediately, setting down her kettle and following.

When she saw Maximus curled on her towels, fast asleep, she didn't gasp or exclaim. She simply stood, hands clasped, nodding as if this confirmed a suspicion she'd long harbored.

"So they did take him," she whispered. "I told Lily something wasn't right about that Sylvia woman."

Goliath meowed again, more urgently this time.

Hilda nodded. "I understand. You need help getting him home." She checked her watch. "It's not even six yet. The streets will be empty."

She moved with surprising efficiency for a woman her age, retrieving a leash from a drawer and gently waking Maximus. The Poodle startled, then relaxed as Hilda spoke to him in soothing tones.

"It's all right, old boy. We're going to get you back to Lily now. Can you stand?"

Maximus rose, his tail wagging with renewed vigor. Whatever sedative had been in his system appeared to have fully worn off. Hilda attached the leash and checked the front window.

"Coast is clear," she reported. "Let's move quickly."

The three of them slipped out the back door and took the scenic route through the community garden, avoiding the main streets. Goliath led, Hilda and Maximus followed at a brisk pace. The snow had stopped, leaving a pristine white blanket over everything, their footprints the only blemish on its surface.

They were one block from the salon when Goliath spotted it—a silver Volvo, dented on one side, idling at the corner. He froze, hackles rising.

Hilda saw it too and quickly pulled Maximus behind a hedge. "That's Sylvia's car," she whispered.

They watched as the Volvo cruised slowly down the street, passing the salon once, then turning around to pass it again. Inside, they could make out Sylvia's distinctive silhouette, her face tense and drawn.

The Purr-fect Suspect

"She's looking for him," Hilda said. "They must have discovered he's gone."

They waited, barely breathing, until the Volvo continued down the street and turned onto the main road. Only then did Hilda exhale.

"We need to hurry. She'll be back."

They emerged from hiding and rushed the final block to the salon. The CLOSED sign was still on the door, but light spilled from within. Lily was already up, probably worried sick about Goliath's nighttime disappearance.

Hilda knocked firmly. There was a moment of silence, then hurried footsteps. The door flew open, and Lily stood there, her face pale with worry, her hair disheveled.

"Hilda? What are you—"

Her words cut off as she saw Maximus. Her eyes widened, filling with tears. She dropped to her knees, arms outstretched.

"Maximus! Oh my God, Maximus!"

The Poodle lunged forward, nearly pulling Hilda off her feet in his eagerness to reach Lily. His entire body wagged with joy as she embraced him, burying her face in his curly coat.

"Where... how did you...?" Lily looked up at Hilda, confusion and gratitude warring on her face.

Hilda gestured to Goliath, who was calmly grooming a paw on the welcome mat. "Ask your cat. He's the real hero. I just helped with the final leg."

Lily's gaze shifted to Goliath, fresh tears spilling over. "Goliath? You found him?"

Goliath paused his grooming to give her a slow blink—a rare display of affection from the usually stoic cat.

Hilda stepped inside, closing the door firmly behind her. "We need to call the police. And Evelyn. But first, get Maximus some water and food. He looks like he hasn't eaten properly in days."

While Lily busied herself with caring for Maximus, Hilda explained what little she knew—how she'd woken to find Goliath and the Poodle in her utility room, and their narrow escape from Sylvia's searching car.

"I don't know where they were keeping him," she finished, "but I'd bet my library card it was somewhere on Sylvia's property. And I'd wager Tony Blackwood was in on it too."

Lily looked up from where she was gently examining Maximus for injuries. "I knew something was off about those two. The way they've been hovering around the salon all week, asking about the show..."

"Well, they've shown their hand now," Hilda said grimly. "The question is, what are we going to do about it?"

Lily's expression hardened with determination. "First, we make sure Maximus is safe and healthy. Then we prove exactly who took him and why."

Goliath, who had settled on the counter to observe the proceedings, gave a soft meow of approval. The hunt wasn't over—not by a long shot. But they'd won this battle, and with the evidence they had gathered, they would soon win the war.

Maximus looked up from his water bowl, his eyes meeting Goliath's across the room. There was a new understanding between them, a bond forged in danger and escape. The Poodle gave a slow, deliberate nod, as if acknowledging a debt that could never fully be repaid.

Goliath returned the nod, equally solemn. Then he stretched, yawned, and curled into a comfortable ball. He'd earned his rest. Tomorrow would bring new challenges, but for now, they were safe. Maximus was home, and the countdown to the Holiday Dog Show could resume.

The game was afoot, and Goliath was just getting started.

Chapter 11

A Surprising Lead

Sunlight streamed through the windows of Lily's grooming salon, illuminating particles of dust and dog hair suspended in the morning air. It was barely seven, but Lily had been awake for hours, her mind whirring with the events of the previous night. Maximus was safe—relatively speaking—at Dr. Rivera's veterinary clinic, where he was being examined for any lasting effects from his ordeal. Evelyn was with him, a sentinel in designer boots, refusing to leave his side.

Lily moved methodically around the salon, setting things back in order. The break-in had left a mess that went beyond physical disarray; it had shattered the sense of safety that once permeated the space. Each item she put back felt like reclaiming a small piece of that security.

The bell above the door jingled, and Lily looked up to see Officer Reynolds entering, his expression serious but not unfriendly.

"Morning, Miss Green," he said, removing his hat. "Hope I'm not too early."

"Not at all," Lily replied, gesturing to the small sitting area near the window. "I've been up since five. Coffee?"

"Please."

Lily poured two mugs from the pot she'd brewed earlier, then joined Reynolds in the sitting area. Goliath, who had been perched on the windowsill observing the street, hopped down and positioned himself at Lily's feet, his eyes fixed on the officer with unsettling intensity.

"That's quite a cat," Reynolds observed, accepting the mug Lily offered.

"He's one of a kind," Lily agreed. "And currently the only one I trust completely in this town."

Reynolds raised an eyebrow. "Strong words."

"It's been a strong few days," Lily said, taking a sip of her coffee. "Any news on Sylvia and Tony?"

"That's partly why I'm here," Reynolds said, leaning forward. "We conducted a preliminary search of Sylvia's property last night, specifically that shed where you found Maximus."

"And?" Lily prompted when he paused.

"We found evidence that substantiates your story—pet-grade sedatives, a timeline matching Maximus's grooming appointments, even some of his fur. But here's where it gets interesting." Reynolds pulled out a small notebook. "We also found materials related to other dogs that have gone missing over the past month."

Lily's eyes widened. "Other dogs? Like a coordinated series of kidnappings?"

"More like trial runs," Reynolds said grimly. "We think they were practicing—refining their techniques before going after a high-profile target like Maximus."

"That's... methodical," Lily said, suppressing a shudder. "Where are those other dogs now?"

"That's the good news. Most were released in different neighborhoods after a day or two, disorientated but unharmed. Their owners assumed they'd wandered off and found their way back."

"And they never connected it to Tony or Sylvia," Lily concluded.

"Exactly. But now we have a pattern, and with the evidence from the shed, we have enough to hold them while we build our case."

Lily considered this information, absently stroking Goliath's head. The cat had moved to her lap during their conversation, a rare display of affection that spoke to the gravity of the situation.

"I assume you're here for my formal statement?" she asked.

Reynolds nodded. "And to warn you. Tony made bail this morning."

The news hit Lily like a splash of cold water. "Already? How is that possible?"

"He has connections," Reynolds said, his mouth twisting in distaste. "And his lawyer is arguing that the evidence is circumstantial."

"What about Sylvia?"

"Still in custody. Her bail hearing is this afternoon, but frankly, I expect she'll be out by dinner."

Lily's grip tightened on her mug. "So they're both going to walk?"

"For now," Reynolds said firmly. "But the investigation is ongoing. We've seized their phones and computers, and we're following the money. People like that always leave a trail."

"And in the meantime, they're free to come after Maximus again," Lily pointed out. "The Holiday Dog Show is tomorrow."

"We'll have officers at the show," Reynolds assured her. "And Dr. Rivera has agreed to keep Maximus under observation until then, with security."

"I should be there," Lily said, already considering her schedule. "I need to finish his grooming anyway, and I don't trust anyone else to handle him right now."

"That's between you and Mrs. Kensington," Reynolds said. "But be careful. Tony wasn't happy when we brought him in, and he mentioned your name specifically."

Goliath's ears flattened against his head, and a low growl rumbled in his chest.

"Smart cat," Reynolds observed again. "Seems to understand exactly what we're saying."

"You have no idea," Lily murmured.

After taking her formal statement and asking a few more questions about the rescue, Reynolds left, promising to keep her updated on any developments. Lily locked the door behind him and leaned against it, her mind racing.

"We're not done, are we?" she asked Goliath. "They're still out there, and they still have a plan."

Goliath meowed once, his tail swishing with clear agitation.

"Right," Lily said, pushing away from the door with renewed determination. "Let's make some calls."

She spent the next hour on the phone, first with Dr. Rivera to arrange a time to groom Maximus at the clinic, then with Evelyn to update her on Reynolds's visit, and finally with Mrs. Whiskers, who listened without interruption before offering a single, cryptic piece of advice:

"Follow the money, dear. It always leads back to the source."

After hanging up, Lily turned to find Goliath sitting by the door, his posture expectant.

"Ready to go?" she asked, reaching for her coat. "We have a lot to do before tomorrow."

The drive to Willow Creek Veterinary Clinic took less than ten minutes, but Lily's mind wandered far during the journey. She played through every interaction she'd had with Tony and Sylvia over the past months, searching for clues she might have missed. Had there been hints of their plot? Signs she should have recognized?

"I should have seen it coming," she said aloud as she pulled into the clinic's parking lot. "They were too interested in Maximus's schedule, too eager to 'help' with the show."

Goliath, who had insisted on accompanying her despite his usual dislike of car rides, made a dismissive noise from the carrier in the passenger seat.

"You're right," Lily agreed, interpreting his response as absolution. "No point in second-guessing now. We found him, that's what matters."

The clinic was quiet when they entered, the waiting room empty except for a teenage receptionist who smiled in recognition.

"Miss Green! Dr. Rivera is expecting you. She's with Maximus and Mrs. Kensington in the private suite at the end of the hall."

Lily thanked her and made her way down the corridor, Goliath's carrier swinging gently at her side. She found the door to the private suite open, revealing a comfortable room that looked more like a hotel suite than a veterinary facility.

Maximus was awake, resting on a plush dog bed near a window that overlooked a small garden. He looked up as Lily entered, his tail giving a tentative wag. Evelyn sat in an armchair beside him, her usually impeccable appearance slightly rumpled from a night of vigil.

"Lily," she said, standing to greet her. "Thank goodness. I was beginning to think we'd have to present him as-is tomorrow."

Despite the complaint, there was warmth in Evelyn's voice, and Lily saw genuine gratitude in her eyes.

"He doesn't look too bad," Lily observed, setting down Goliath's carrier and opening the door. "But we can definitely get him show-ready."

Goliath emerged cautiously, surveying the room before approaching Maximus with deliberate steps. The Poodle watched him, head cocked in what seemed like recognition. There was a moment of silent communication between the two animals, then Goliath settled a few feet away, apparently satisfied with whatever assessment he'd made.

"Dr. Rivera says he's physically fine," Evelyn reported, her hand absently stroking Maximus's curly head. "The sedative they used was mild, meant to keep him quiet rather than unconscious. He was well-fed and watered."

"They wanted him healthy for the show," Lily deduced. "Just... not present until after their own dogs had competed."

"Exactly," Evelyn's mouth tightened. "A despicable plan, but not one intended to harm him permanently. Small mercies, I suppose."

Lily began unpacking her grooming supplies, laying them out on a nearby table with practiced efficiency. "Officer Reynolds told me Tony made bail," she said, keeping her voice neutral.

"Yes," Evelyn's tone could have frozen water. "His lawyer is Herbert Livingston, an old family friend. Very connected."

"And Sylvia?"

"Her hearing is at two. I've asked my own attorney to attend, though I doubt it will make a difference. The system favors those with resources."

Lily nodded, remembering Mrs. Whiskers's words. Follow the money. "Have you known Tony a long time?" she asked, trying to sound casual as she examined Maximus's coat.

Evelyn hesitated, then sighed. "We were business partners, years ago. Before he... Well, let's just say the split was not amicable."

"He stole from you," Lily guessed.

"Clients, mostly," Evelyn confirmed. "And a breeding technique I'd developed. Not illegal, strictly speaking, but deeply unethical."

Lily processed this as she began gently brushing Maximus, working out the tangles that had formed during his captivity. "And Sylvia? Where does she fit in?"

"She approached me first, actually," Evelyn said, her tone contemplative. "About three years ago. Wanted to open a high-end grooming salon, asked for my backing. I declined—I already had you, and your work has always been exemplary."

Lily felt a flush of pride at the compliment, unexpected from the usually reserved Evelyn.

"Six months later, she opened Paws and Whiskers directly across from your salon," Evelyn continued. "With Tony's financial backing, though they tried to hide that connection."

"So she had a grudge against both of us," Lily concluded. "Me for existing, you for rejecting her."

"A simple but accurate assessment," Evelyn agreed.

They fell into a companionable silence as Lily continued grooming Maximus, who seemed to be enjoying the attention after his ordeal. Goliath remained vigilant, occasionally moving to the window to survey the parking lot before returning to his post near the Poodle.

A soft knock on the door frame interrupted their peaceful routine. Dr. Rivera stepped in, clipboard in hand, her expression apologetic.

"Sorry to disturb you, but there's someone here asking to see Maximus. A Ms. Devereux? She says she's a friend of the family."

Evelyn and Lily exchanged a sharp glance.

"Margot Devereux?" Evelyn asked, her voice suddenly cool.

"Yes," Dr. Rivera confirmed, glancing at her clipboard. "She's quite insistent. Says she has a gift for Maximus's recovery."

"She's Sylvia's sister," Lily said quietly. "And business partner."

Dr. Rivera's eyebrows shot up. "I see. Shall I tell her you're not receiving visitors?"

Evelyn appeared to consider for a moment, then shook her head. "No, I think I'd like to speak with Ms. Devereux." She turned to Lily. "Would you mind continuing without me for a few minutes? I'll meet her in the waiting room."

"Of course," Lily agreed, concern furrowing her brow. "But are you sure that's wise?"

"Sometimes," Evelyn said, rising from her chair with regal poise, "the direct approach yields the most interesting results."

After Evelyn left, Lily continued working on Maximus, but her movements were distracted, her mind in the waiting room with Evelyn and Margot. Goliath seemed equally concerned, moving to the door and sitting there, ears perked toward the hallway.

"I wish I could hear what they're saying," Lily murmured.

As if in response, Goliath slipped out the door and disappeared down the corridor.

"Goliath!" Lily called in a hushed voice, but the cat was already gone.

She considered following him, but Maximus whined softly, drawing her attention back to the task at hand. "You're right," she told the Poodle. "Goliath can take care of himself."

In the waiting room, Evelyn stood facing Margot Devereux, a tall woman with Sylvia's sharp features but none of her sister's artificial warmth. Margot's blonde hair was pulled back in a severe ponytail, and her tailored pantsuit suggested she had come directly from an office.

"Mrs. Kensington," Margot said, her voice cool but not unfriendly. "Thank you for agreeing to see me."

"Curiosity," Evelyn replied. "It's a powerful motivator."

Margot's lips curved in what might have been a smile. "Indeed. I imagine you're curious about my presence here, given the circumstances."

"The circumstances being your sister's arrest for kidnapping my dog? Yes, I admit to some curiosity."

Unnoticed by either woman, Goliath had positioned himself beneath a chair, his green eyes watching intently as the conversation unfolded.

"I want to make it clear that I had no knowledge of Sylvia's plan," Margot said, her tone firm. "What she and Tony did was unconscionable, and I've already provided a statement to the police to that effect."

Evelyn's eyebrow arched in perfect skepticism. "How commendable of you. And yet, you're here, presumably to what—express your sympathies?"

Margot shifted, the first sign of discomfort she'd shown. "Partially, yes. But also to warn you."

"Warn me?" Evelyn's voice remained level, but her posture stiffened.

"Sylvia's bail hearing is this afternoon, as you know. Her lawyer is confident she'll be released." Margot paused, choosing her next words carefully. "She's not going to give up on her plan. The Holiday Dog Show means too much to her."

"Why tell me this?" Evelyn demanded. "Loyalty to family usually trumps moral qualms."

"Because unlike my sister, I understand limits," Margot replied. "Business rivalry is one thing. Criminal acts are another. And frankly, Mrs. Kensington, I'm worried about what she might do next."

Goliath's ears perked up at this, his attention fully focused on Margot.

"She's become... obsessive," Margot continued. "The show, the sponsorships, beating you—it's all she talks about. When Maximus disappeared, she was like a different person. Elated. Triumphant."

"And yet you did nothing," Evelyn observed coldly.

"I didn't know," Margot insisted. "Not until yesterday, when the police came. That's when I found out about the shed, the sedatives... all of it."

"What exactly are you warning me about, Ms. Devereux? That Sylvia might try again?"

Margot nodded. "She and Tony have invested too much to walk away. And they have allies—people who stand to gain if Maximus doesn't compete. The Holiday Dog Show is just the beginning. There are national competitions, endorsement deals..."

"Money," Evelyn said simply. "It all comes back to money."

"Yes," Margot admitted. "And pride. Tony's never forgiven you for what happened between you. And Sylvia... she needs to win. It's pathological."

From his hiding place, Goliath watched as Evelyn considered Margot's words, her expression unreadable. The cat's tail twitched, a sign of his own calculations.

"And what do you want from this exchange of information?" Evelyn asked finally. "Immunity? Gratitude?"

Margot straightened, her pride evidently stung. "Neither. I'm trying to do the right thing. Take it or leave it."

A tense silence stretched between the two women, broken only when the reception door opened and Officer Reynolds entered, his presence immediately commanding attention.

"Mrs. Kensington," he said, nodding to Evelyn before turning to Margot. "Ms. Devereux. I was told I might find you both here."

"Officer," Evelyn acknowledged. "Is there news?"

"Yes, ma'am. We've uncovered new evidence linking both Sylvia Brightwell and Tony Blackwood to the kidnapping and to several other incidents involving show dogs in neighboring counties. The district attorney is considering upgrading the charges."

Margot's face paled slightly. "What kind of evidence?"

"Financial transfers," Reynolds said. "Large sums moving between accounts just before each incident. Including yours, Ms. Devereux."

"That's impossible," Margot protested. "I never—"

"The transfers came from your business account," Reynolds continued implacably. "The one you share with your sister. She may have initiated them, but your signature is on the authorization forms."

Goliath slipped silently from beneath the chair and made his way back to the private suite, his mission accomplished. He found Lily putting the finishing touches on Maximus's coat, the Poodle now looking every inch the champion he was.

"There you are," Lily said as Goliath reentered. "You missed all the excitement. Dr. Rivera says Maximus is cleared to go home with Evelyn today. She's even arranged for a security guard to watch the house tonight, just in case."

Goliath meowed, his tone conveying far more than a simple acknowledgment. Lily paused, studying him.

"You know something," she said. "What did you see out there?"

Before the cat could respond—if such a thing were possible—Evelyn returned, her expression triumphant.

"Officer Reynolds just arrested Margot Devereux," she announced. "She claims she's innocent, but they've found financial records linking her directly to the plan. All three of them were in it together."

Lily's eyes widened. "Three? But I thought—"

"So did I," Evelyn said. "But it appears Margot was more involved than she wanted us to believe. She came here hoping to cast suspicion elsewhere, but Reynolds was a step ahead."

"That's... incredible," Lily said, still processing the news. "So it's over? All of them are in custody?"

"Tony's still out on bail," Evelyn reminded her. "But with this new evidence against all three of them, Reynolds says it's unlikely the judge will allow him to remain free. They're working on a revocation hearing for first thing tomorrow morning."

"Just in time for the show," Lily observed, running her fingers through Maximus's freshly-groomed coat one last time.

"Indeed." Evelyn's expression softened as she took in the transformation. "He looks magnificent, Lily. You've outdone yourself."

"Just doing what I love," Lily said modestly. "And making sure our champion is ready for his moment."

Evelyn knelt beside Maximus, taking his face in her hands with a tenderness few people ever witnessed from the usually austere woman. "You've been through quite an ordeal, haven't you?" she murmured. "But you're safe now. And tomorrow, you'll show everyone why you're the best."

Maximus licked her cheek, his tail wagging with enthusiasm. Whatever trauma he had endured seemed largely forgotten in the face of his owner's affection and Lily's familiar grooming routine.

"I've arranged for private security at my home tonight," Evelyn said, standing up and brushing dog hair from her slacks. "An excessive precaution, perhaps, but I'm not taking any chances. Not with Tony still out there."

"I think that's very wise," Lily agreed. She began packing away her grooming tools, her movements efficient but unhurried. "What time should I meet you at the show tomorrow?"

"Early," Evelyn said decisively. "Say, seven? The judging doesn't start until ten, but I want to get Maximus settled and comfortable with the environment."

"Seven it is," Lily confirmed. "I'll bring my emergency kit, just in case."

As they finished their preparations to leave the clinic, Goliath hopped into his carrier without his usual protest, seemingly satisfied with the day's developments. Lily secured the latch, then turned to Dr. Rivera, who had returned to check on them.

"Thank you for everything," she said warmly. "For taking care of Maximus and for accommodating us today."

"All part of the job," Dr. Rivera replied with a smile. "And frankly, the most exciting case I've had in years. Small-town veterinary practice doesn't usually involve kidnappings and police investigations."

"Let's hope it doesn't become a trend," Evelyn said dryly.

They said their goodbyes, and Lily headed for her car, carrier in one hand, grooming case in the other. The afternoon sun was beginning its descent, casting long shadows across the parking lot. As she loaded her things into the trunk, she felt a strange prickling at the back of her neck—the unmistakable sensation of being watched.

She turned slowly, scanning the lot, but saw only a few empty cars and a delivery van at the far end. Still, the feeling persisted. Goliath seemed to sense it too; a low growl emanated from his carrier.

"I know," Lily murmured. "Something feels off."

She closed the trunk and quickly got in the driver's seat, locking the doors immediately. As she started the engine, she noticed movement in her rearview mirror—someone in the delivery van, perhaps? But when she looked more directly, there was nothing to see.

Shaking off the paranoia, Lily pulled out of the parking lot and headed back toward town. The salon was closed for the day, but she had paperwork to catch up on, and frankly, she didn't want to be alone in her apartment above the shop. Not with Tony Blackwood still at large and potentially harboring a grudge.

The drive back was uneventful, the streets of Willow Creek quiet in the late afternoon lull. Shopkeepers were beginning to close up for the day, and the first string of holiday lights flickered to life along Main Street.

As Lily parked in her usual spot behind the salon, she saw Mrs. Whiskers sitting on the back steps, a thermos in her gloved hands.

"Thought you might need some fortification," the librarian called as Lily got out of the car. "It's been quite a day, from what I hear."

"News travels fast," Lily observed, retrieving Goliath's carrier from the passenger seat.

"Small town," Mrs. Whiskers replied with a shrug. "And I have excellent sources."

She held up the thermos as Lily approached. "Chamomile with a touch of honey. Good for the nerves."

"Thank you," Lily said sincerely, unlocking the back door to let them in. "I could use a friendly face right now."

Once inside, Lily released Goliath from his carrier, and the cat immediately began a thorough inspection of the premises, as if checking for intruders or changes since they'd left. Mrs. Whiskers settled at the small table in the break room, pouring tea into two mugs with practiced precision.

"So," she said as Lily sat across from her. "Margot Devereux. I had my suspicions about her."

"You never mentioned her in your notes," Lily pointed out, accepting a steaming mug gratefully.

"I prefer to work with evidence, not speculation," Mrs. Whiskers said. "But there was something about her—too polished, too controlled. And her relationship with her sister seemed... complicated."

"Well, they're all in it together now," Lily said, blowing gently on her tea before taking a sip. "Though I still can't believe they went to such extremes over a dog show."

"It's rarely about what it appears to be on the surface," Mrs. Whiskers mused. "The dog show is prestigious, certainly, but there's more at stake."

"Money," Lily supplied, remembering Evelyn's words.

"Precisely. The winner of the Holiday Dog Show automatically qualifies for the National Championship in February. The exposure alone is worth thousands in breeding fees and endorsement deals. And there are rumors that Canine Elite is looking for a new brand ambassador for their luxury pet food line."

"Canine Elite?" Lily raised her eyebrows. "They're huge."

"A seven-figure contract, from what I've heard," Mrs. Whiskers said, sipping her tea. "Now that's motivation."

Goliath rejoined them, jumping onto an empty chair and sitting tall, his green eyes fixed on Mrs. Whiskers with unusual intensity.

"Your cat thinks I know more than I'm saying," the librarian observed with a small smile. "He's not wrong."

Lily looked between them, sensing the undercurrent of communication. "What aren't you telling me?"

Mrs. Whiskers set down her mug. "There's been talk—nothing confirmed, mind you—that someone has been buying up property around town. Pet-related businesses specifically. The old feed store, that vacant lot behind the park where they used to hold the summer pet fair, and there's an offer on the building next to your salon."

"Who would want those properties?" Lily asked, confused.

"Someone planning to consolidate the local pet industry," Mrs. Whiskers suggested. "Create a monopoly of sorts. Control everything from food to grooming to show competitions."

"That's... ambitious," Lily said. "You think Tony and Sylvia are behind it?"

"I think," Mrs. Whiskers said carefully, "that you should be very careful at tomorrow's show. With Tony still free and so much at stake, there's no telling what might happen."

Goliath meowed, a sound of clear agreement that made both women turn to look at him.

"He understands every word, doesn't he?" Mrs. Whiskers asked, her eyes glinting with amusement.

"Sometimes I think he understands more than I do," Lily admitted.

The Purr-fect Suspect

They finished their tea in companionable silence, each lost in their thoughts about the coming day. As Mrs. Whiskers prepared to leave, she paused at the door.

"Remember what I told you the first time we discussed this," she said. "Trust your instincts. And trust that cat of yours."

"I will," Lily promised. "And thank you—for the tea and the wisdom."

After Mrs. Whiskers left, Lily locked the door securely and went through her closing routine, double-checking each window and entrance. Goliath followed her, occasionally rubbing against her legs, as if offering reassurance.

"One more day," she told him as they headed upstairs to her apartment. "One more day, and then this will all be over."

As they settled in for the night, Lily took comfort in Goliath's solid presence at the foot of her bed. Tomorrow would bring resolution, one way or another. Maximus would compete, the truth would come to light, and justice would be served.

Or so she hoped. But even in her optimism, Lily couldn't quite shake the feeling that they were missing something important—something that had been right in front of them all along.

Goliath, curled in a tight ball with his eyes half-closed, kept his own counsel. But his ears remained perked, alert to every sound outside their window, every creak in the old building.

Tomorrow would indeed bring resolution. But not, perhaps, in the way any of them expected.

Chapter 12

The Librarian's Secret

Lily pushed open the library door, the soft whoosh of air accompanied by the jingle of a bell. The scent of old paper and ink greeted her, a familiar comfort. Her eyes flitted over the rows of books, towering like sentinels in the quiet space. She spotted Hilda at the librarian's desk, busy with a stack of returns. Lily's footsteps echoed softly on the wooden floor, each step building a sense of anticipation.

Hilda looked up as Lily approached, a flicker of tension crossing her face. She adjusted her wire-rimmed glasses and offered a polite, if reserved, smile.

"Lily," Hilda said, stacking the last book. "What brings you here?"

"I was just in the neighborhood," Lily lied, her tone breezy. "Thought I'd stop by and see how you're doing."

Hilda's lips pressed into a thin line. "I'm well, thank you. Busy, as always."

Lily leaned against the counter, studying Hilda's face. The older woman had always been an enigma to the townspeople, her quiet demeanor masking a sharp intellect. Lily respected her, even if she didn't fully understand her.

"Have you heard about the Holiday Dog Show?" Lily said, keeping her voice casual. "It's going to be quite the event this year."

Hilda's fingers fidgeted with the edge of a book, her eyes momentarily darting away. "Yes, I believe I saw a flyer."

"Mrs. Kensington is really pulling out all the stops," Lily continued. "She even has a special category for rescued pets now. It's wonderful how much she cares about the animals."

The Purr-fect Suspect

Hilda's gaze snapped back to Lily, a spark of something—anger?—flickering in her eyes. "Mrs. Kensington is very... involved," she said, her voice tight.

Lily noted the change in Hilda's demeanor. She had a keen eye for these things, the subtle shifts that indicated more than what words conveyed. "You used to be quite involved yourself, didn't you? I remember seeing you at the shows, always with a book and a thermos of tea."

Hilda shrugged. "That was a long time ago."

Lily didn't miss the way Hilda's eyes darted to the side whenever Mrs. Kensington's name was mentioned. There was history here, she realized. Maybe more than just history.

Outside, Goliath slunk through the shadows, his movements fluid and silent. The large Tom cat paused in front of Hilda's house, his green eyes taking in the familiar surroundings. The house was dark, save for a faint glow from an upstairs window. He leapt onto the windowsill and tested the glass with a paw. It slid open, just enough for him to squeeze through.

Inside, Goliath's nose twitched, his senses on high alert. He padded through the dimly lit rooms, his eyes flicking from side to side. Everything seemed in order, but he knew better than to trust appearances. He was looking for something specific, a clue that would tie everything together.

Back at the library, Lily pressed on. "It's a shame you don't participate anymore. Your knowledge and experience would be such an asset, especially for the new competitors."

Hilda's hands were clasped tightly in front of her, knuckles white. "People move on. Interests change."

"Has something changed for you, Hilda?" Lily asked, her tone soft but probing. "You were so passionate about it. It seems like you just... disappeared."

Hilda's response was a beat too slow. "I have other commitments now."

Lily studied Hilda's face, searching for cracks in the façade. She found them in the tightness around Hilda's mouth, the way her shoulders hunched ever so slightly. "Commitments or conflicts?" she asked, more pointedly.

Hilda's eyes flashed with something dangerous. "Is there a point to this, Lily?"

Lily held up her hands in a placating gesture. "I'm just curious, that's all. You know how small towns are. People notice when someone drops out of something they used to love."

"Curiosity can be dangerous," Hilda said, her voice cold.

In Hilda's house, Goliath paused at the end of a hallway. A door was slightly ajar, a sliver of light cutting through the darkness. He approached it cautiously, ears perked for any sound from within. He nudged the door open with his nose, and it swung inward with a creak.

The room was a shrine to the dog show. Ribbons and trophies lined the walls, each one gleaming in the soft light. Photographs were interspersed among them, capturing moments of triumph and joy. Goliath took it all in, his eyes narrowing as he pieced together the implications.

In the center of the room stood a large kennel. Inside, a white poodle lay on a bed of blankets, its posture despondent. Goliath recognized the dog immediately: Maximus, the champion Poodle. He approached the kennel, his movements slow and deliberate.

Maximus lifted his head, eyes dull with resignation. Goliath studied the poodle, his sharp mind working through the possibilities. This was more than a temporary hiding place. The care with which the room was maintained, the sheer amount of memorabilia—it all pointed to something deeper.

"Lily," Hilda said, breaking the silence. "I appreciate your concern, but I really must get back to work."

Lily sensed she was at a breaking point. One more push, and Hilda might just spill everything. But was she ready to hear it? Prepared to deal with whatever confession came out?

"I understand," Lily said, backing off. "Just one last thing—I saw that Maximus is missing. Do you think he'll turn up in time for the show?"

Hilda's face went pale. "Dogs go missing all the time. I'm sure he's fine."

"Are you?" Lily asked, holding Hilda's gaze. The older woman looked away, unable to meet her eyes.

"We can hope," Hilda said, almost whispering.

Lily straightened, her mind racing. "Take care, Hilda. We'll see you at the show."

The Purr-fect Suspect

She walked away slowly, her thoughts a whirlwind of suspicions and half-formed theories. At the door, she turned back. Hilda was still at the desk, staring at the stack of books in front of her, motionless.

Goliath slipped through the window and onto the street, his movements hurried but precise. He knew time was short. The dog show was only days away, and if they didn't act quickly, Maximus might never be seen again. He had to get to Lily, to make her understand the gravity of the situation.

Lily stood by her car, fumbling for her keys. She jumped as Goliath appeared from the shadows, his green eyes locking onto hers. She opened the door, and Goliath leapt into the passenger seat, his fur bristling with urgency.

"Well?" she said, sliding into the driver's seat. "Did you find anything?"

Goliath stared at her, unblinking. Lily sighed. "Of course you did."

She started the car, the engine's rumble breaking the night's stillness. "I don't know what to think," she said, more to herself than to Goliath. "Hilda seems… conflicted. Like she wants to tell me something but can't."

Goliath settled into his seat, his eyes never leaving Lily. She glanced over at him, taking in his intense gaze. "You really think she's capable of this? Stealing Maximus just to sabotage Mrs. Kensington?"

The cat didn't answer, but Lily could almost hear his thoughts. They were the same as hers.

"I guess we don't have a choice," she said, her grip tightening on the steering wheel. "If we don't do something, the whole town will turn on her. We need proof, one way or the other."

She drove in silence, her mind flipping through the night's events like the pages of a book. Goliath stretched and yawned, his tension momentarily releasing.

As they neared Lily's house, she spoke again. "We'll tell the police anonymously. That way, if we're wrong…"

She trailed off, knowing that being wrong was the least of their worries. If they were right, it would tear the community apart. But if they were wrong and did nothing, it would destroy an innocent woman.

Lily parked in her driveway and turned off the car. She didn't move to get out, instead sitting in the darkness, thinking. Goliath watched her, waiting.

"We're doing the right thing," she said, as if trying to convince herself. "Aren't we?"

With that, she opened her door and stepped out. Goliath followed, his large frame moving gracefully to the ground. They walked to the front door together, a silent team with a heavy burden.

Inside, Lily went to the kitchen and picked up the phone. She hesitated, looking at Goliath who had settled on the counter, his eyes half-closed but still alert. She dialed the number slowly, each beep sounding like a gunshot in the quiet house.

"Stanton Police Department," a voice crackled through the receiver. "How can I help you?"

Lily's mouth went dry. She opened and closed it, struggling to find the words. Goliath's eyes were on her, piercing through the dim light of the kitchen.

"I... I need to report something," she said, her voice shaking. "It's about the missing dog, Maximus."

The line was silent for a moment, then the dispatcher spoke. "Go ahead."

Lily took a deep breath. "He's at Hilda Farnsworth's house. In the back room, with all the dog show trophies."

The dispatcher started to ask a question, but Lily cut him off. "She's just keeping him safe. She would never hurt him. Please, you have to believe that."

She slammed the receiver down, her hands trembling. Goliath stretched, his claws scraping the countertop, and jumped to the floor. He rubbed against Lily's leg, a rare show of affection.

"We did what we had to," she said, looking down at the cat. "Now we wait."

The next morning, news spread quickly through the town. The police had found Maximus, safe and sound, in Hilda's makeshift kennel. Speculation ran rampant: Had Hilda stolen him? Was she planning to claim the prize money? Or was it something more personal, a vendetta against Mrs. Kensington?

Lily listened to the gossip with a heavy heart. She and Goliath had hoped that an anonymous tip would spare Hilda immediate scrutiny, but in a town as small as Stanton, nothing stayed quiet for long.

The Purr-fect Suspect

"Hilda would never take a dog," one of Lily's regulars claimed as she paid for her newly groomed terrier. "She's the most honest person I know."

Lily hoped that was true. She remained silent, not wanting to add to the speculation. As soon as the customer left, she locked the front door and flipped the sign to "Closed." Goliath, who had been lounging on the reception desk, stretched and hopped down.

"We need to talk to her," Lily said. "If anyone can explain why she did it, it's Hilda."

She changed into a warm jacket and grabbed Goliath's leash. He resisted as she tried to clip it onto his collar, swatting at her hands with his large paws.

"Just in case," she said, managing to secure the leash after a brief struggle. "You know how Hilda feels about stray animals."

They walked the short distance to the library. The cold air bit at Lily's cheeks, and she buried her hands deep in her pockets. Goliath trotted beside her, his disdain for the leash evident in his stiff-legged walk.

The library was empty when they arrived. Lily noted that the usual warmth of the space was lacking; even the Christmas decorations seemed subdued. She made her way to the back, where a small reading nook offered a view of the snow-covered town square. Hilda sat alone, a book open in her lap, though her eyes were distant and unfocused.

"Hilda," Lily said softly. The older woman looked up, and for a moment Lily thought she saw a flash of fear in Hilda's eyes. It quickly dissolved into resignation.

"Lily," Hilda said, closing her book. "I'm surprised you're talking to me."

Lily unclipped Goliath's leash. The cat shook himself and sauntered over to Hilda, sitting just out of reach. "We need to understand," Lily said. "Why you took him."

Hilda sighed and removed her glasses, rubbing the bridge of her nose. "I didn't take him. He was left on my doorstep. Abandoned."

"By who?" Lily asked, though she suspected the answer.

Hilda put her glasses back on, her eyes now hard. "Someone who thought I could keep him safe. Someone who knows how these things work."

"Mrs. Kensington."

Hilda didn't confirm or deny, but the silence spoke volumes.

"Why would she abandon Maximus?" Lily asked. "He's her pride and joy."

"Is he?" Hilda said, her voice laden with bitterness. "Do you think she got where she is by playing fair? By caring for every animal like it was her own?"

Lily remembered Hilda's words from the night before: Curiosity can be dangerous. She was starting to see just how deep this went, and it scared her.

"Hilda, we only want to help. The police—"

"The police will do what they always do," Hilda interrupted. "They'll listen to whoever shouts the loudest. Don't worry, Lily. I know how to take care of myself."

Lily didn't doubt that Hilda could handle whatever was coming. But should she have to? That was the question gnawing at her.

"Please," Lily said. "Let us help you. We can talk to—"

"No," Hilda said firmly. "But thank you for the offer."

Lily knew a dismissal when she heard one. She called to Goliath, who stood and stretched but lingered a moment, as if expecting Hilda to say something more. When she didn't, he padded over to Lily.

"Take care, Hilda," Lily said as she walked away. She glanced back once, seeing Hilda staring out the window, her book unopened in her lap.

The next few days were a blur for Lily. The Holiday Dog Show consumed the town, with last-minute preparations and endless excitement. Maximus's return had only heightened the fervor, and people spoke of little else.

Lily worked long hours, grooming dozens of dogs in preparation for the big event. Each night, she collapsed into bed, her body aching and her mind racing with thoughts of Hilda, Maximus, and the looming show.

On the morning of the dog show, Lily woke to a flurry of text messages. One caught her eye immediately: "Can you believe Hilda is out on bail? Unbelievable!"

She sat up in bed, her heart sinking. They'd arrested her. Goliath, who had been sleeping at her feet, stretched and walked up to nuzzle her. She stroked his fur absently, her mind whirling.

"We have to go," she said to Goliath. "We have to stop this."

The Purr-fect Suspect

She dressed quickly and grabbed Goliath's carrier. The cat eyed it warily but didn't resist as she gently placed him inside. "It's for your own good," she said. "You know Hilda isn't your biggest fan right now."

Lily drove to the town hall, where the dog show was already in full swing. The parking lot was packed, and she had to squeeze her small car into a tight spot near the back. She left Goliath in the carrier, cracking a window for air.

The main hall was a cacophony of barks and voices. Lily weaved through the crowd, her eyes scanning for familiar faces. She spotted Mrs. Kensington near the stage, where a line of dogs waited to be judged. Maximus stood proudly at her side, his coat shimmering like freshly fallen snow.

"Penelope," Lily called. Mrs. Kensington turned, a wide smile breaking across her face.

"Lily, darling! Can you believe the turnout? It's marvelous!"

Lily forced a smile. "It's wonderful. I'm so glad Maximus is back. He looks amazing."

Mrs. Kensington stroked the poodle's head affectionately. "He's a survivor, this one. We were so worried."

"I heard the police have a suspect," Lily said, watching Penelope's reaction closely. "Someone said Hilda Farnsworth was arrested."

Penelope's smile didn't waver, but her eyes took on a steely glint. "It's tragic, really. Hilda was such a fixture in the community. I never would have suspected her."

"Do you think she's guilty?"

Penelope shrugged, a delicate gesture that seemed practiced. "The evidence is compelling. But who can say? I'm just grateful Maximus is safe."

Lily's stomach churned. She needed to get away, to think. "I have to check on a client's dog," she lied. "I'll see you later."

She made her way back to her car, her thoughts a tangled mess. How could Penelope be so calm, so confident, when Hilda's life was in ruins?

In the car, Goliath meowed plaintively. Lily opened the carrier, and the cat stretched out, then jumped onto her lap.

"What are we going to do?" she asked him. "If Hilda goes down for this, and she's innocent…"

Goliath stared at her, his green eyes unblinking. Lily sighed. "I know. We need proof. Real proof."

She started the car and drove slowly through the residential streets, avoiding the main thoroughfare. As she passed Hilda's house, she noticed a figure on the porch. It was Hilda, sitting in a wooden rocking chair, her hands clasped in her lap. She looked smaller than Lily had ever seen her, almost frail.

Lily pulled over to the curb and killed the engine. She hesitated, unsure if she should approach. Goliath watched intently, as if willing her to make a decision.

"I just want to talk," Lily said as she walked up the driveway. Hilda looked at her, and Lily saw the deep lines of fatigue etched into the older woman's face.

"Talking seems to be what we're best at," Hilda said, not unkindly.

Lily stood at the bottom of the porch steps, not daring to come closer without an invitation. "I'm sorry about… everything. We never thought it would go this far."

Hilda's eyes clouded with confusion. "We?"

Lily took a deep breath. "I called the police. Anonymously. We thought… we hoped that if they found Maximus, it would clear things up."

Hilda leaned back in her chair, closing her eyes. "Well, that explains a lot."

"Explains, but doesn't excuse," Lily said, her voice heavy with guilt. "We just wanted to make sure the truth came out. We didn't want to accuse you—"

"But you did," Hilda said, opening her eyes. "You accused me because you assumed I was the one who took him. Because you couldn't imagine that someone like Penelope would ever stoop so low."

LLily's breath caught in her throat. She hadn't considered that Hilda might know the whole story, or that she would be this direct.

"Hilda," Lily started, then paused. "We just didn't understand why you would take such a risk."

"A risk," Hilda repeated, almost to herself. "Lily, do you know why I started this library? Why I put every penny I had into it?"

Lily stayed silent, unsure where this was going.

The Purr-fect Suspect

"Because I believed in this community. I believed that if you gave people access to knowledge, to the truth, they would make better decisions. That they'd be wiser, more compassionate."

Hilda looked straight at Lily, and the younger woman felt the full weight of that gaze. "But knowledge means nothing without understanding, and facts are useless without context. The truth is often more complicated than people are willing to accept."

Lily thought of all the times she'd come to the library, of the books Hilda had recommended, of the quiet moments in the reading nook. She realized that Hilda had always been more than just a keeper of books; she'd been a steward of the community's conscience.

"We're not as wise as we think we are," Hilda continued. "But we can learn. That's the hope, anyway."

Lily's mind raced. She needed to fix this, to make Hilda see that they were on the same side—seeking the truth, even when it was uncomfortable.

"We're still learning," Lily said. "Hilda, we know that Penelope has been... less than honest. But without real evidence—"

"Evidence," Hilda interrupted, her voice tinged with irony. "Yes, that's what you need, isn't it? Something tangible. Something you can point to and say, 'This is the truth.'"

Lily waited, sensing that Hilda was on the verge of revealing something important.

"Come inside," Hilda said, standing slowly. "There's something you need to see."

Lily followed Hilda into the house. The interior was as she remembered it from her childhood visits: cozy, with walls lined with bookshelves and an eclectic mix of furniture. Hilda led her to the kitchen, where a large teakettle sat on the stove.

"Tea?" Hilda asked. Lily nodded, though she was too anxious to think about drinking anything.

As Hilda busied herself with the teakettle, Lily's eyes wandered. She noticed a stack of old newspapers on the kitchen table, all meticulously organized. The top one had a headline that read, "Local Library Celebrates 20 Years." There was a photo of Hilda, younger and smiling, surrounded by townspeople.

Hilda poured two cups of tea and handed one to Lily. "Sit," she said, motioning to the table. Lily obeyed, warm ceramic in her hands, the steam rising to meet her face.

Hilda took a seat and sipped her tea slowly. "The community has changed," she said, almost wistfully. "People have changed. Or maybe they've just stayed the same, and I'm the one who changed."

Lily waited, the tension in her chest growing.

"I kept these," Hilda said, gesturing to the newspapers. "They're a record of sorts. A way to remember how things were. How we were."

Lily set her tea down and picked up the top paper, flipping through it carefully. Each page was a time capsule, filled with articles about local events, obituaries, and school achievements.

"Hilda, I don't understand—"

"Look at the next one," Hilda said, cutting her off.

Lily did as she was told. The second paper in the stack was older, yellowed with age. Its headline read, "Champion Poodle Wins Again!" There was a picture of a young Penelope Kensington, beaming, with a poodle that looked strikingly like Maximus.

"Penelope's first win," Hilda said. "That dog was named Achilles. He was the spitting image of Maximus, wasn't he?"

Lily's eyes widened as she began to understand. "They're not just similar. It's like they're the same dog."

Hilda nodded slowly. "The same dog, the same trophies, the same photos. Penelope has been playing this game for a long time."

Lily's mind raced. If what Hilda was suggesting was true, it meant that Penelope hadn't just been dishonest—she'd been fraudulent for decades.

"Why are you showing me this?" Lily asked. "Why not take it to the police?"

Hilda leaned back in her chair, her eyes tired. "Because the police deal in facts, not inferences. In the court of public opinion, this might be enough to cast doubt. But in a real court? It's just a story."

Lily thought of all the stories she'd read, of how the best ones revealed deeper truths about life, about people. She realized that Hilda wasn't just trying to save herself; she was trying to teach Lily something.

"So what do we do?" Lily asked. "Just let her get away with it?"

Hilda finished her tea and set the cup down gently. "The dog show is tonight. If Maximus wins, the cycle continues. If he loses…"

The Purr-fect Suspect

Lily understood. If Maximus lost, it would be a break in the unchanging line of poodles. It would raise questions, create suspicion.

"But who could beat him?" Lily said. "He's perfect."

A small, almost imperceptible smile touched Hilda's lips. "Perfection is a fragile thing. It doesn't take much to tip the balance."

Lily's thoughts turned to the dogs she'd groomed over the years, to the love and care their owners lavished on them. Maximus was beautiful, but he had the look of something crafted, not nurtured.

She stood, her mind made up. "Thank you, Hilda. For everything."

Hilda remained seated, her hands now resting on the stack of newspapers. "Lily," she said as the younger woman started to walk away. "Remember that understanding is harder than knowing."

Lily paused, then nodded. "I'll remember."

She left Hilda's house, her thoughts a maelstrom. In the car, Goliath waited patiently, his green eyes tracking Lily as she slid into the driver's seat.

"We have a plan," she told him. "But it's going to take all of us."

Lily drove home, her mind running through every detail they would need to account for. When they arrived, she took Goliath inside and let him out of the carrier. He stretched and yawned, then trotted to the kitchen, expecting a treat.

"Not yet," Lily called to him. "We need to practice."

She went to her bedroom and retrieved a small grooming kit. Goliath eyed it warily as she brought it into the living room.

"Come here," she said, patting the couch. Goliath hesitated, then jumped up, his body tensing.

Lily opened the kit and took out a brush. "If we're going to pull this off, you need to look your best."

Goliath growled low in his throat but didn't move as Lily started to brush his fur. She worked slowly, methodically, talking to him the whole time.

"You'll only be in for a few minutes," she said. "Just long enough to stir things up. Once the judges get a good look, we'll make the switch."

Goliath flicked his tail, clearly unhappy, but Lily knew he understood. They'd been through enough together that she could almost read his thoughts.

When she finished brushing, Goliath's black and white fur gleamed. He looked regal, like a miniature lion.

"Perfect," she said, admiring her work. "Now for the collar."

She took out a red velvet collar with a small bell attached. Goliath sniffed it and swatted at the bell, making it jingle. Lily fastened it around his neck, and Goliath sat up proudly, his disapproval melting into vanity.

"You look like a Christmas ornament," Lily said, smiling for the first time in days. "Okay, now the carrier."

Goliath's ears flattened against his skull, and he sank lower on the couch, his once-proud posture dissolving into a puddle of reluctant fur. He eyed the carrier with a mix of dread and resignation, like a condemned prisoner staring at the gallows. His tail flicked once, twice, then curled tightly around his body as if to protect himself from the impending doom.

Lily noticed his growing tension and sighed. "Goliath, you know this is important," she said, her voice softening. "We've been through worse, haven't we?"

She reached out to stroke his head, but he turned away, his green eyes now slits of defiance. The bell on his collar tinkled with the movement, a mocking echo of festive cheer in the otherwise somber room.

"Remember when we had to sneak you into the vet's office? You were braver than this," Lily said, trying to coax him with memories of their past exploits. She knew he hated the carrier, but they didn't have time for a standoff. The plan hinged on Goliath playing his part, and she needed him to understand that this was more than just another inconvenient trip.

Goliath stretched out one paw, then another, as if he were about to make a slow, deliberate move. Instead, he slumped back into the cushions, his whole body a picture of feline martyrdom.

"Just to see if it fits," Lily said. "Come on."

She brought the carrier over and opened it. Goliath eyed it, then slowly, reluctantly, crawled in. He filled the carrier completely, his large frame pressing against the sides.

Lily closed the door and lifted it, swaying it gently from side to side. Goliath's green eyes tracked her movements, his body rigid.

"How is it?" she asked. "Not too tight?"

Goliath didn't respond, but Lily could tell he was uncomfortable. Still, it would have to do.

The Purr-fect Suspect

She set the carrier down and opened it, letting Goliath stretch and shake himself free. He leapt to the floor and padded away, his dignity slightly bruised.

"We're ready," Lily said, more to herself than to Goliath. "I hope."

The hours until the dog show crawled by. Lily tried to distract herself with chores, but her mind kept circling back to the plan, to all the things that could go wrong. What if the judges recognized Goliath? What if Penelope suspected something and called them out? What if Hilda was wrong, and none of this made a difference?

When it was finally time to leave, Lily loaded Goliath into the carrier and grabbed her coat. The evening had turned bitterly cold, and she could see her breath as she walked to the car.

The drive to the town hall was silent. Lily didn't play the radio, and Goliath made no sounds from his carrier. It was as if both of them were conserving their energy for what was to come.

The parking lot was still full, but Lily managed to find a spot not too far from the entrance. She left Goliath in the car temporarily, knowing the chaos inside would be too much for him.

The main hall was even more crowded than before. The air was thick with the smell of dogs and sweat, and the noise was nearly unbearable. Lily pushed her way through the crowd, making her way to the staging area behind the main floor.

She found Mrs. Kensington sitting in a lounge area, feeding Maximus small treats from a bag. The poodle sat perfectly still, his posture straight, like a soldier at attention.

"Penelope," Lily said. Mrs. Kensington looked up, a bit of surprise in her eyes.

"Lily! Have you come to wish us luck?"

Lily hesitated, then said, "I have a proposal."

Penelope raised an eyebrow, curious. "Oh?"

"Maximus is a shoo-in," Lily said. "Everyone knows it. But I was thinking… it might be good for the community if he had some real competition."

Penelope's expression shifted to one of amusement. "And who do you propose could compete with Maximus?"

Lily took a deep breath. "My cat."

Penelope laughed, a high, tinkling sound. "Lily, this is a dog show. Are you serious?"

"Completely," Lily said. "Goliath has the poise, the grooming, the presence. Just look at him."

She pointed to the glass doors that led to the parking lot. Penelope stood and walked over, peering outside. Lily joined her, and together they looked at Lily's car. Goliath sat in the carrier, his head held high, the red collar adding a touch of elegance.

Penelope's eyes narrowed. "He's beautiful, I'll give you that. But this is ridiculous."

"Is it?" Lily said. "The crowd would love it. Imagine the drama, the excitement. And if Maximus wins against such an unusual challenger, it will make his victory even sweeter."

Lily could see the wheels turning in Penelope's mind. She was a showman at heart, and the idea of added spectacle was clearly tempting her.

"It's not up to me," Penelope said finally. "The judges would have to agree."

Lily smiled. "Leave that to me."

She turned to walk away, but Penelope called after her. "Lily, why are you doing this?"

Lily paused and looked back. "Because I care about the community. Just like you."

She left the main hall and went to her car, opening the door to let in the frigid air. Goliath looked up at her, his eyes questioning.

"They're going for it," she said, her breath visible in the cold. "We just need to convince the judges."

She closed the door and walked around to the trunk, opening it and rummaging through a bag. She pulled out a small container and opened it, revealing a mix of herbs and cotton balls.

"Lucky I had this left over from Halloween," she said as she got back into the car. "Hold still."

She took a cotton ball and dipped it into the mixture, then carefully rubbed it on Goliath's fur. The cat flinched at first, then settled as the herbs released a warm, smoky fragrance.

"This will mask your scent," Lily said. "We can't have the dogs going crazy around you."

When she finished, Goliath's fur had taken on a subtle, dull hue, as if covered in a fine layer of ash. The aroma of the herbs filled the car, giving it a cozy, almost magical atmosphere.

The Purr-fect Suspect

"Now we just wait," Lily said, leaning back in her seat. She closed her eyes, trying to calm the storm in her mind. Goliath curled up in his carrier, the warmth of the herbs seeping into his muscles.

An hour passed. Lily dozed intermittently, her dreams a confusing mix of dogs and books and Hilda's stern, knowing gaze. She woke with a start when someone knocked on the car window.

"Lily!" a voice shouted. She looked out to see a young man wearing an official-looking badge. "The judges want to speak with you."

Lily cracked the door, letting in a rush of cold air. "Be right there," she said, her voice groggy.

The man walked away, and Lily closed the door, rubbing her hands together to warm them. "This is it," she said to Goliath. "Stay calm."

She got out of the car and retrieved Goliath's carrier, then made her way back into the town hall. The noise had died down a bit, and Lily saw that many of the preliminary rounds were finished. Dogs and their owners lounged in makeshift rest areas, looking tired but content.

Lily walked to the judges' table, where three older individuals sat with clipboards and pens. One of them, a woman with silver hair pulled into a tight bun, beckoned Lily over.

"We've been told of your… proposal," the woman said, her tone neutral. "May we see the cat?"

Lily placed the carrier on the table and opened the door. Goliath stepped out cautiously, his movements slow and deliberate. He stood on the table, stretching his full length, then sat down, his tail curling around his paws.

The judges leaned in, examining Goliath from different angles. One of them, a man with a thick mustache, reached out to touch Goliath's fur. The cat allowed it, his eyes half-closed in an expression of regal indifference.

"He's certainly well-groomed," the mustachioed judge said. "But this is highly unorthodox."

The silver-haired woman spoke again. "Why do you want to enter him? What do you hope to achieve?"

Lily had prepared for this question. "It's for charity," she said. "The increased interest and ticket sales will benefit the animal shelter. Plus, it's all in good fun. We just want to add a little excitement to the competition."

The judges conferred in hushed tones, their faces serious. Lily's heart pounded in her chest. This was the linchpin of their plan; without the judges' approval, everything would fall apart.

The silver-haired woman turned back to Lily. "Very well. We'll allow it, but he will be judged by the same standards as the dogs. If he causes any disruption, he will be disqualified immediately."

Lily let out a breath she didn't realize she was holding. "Thank you," she said. "You won't regret it."

She carefully placed Goliath back into the carrier and closed the door. As she walked away, she felt a rush of adrenaline. They had a chance now, a real chance.

Outside, she took Goliath to her car and started the engine to warm them up. "You were perfect," she told him. "Now we just need to get through the final round."

She thought about calling Zoe, about telling her everything. Zoe would probably think they were crazy, but she would understand. Instead, Lily pulled out her phone and stared at it, conflicted.

She dialed a number and waited. After a few rings, a voice answered. "Stanton Police Department."

Lily hesitated, then spoke. "This is about the Farnsworth case. You need to know that Hilda is innocent. Please, you have to look at Penelope Kensington. She's the one who—"

The line went dead. Lily looked at her phone and saw that the battery had died. She cursed under her breath, then slumped back in her seat.

"Let's hope they believe us," she said to Goliath. "And that we're not too late."

The final round of the dog show was set to begin. Lily made her way back inside, carrying Goliath's carrier with a sense of purpose. The main hall had taken on a festive atmosphere, with Christmas lights casting a warm glow over the proceedings. A large crowd had gathered around the main stage, and the air was thick with anticipation.

Lily found a spot near the stage and set Goliath's carrier on a chair. She peeked in, and Goliath looked up at her, his eyes calm and focused.

"Just a little longer," she said. "We can do this."

The announcer took to the stage, a tall man in a tuxedo holding a microphone. "Ladies and gentlemen, thank you for your patience. We are now ready to begin the final round of the Holiday Dog Show!"

The Purr-fect Suspect

The crowd erupted in applause and cheers. Lily's hands tingled with nervous energy.

The announcer continued, "This year, we have a special surprise. In addition to our usual canine competitors, we have a very special entry. Please welcome Goliath, the cat!"

Lily held her breath as the crowd reacted with a mix of gasps, laughter, and murmurs. She unlatched Goliath's carrier, and the cat stepped out onto the chair, stretching and yawning as if he owned the place.

Lily had to admit, he looked stunning. The dull, herb-infused fur had given way to a glossy sheen, and the red collar made him look like a piece of living Christmas decoration.

The announcer spoke again. "Goliath will be competing against our reigning champion, Maximus, in a head-to-head showdown. May the best animal win!"

Lily's gaze shifted quickly to Mrs. Kensington, seated a few rows back from the stage. Penelope's face was rigid, a mask of controlled emotion that betrayed the high stakes she felt. Her eyes were laser-focused on the stage, unblinking, as if willing it to conform to her desires. Maximus sat at her feet, the picture of canine perfection, his posture as straight and unyielding as a marble statue.

A volunteer in a festive sweater hurried over to Lily and handed her a small slip of paper. "This is the order," the volunteer said before rushing off to tend to other tasks.

Lily's fingers closed around the paper, crumpling it slightly. She didn't look at it right away. Instead, she let her eyes wander back to Penelope, wondering how the woman could remain so composed, so statuesque, in the face of this unexpected twist. Penelope had the demeanor of someone used to winning, and Lily suspected that even she was beginning to feel the strain of this new, unpredictable element.

The crowd buzzed with excitement and speculation. Whispers of "Can a cat really compete?" and "This is going to be interesting!" floated through the air. The festive atmosphere took on a sharper edge, like tinsel with a hidden wire, as people settled in for what promised to be a dramatic finale.

Lily thought about the risk they were taking. It wasn't just about the show; it was about buying time, about creating a diversion that would hopefully lead to something greater. She believed in Goliath's abilities, but more than that, she believed in the cause they were fighting for. Still, the what-ifs gnawed at her. What if the crowd turned against them? What if Goliath panicked? What if this whole gambit failed, and they were left with nothing?

She took a moment to steady herself, inhaling the mix of pine and dog that filled the hall. Her eyes flicked back to the stage, where a large Christmas tree adorned with ribbons and ornaments cast a soft glow over the proceedings. This was Willow Creek's big event, and they had managed to turn it into a spectacle. Whether that was a good thing or a bad thing remained to be seen.

With a slow, deliberate motion, Lily uncrumpled the slip of paper in her hand and looked at it. The order was simple, but it carried the weight of a hundred possibilities. First, Goliath would have to demonstrate basic obedience skills. Then, Maximus would perform a series of tricks. Finally, there would be a joint appearance where both animals displayed their poise and presence.

She took a deep breath, letting the air fill her lungs and stretch her ribcage. This was it. Every moment had led them here, and there was no turning back.

Chapter 13

Race Against Time

Goliath perched atop a parked car, the old sedan's hood warm beneath his paws despite the morning chill. He had the high ground now, a brief reprieve from the chaos unfolding below. His green eyes cut through the sea of humans hurrying about the town square, all frantically preparing for the Holiday Dog Show that would begin in less than five hours. His tail lashed once, twice. Still no sign of Lily.

From his elevated position, Goliath could see the pavilion where judges were setting up their tables. Workers strung garlands of twinkling lights across the bandstand. Volunteers arranged rows of chairs before the main stage. The whole town was caught in the frenzy of pre-show excitement, oblivious to the tension hanging over the day like a storm cloud.

Only hours ago, they had rescued Maximus from Sylvia's shed, but their triumph was short-lived. While Lily had rushed the Poodle to the vet for examination, Goliath had remained at the salon, keeping watch. That's when he'd overheard Tony and Sylvia outside, their hushed voices carrying through the mail slot.

"She can't prove anything," Sylvia had hissed. "It's our word against hers."

"Maximus recognized us," Tony had argued. "And that damn cat saw everything."

"A cat can't testify," Sylvia had retorted. "We stick to the plan. When Maximus doesn't show up for the competition, Evelyn will be disqualified. That's all that matters."

They didn't know Maximus had been rescued. And more importantly, they had a new scheme brewing—one that Goliath needed to uncover before it was too late.

The sound of an approaching vehicle caught his attention. Lily's ancient blue Subaru pulled into a parking spot near the square, and Goliath's hackles lowered slightly. She was back, finally. But she was alone. Where was Maximus?

Goliath leapt down from the car roof, narrowly avoiding a child who lunged for his tail. He darted across the square, weaving through the forest of human legs with practiced ease, and reached Lily just as she was locking her car.

"Goliath!" she exclaimed, bending to scratch behind his ears. "I've been looking everywhere for you."

He butted his head against her ankle, then looked pointedly back toward the square.

"The vet says Maximus will be fine," Lily said, as if reading his concern. "They sedated him, but there's no permanent damage. Dr. Rivera is keeping him for a few more hours just to be safe. Evelyn is with him."

Goliath meowed, an unusual vocalization for the normally stoic cat.

"I know," Lily continued, her voice dropping to a whisper. "We need evidence linking Tony and Sylvia to the kidnapping. The police won't pursue it without proof."

She bent lower, her voice barely audible. "I have a plan, but I need your help."

Goliath's ears perked forward as Lily outlined her strategy. They needed to get into Sylvia's office and find anything that might connect her to Maximus's abduction—receipts, notes, anything. And they needed to do it now, while Sylvia was busy helping set up her booth at the show.

"If we don't find evidence by noon," Lily said, "they'll get away with it. And I'm afraid they might try something else to keep Maximus from competing."

Goliath's tail flicked. He understood the stakes better than Lily knew.

The Purr-fect Suspect

Together, they made their way to Paws and Whiskers, Sylvia's upscale grooming salon. As expected, the shop was closed for the holiday show, but the lights in the back office remained on. Lily approached the rear entrance, the one used for deliveries, and tried the handle. Locked.

"Of course," she muttered, disappointed but not surprised.

Goliath nudged her leg, then trotted to a narrow window a few feet off the ground. The window was open a crack, likely to provide ventilation for the shop while it was closed. With a graceful leap, Goliath landed on the window ledge and pushed at the glass with his head, widening the gap.

"Brilliant," Lily whispered.

Goliath slipped inside, disappearing into the dimly lit interior. After a moment, Lily heard the click of the back door unlocking, and Goliath reappeared, looking quite pleased with himself.

"Remind me never to underestimate you," Lily said, easing the door open.

Inside, the salon smelled of expensive pet shampoos and designer scents—nothing like the homey, lived-in aroma of Lily's shop. Everything was sleek, modern, and sterile. They moved quietly to the office at the back, where a glass desk and ergonomic chair dominated the small space.

"Start looking," Lily said, as she began rifling through the desk drawers. "We need anything that connects them to Maximus."

Goliath leapt onto a shelf lined with binders and began nudging them with his nose, as if he understood exactly what they were searching for. One binder fell open onto the desk, revealing invoices for special supplies—including a sedative typically used for show dogs.

"Interesting," Lily murmured, snapping a photo with her phone. "But not conclusive."

They continued searching, the minutes ticking by with agonizing slowness. Lily found nothing of note in the desk, and was about to check the filing cabinet when Goliath let out a soft chirp—his version of "come look."

He had pushed open a cabinet door near the floor, revealing a small safe. The door of the safe was ajar, as if someone had recently accessed it and failed to secure it properly.

"What have we here?" Lily said, kneeling to investigate.

Inside the safe were several folders, a stack of cash, and a small leather notebook. Lily extracted the notebook and opened it, her eyes widening as she scanned the pages.

"Goliath, you're a genius," she breathed.

The notebook contained detailed notes about Maximus—his routine, his schedule, when he visited Lily's salon. There were even notes about which foods would most effectively mask the taste of sedatives. The final entry, dated just before Maximus went missing, read: "Transport arranged. T will provide the van."

"This is it," Lily said, snapping photos of each page. "This proves they planned it."

A noise from the front of the salon made them both freeze. The bell over the door jingled, followed by the sound of voices—Sylvia's distinctive tone, and another, deeper voice that could only be Tony's.

"They're back," Lily whispered, her face paling.

Goliath moved swiftly to the door, peering around the corner. Sylvia and Tony were in the reception area, arguing in hushed but intense tones.

"You said you took care of it," Sylvia was saying.

"I did," Tony replied. "But that blasted cat complicated things. And now the vet's involved."

"If Maximus competes, we're finished," Sylvia hissed. "Do you understand? Years of planning, down the drain."

Goliath darted back to Lily, who was frantically trying to replace everything exactly as they'd found it. He nudged her leg urgently, then made for the back door.

"Coming," she whispered, carefully closing the safe and the cabinet.

They slipped out the back door just as the voices grew louder, approaching the office. Lily pulled the door shut with excruciating slowness, wincing at the soft click of the latch.

Once outside, they didn't waste time. They moved quickly but calmly down the alley, trying not to draw attention. Only when they were a block away did Lily let out the breath she'd been holding.

"That was too close," she said, her voice shaking. "But we got what we needed."

Goliath meowed, his tail twitching anxiously.

The Purr-fect Suspect

"You're right," Lily agreed, as if they were having an actual conversation. "We need to get this to the police right away."

Goliath perched atop a parked car, the old sedan's hood warm beneath his paws despite the morning chill. He had the high ground now, a brief reprieve from the chaos unfolding below. His green eyes cut through the sea of humans hurrying about the town square, all frantically preparing for the Holiday Dog Show that would begin in less than five hours. His tail lashed once, twice. Still no sign of Lily.

From his elevated position, Goliath could see the pavilion where judges were setting up their tables. Workers strung garlands of twinkling lights across the bandstand. Volunteers arranged rows of chairs before the main stage. The whole town was caught in the frenzy of pre-show excitement, oblivious to the tension hanging over the day like a storm cloud.

Only hours ago, they had rescued Maximus from Sylvia's shed, but their triumph was short-lived. While Lily had rushed the Poodle to the vet for examination, Goliath had remained at the salon, keeping watch. That's when he'd overheard Tony and Sylvia outside, their hushed voices carrying through the mail slot.

"She can't prove anything," Sylvia had hissed. "It's our word against hers."

"Maximus recognized us," Tony had argued. "And that damn cat saw everything."

"A cat can't testify," Sylvia had retorted. "We stick to the plan. When Maximus doesn't show up for the competition, Evelyn will be disqualified. That's all that matters."

They didn't know Maximus had been rescued. And more importantly, they had a new scheme brewing—one that Goliath needed to uncover before it was too late.

The sound of an approaching vehicle caught his attention. Lily's ancient blue Subaru pulled into a parking spot near the square, and Goliath's hackles lowered slightly. She was back, finally. But she was alone. Where was Maximus?

Goliath leapt down from the car roof, narrowly avoiding a child who lunged for his tail. He darted across the square, weaving through the forest of human legs with practiced ease, and reached Lily just as she was locking her car.

"Goliath!" she exclaimed, bending to scratch behind his ears. "I've been looking everywhere for you."

He butted his head against her ankle, then looked pointedly back toward the square.

"The vet says Maximus will be fine," Lily said, as if reading his concern. "They sedated him, but there's no permanent damage. Dr. Rivera is keeping him for a few more hours just to be safe. Evelyn is with him."

Goliath meowed, an unusual vocalization for the normally stoic cat.

"I know," Lily continued, her voice dropping to a whisper. "We need evidence linking Tony and Sylvia to the kidnapping. The police won't pursue it without proof."

She bent lower, her voice barely audible. "I have a plan, but I need your help."

Goliath's ears perked forward as Lily outlined her strategy. They needed to get into Sylvia's office and find anything that might connect her to Maximus's abduction—receipts, notes, anything. And they needed to do it now, while Sylvia was busy helping set up her booth at the show.

"If we don't find evidence by noon," Lily said, "they'll get away with it. And I'm afraid they might try something else to keep Maximus from competing."

Goliath's tail flicked. He understood the stakes better than Lily knew.

Together, they made their way to Paws and Whiskers, Sylvia's upscale grooming salon. As expected, the shop was closed for the holiday show, but the lights in the back office remained on. Lily approached the rear entrance, the one used for deliveries, and tried the handle. Locked.

"Of course," she muttered, disappointed but not surprised.

Goliath nudged her leg, then trotted to a narrow window a few feet off the ground. The window was open a crack, likely to provide ventilation for the shop while it was closed. With a graceful leap, Goliath landed on the window ledge and pushed at the glass with his head, widening the gap.

"Brilliant," Lily whispered.

Goliath slipped inside, disappearing into the dimly lit interior. After a moment, Lily heard the click of the back door unlocking, and Goliath reappeared, looking quite pleased with himself.

"Remind me never to underestimate you," Lily said, easing the door open.

Inside, the salon smelled of expensive pet shampoos and designer scents—nothing like the homey, lived-in aroma of Lily's shop. Everything was sleek, modern, and sterile. They moved quietly to the office at the back, where a glass desk and ergonomic chair dominated the small space.

"Start looking," Lily said, as she began rifling through the desk drawers. "We need anything that connects them to Maximus."

Goliath leapt onto a shelf lined with binders and began nudging them with his nose, as if he understood exactly what they were searching for. One binder fell open onto the desk, revealing invoices for special supplies—including a sedative typically used for show dogs.

"Interesting," Lily murmured, snapping a photo with her phone. "But not conclusive."

They continued searching, the minutes ticking by with agonizing slowness. Lily found nothing of note in the desk, and was about to check the filing cabinet when Goliath let out a soft chirp—his version of "come look."

He had pushed open a cabinet door near the floor, revealing a small safe. The door of the safe was ajar, as if someone had recently accessed it and failed to secure it properly.

"What have we here?" Lily said, kneeling to investigate.

Inside the safe were several folders, a stack of cash, and a small leather notebook. Lily extracted the notebook and opened it, her eyes widening as she scanned the pages.

"Goliath, you're a genius," she breathed.

The notebook contained detailed notes about Maximus—his routine, his schedule, when he visited Lily's salon. There were even notes about which foods would most effectively mask the taste of sedatives. The final entry, dated just before Maximus went missing, read: "Transport arranged. T will provide the van."

"This is it," Lily said, snapping photos of each page. "This proves they planned it."

A noise from the front of the salon made them both freeze. The bell over the door jingled, followed by the sound of voices—Sylvia's distinctive tone, and another, deeper voice that could only be Tony's.

"They're back," Lily whispered, her face paling.

Goliath moved swiftly to the door, peering around the corner. Sylvia and Tony were in the reception area, arguing in hushed but intense tones.

"You said you took care of it," Sylvia was saying.

"I did," Tony replied. "But that blasted cat complicated things. And now the vet's involved."

"If Maximus competes, we're finished," Sylvia hissed. "Do you understand? Years of planning, down the drain."

Goliath darted back to Lily, who was frantically trying to replace everything exactly as they'd found it. He nudged her leg urgently, then made for the back door.

"Coming," she whispered, carefully closing the safe and the cabinet.

They slipped out the back door just as the voices grew louder, approaching the office. Lily pulled the door shut with excruciating slowness, wincing at the soft click of the latch.

Once outside, they didn't waste time. They moved quickly but calmly down the alley, trying not to draw attention. Only when they were a block away did Lily let out the breath she'd been holding.

"That was too close," she said, her voice shaking. "But we got what we needed."

Goliath meowed, his tail twitching anxiously.

"You're right," Lily agreed, as if they were having an actual conversation. "We need to get this to the police right away. And we need to make sure Maximus is safe for the show."

They hurried toward the police station, but as they rounded the corner of Main Street, they spotted Officer Reynolds climbing into his cruiser.

"Officer!" Lily called out, waving frantically.

Reynolds looked up, his expression shifting from surprise to mild annoyance. "Ms. Green. What can I do for you?"

"We have evidence," Lily said, breathless from running. "About Maximus's kidnapping."

Reynolds sighed. "We've been over this. The dog was found, no permanent harm done. Case closed."

"But it wasn't an accident," Lily insisted, holding up her phone. "I have proof that Sylvia Brightwell and Tony Blackwood planned the whole thing. Look."

The Purr-fect Suspect

Reynolds took the phone reluctantly, scrolling through the photos with growing interest. His eyebrows rose as he reached the final entries.

"Where did you get these?" he asked, his tone now professional, all traces of dismissal gone.

"From Sylvia's office," Lily admitted. "The safe was open, and—"

"So you broke in?" Reynolds interrupted, handing the phone back. "Ms. Green, that's illegal entry. This evidence is inadmissible."

Lily's face fell. "But they kidnapped Maximus! They drugged him! They're planning something else—I heard them!"

Reynolds held up a hand. "I understand you're upset, but I can't act on illegally obtained evidence." He softened slightly at Lily's crestfallen expression. "Look, keep an eye out at the show. If you see anything suspicious, call me directly. I'll be patrolling the area all day."

He handed her his card, then climbed into his cruiser and drove away, leaving Lily standing helplessly on the sidewalk.

"Unbelievable," she muttered.

Goliath meowed in what sounded remarkably like agreement.

Lily checked her watch. It was nearly 11:00 AM. The show would begin at 2:00 PM, with champions like Maximus scheduled to appear at 3:30 PM. Not much time to come up with a new plan.

"We need to warn Evelyn," Lily decided. "And we need to get to the vet's office to check on Maximus."

They made their way to Willow Creek Veterinary Clinic, a small but well-equipped facility on the edge of town. Inside, the waiting room was mercifully empty except for a woman with a cat carrier and an elderly man with a parrot.

The receptionist recognized Lily immediately. "Dr. Rivera is just finishing up with Maximus. Mrs. Kensington is with him."

"Can I join them? It's urgent," Lily said.

The receptionist nodded and buzzed her through to the exam rooms. Lily followed the corridor, Goliath trotting at her heels despite the "No Pets in Exam Areas" sign.

They found Evelyn in room three, watching as Dr. Rivera, a woman in her fifties with salt-and-pepper hair, checked Maximus's reflexes. The Poodle looked alert and much improved, his tail wagging as Lily entered.

"Lily," Evelyn acknowledged with a small nod. "Dr. Rivera says Maximus is recovering well."

"The sedative is completely out of his system," the vet confirmed. "He's in excellent health, all things considered. I see no reason why he can't compete today."

"That's fantastic," Lily said, relief washing over her. "But we may have a problem."

She quickly explained what she and Goliath had discovered—the notebook, the overheard conversation, Officer Reynolds's dismissal of their evidence.

Evelyn's face hardened with each word. "You're saying they're planning something else? To keep Maximus from competing?"

"That's what it sounded like," Lily confirmed. "Sylvia said, 'If Maximus competes, we're finished.'"

Dr. Rivera frowned. "I don't like the sound of that. Perhaps Maximus should skip the show, just to be safe."

"Absolutely not," Evelyn said firmly. "I will not let them win through intimidation. Maximus will compete, and he will win—fairly, as he always has."

She turned to Lily, her expression softening slightly. "Thank you for bringing this to my attention. I'll make sure Maximus is never left alone until after the show."

"What about the police?" Lily asked.

"Leave that to me," Evelyn said, a dangerous gleam in her eye. "I have friends on the town council, remember? One call from me, and Chief Davis will take this very seriously indeed."

Lily nodded, relieved to have Evelyn's support. "When will Maximus be released?"

"Right now," Dr. Rivera said, handing Evelyn the leash. "Just keep him calm, make sure he drinks plenty of water, and bring him back if you notice any unusual behavior."

"I will," Evelyn promised, taking the leash. "Thank you, Doctor."

They left the clinic together, Maximus walking tall and proud between them, seemingly unaffected by his ordeal. The Poodle noticed Goliath and paused, his tail wagging tentatively.

Evelyn watched with interest as Goliath approached Maximus. The cat circled the Poodle once, then sat directly in front of him, their eyes meeting. There was a moment of silent communication, then Goliath stood and began walking toward the show grounds, looking back as if expecting them to follow.

The Purr-fect Suspect

"Well," Evelyn said, raising an eyebrow. "It seems our escort is ready."

Lily smiled. "Goliath takes his responsibilities very seriously."

They made their way to the town square, where the Holiday Dog Show was now in full swing. The afternoon sun sparkled on fresh snow, and the air was filled with barking, laughter, and holiday music. Under different circumstances, it would have been a perfect scene.

But as they approached the registration table, Lily's anxiety returned. She scanned the crowd, spotting Sylvia by her booth, chatting with a group of admirers. Tony was nowhere to be seen.

"I'll get Maximus checked in," Evelyn said. "Keep an eye out for anything suspicious."

Lily nodded and knelt to address Goliath. "Stay with Maximus," she whispered. "Don't let him out of your sight."

Goliath blinked slowly, then positioned himself beside the Poodle, his posture alert and watchful.

As Evelyn led Maximus to the registration table, whispers rippled through the crowd. Everyone had heard about the champion's disappearance, and his return was causing quite a stir. Phones appeared, taking photos and videos.

Lily noticed Sylvia freeze mid-conversation, her face paling as she spotted Maximus. Their eyes met across the square, and Lily saw something flicker in Sylvia's expression—shock, then anger, then a cold determination that made Lily's blood run cold.

Sylvia excused herself from her admirers and slipped away, heading toward the parking area. Lily hesitated, torn between following Sylvia and staying near Maximus.

The decision was made for her when Goliath suddenly shot away from Maximus's side, darting through the crowd after Sylvia.

"Goliath!" Lily called, but the cat was already gone.

She turned to see Evelyn and Maximus surrounded by well-wishers, safely in the spotlight of public attention. Making a split-second decision, Lily plunged into the crowd, following Goliath's path.

She caught glimpses of his black and white coat as he wove between legs and obstacles, staying just within sight. The cat led her to the edge of the square, where the competitors' vans and grooming stations were set up.

There, partially hidden between two large vans, stood Sylvia and Tony, their heads bent together in urgent conversation. Lily ducked behind a nearby food cart, straining to hear.

"—can't believe they found him," Sylvia was saying. "This ruins everything."

"Not necessarily," Tony replied, his voice low and tense. "Plan B is already in motion."

"Are you sure it'll work? Richards wasn't exactly confident."

"It'll work," Tony assured her. "A few drops in his water before the show, and Maximus will be disqualified for erratic behavior. No one will connect it to us."

Lily's heart raced. They were planning to drug Maximus again, right before his competition time! She had to warn Evelyn.

She backed away slowly, careful not to make a sound. But as she turned to hurry back to the main square, she bumped into someone—Officer Reynolds.

"Ms. Green," he said, eyes narrowing. "What are you doing back here?"

"Officer," Lily whispered urgently. "They're going to drug Maximus. I just overheard them. We need to stop them!"

Reynolds looked past her to where Sylvia and Tony were still huddled in conversation. His expression shifted from skepticism to concern.

"Stay here," he ordered quietly. "Don't move."

He walked casually toward the pair, hand resting near his service weapon. "Ms. Brightwell, Mr. Blackwood," he called. "Mind if I have a word?"

Lily watched as they turned, startled by the officer's approach. What happened next unfolded with stunning speed.

Tony bolted, shoving past Reynolds and sprinting toward the parking lot. Sylvia tried to follow, but the officer caught her arm, holding her in place.

"Anthony Blackwood!" Reynolds bellowed. "Stop right there!"

Tony ignored the command, jumping into a waiting van. The engine roared to life, and the van lurched forward, narrowly missing a group of spectators as it sped away.

The Purr-fect Suspect

Reynolds spoke rapidly into his radio, calling for backup and giving a description of the fleeing van. Meanwhile, Sylvia struggled in his grip, her face contorted with fury.

"This is harassment!" she shouted. "I've done nothing wrong!"

"Then you won't mind emptying your pockets," Reynolds replied calmly.

Lily stepped forward, Goliath appearing at her side. The cat's eyes were fixed on Sylvia, his tail lashing with barely contained aggression.

"Check her right jacket pocket," Lily suggested. "That's where she put whatever they were talking about."

Reynolds did so, despite Sylvia's protests. From the pocket, he withdrew a small vial of clear liquid, unlabeled and suspicious.

"Care to explain what this is, Ms. Brightwell?" he asked.

Sylvia's defiance crumbled. "It's just water," she claimed weakly.

"We'll let the lab determine that," Reynolds said, securing the vial in an evidence bag. "In the meantime, I'm bringing you in for questioning regarding the kidnapping of Maximus Kensington and conspiracy to harm an animal."

As he led a protesting Sylvia away, Lily knelt and stroked Goliath's fur. "You did it," she whispered. "We did it."

The cat's purr rumbled like distant thunder—a rare sound from the stoic feline. He looked up at Lily with what she could have sworn was satisfaction, then stood and trotted back toward the main square, clearly expecting her to follow.

They returned to find Evelyn and Maximus still at the registration table, now surrounded by a small crowd of officials. Evelyn's face lit up when she spotted Lily.

"There you are!" she called. "What happened? You disappeared so suddenly."

Lily quickly explained the situation. Evelyn's expression darkened as she heard about Tony's escape and Sylvia's arrest.

"The nerve," she muttered. "To think they would stoop so low."

"Officer Reynolds has the vial they were going to use," Lily said. "And I think they'll find Tony soon enough."

Evelyn nodded, then her features softened into a genuine smile. "Thank you, Lily. For everything." She looked down at Goliath, who sat regally beside Maximus. "And thank you too, Detective Cat."

The head judge approached, clipboard in hand. "Mrs. Kensington? We're ready for Maximus's pre-show inspection."

"Of course," Evelyn said, straightening her shoulders. "Let's proceed."

As they walked toward the judging area, Evelyn leaned closer to Lily. "When this is all over, I want to talk to you about expanding your business. I think Willow Creek could use a permanent pet detective service, don't you?"

Lily's eyes widened in surprise, then she smiled, looking down at Goliath. "I think that's an excellent idea."

The cat's only response was a slow, deliberate blink—but somehow, it felt like the most enthusiastic endorsement in the world.

With just hours until Maximus was due to perform, they had uncovered a plot, prevented a disaster, and set in motion the wheels of justice. Not bad for a morning's work.

Now all that remained was for Maximus to win the Holiday Dog Show—a foregone conclusion, really. And after that? Well, Willow Creek's first pet detective agency awaited, and Lily had a feeling their adventures were just beginning.

Chapter 14

The Great Escape

Goliath sliced through the sea of legs like a shark in knee-high waves. The Holiday Dog Show churned with human and canine bodies, a roiling cauldron of barking, yapping, and overexcited squeals. The air crackled with the static of too much wool and too much ego. He hated every minute of it.

His green eyes darted left and right, scanning for a familiar human silhouette. Where was she? He paused, ears flicking, as a toddler with a Great Dane attempted to pat him on the head. The toddler cried; the Dane barked. Goliath glared them both into submission and moved on.

"Lulu! Heel, girl!" a woman in a Santa hat shrieked. A Corgi in reindeer antlers bolted past, almost toppling Goliath. He dug his claws into the carpet, cursing his luck. This was Lily's territory. He should be safe here, even if he had to endure the stench of wet dog and hot cocoa. But without Lily, he was just another stray, and time was ticking.

Near the agility course, he spotted a booth overflowing with gift baskets. Lily stood behind it, her curly brown hair frizzed with static, her smile as warm as an overbaked biscuit. Relief washed over him like catnip. He bounded toward her, tail up, just as a Border Collie intercepted him. A snarl, a hiss, and the Collie backed down, its owner none the wiser.

"Goliath!" Lily exclaimed, bending to scoop him up. "I was starting to worry."

He butted her chest with his head, a rare show of affection. She scratched behind his ears, and for a moment, he almost forgot the dire situation.

"Did you find him?" she asked, eyes wide with hope.

Goliath let out a plaintive meow. No, he hadn't found Maximus, but he'd found something else. Something that might lead them to him.

Lily's face fell. "We're running out of time. Mrs. Kensington will be here any minute, and if Maximus isn't—"

She didn't finish the sentence. She didn't have to. Goliath knew what was at stake. The Holiday Dog Show was the biggest event of the year for Willow Creek's pet community. Maximus was the reigning champion, and his sudden disappearance threatened more than just his title. It threatened the fragile alliances that held their small town together.

Lily set Goliath down and grabbed her coat. "We have to go to Hilda's. It's the only lead we've got."

Goliath's tail twitched. He wasn't fond of Hilda or her horde of yappy little mutts, but he knew Lily was right. If they didn't find Maximus soon, all paws would point to them.

"Come on," Lily said, starting for the exit. "We'll be back before the opening ceremony."

Goliath trotted after her, casting one last glance at the chaos of the dog show. He preferred the quiet danger of the streets to this madhouse. At least in the alleyways, he knew who his enemies were.

They pushed through the double doors and into the crisp December air. Snowflakes drifted lazily from a leaden sky, muting the world in a soft, white hush. Goliath took a deep breath, savoring the cold. His fur was thick enough to handle winter's bite, unlike the parade of shivering lapdogs now clogging the parking lot.

Lily fumbled with her keys, then stopped. "Maybe we shouldn't drive. It's only a few blocks, and the streets are slick."

Goliath looked up at her, his whiskers already frosting over. She was stalling, and he knew why. Confronting Hilda was a risky move. The old woman had a temper, and worse, she had connections. If they accused her and were wrong...

"Let's walk," Lily said, stuffing the keys back in her purse. "It'll give us time to think."

She started down the sidewalk, and Goliath followed, his paws leaving tiny, precise prints in the fresh snow. He hoped she was right. He hoped they had enough time to think their way out of this. Because if they didn't, the next set of prints in the snow might be a trail leading straight to the pound.

The streets of Willow Creek were a different world from the dog show. Snow muffled the sounds of the small town, creating an almost eerie silence. Christmas lights twinkled from eaves and porches, their colors subdued by the thickening storm. Goliath padded ahead of Lily, his acute senses on high alert. The quiet should have been comforting, but it only served to amplify the tension.

He thought back to the last time they'd been in such a predicament. It wasn't even six months ago that they'd solved the mystery of the missing catnip stash. That had been child's play compared to this. A kidnapped champion, a ticking clock, and the very real possibility of ruining Lily's reputation. This was a different league.

Lily had been his savior, taking him in when no one else would. She understood him in a way that no human should be able to understand a cat. That's why he went along with her crazy schemes, why he put up with the dogs, why he stayed. She was more than his human; she was his partner. And right now, his partner was in over her head.

They turned onto Maple Street, where the snow lay in pristine drifts, unspoiled by tire tracks or footprints. Goliath's thoughts drifted to Maximus. The big Golden Retriever was a pompous fool, but he didn't deserve this. Who stood to gain from his disappearance? That was the question gnawing at Goliath. If they could answer that, they'd have their culprit.

The Victorian loomed ahead, its pastel paintwork incongruous against the gray sky. Goliath paused at the gate, his fur bristling. Lily stopped beside him, biting her lip.

"We have to be careful," she said, as if Goliath needed reminding. "If Hilda had anything to do with it, we can't just accuse her outright."

Goliath flicked his tail. He knew the stakes. Hilda Sorensen was a fixture in the community, as untouchable as the town's oldest oak. They needed evidence, not just suspicions.

Lily took a deep breath and opened the gate. It squealed on its hinges, loud in the winter stillness. Goliath's ears flattened. He hated this house, with its gaudy yard ornaments and perpetual smell of kibble. Every visit was a test of his limited patience.

They walked up the shoveled path to the front porch. Lily's steps were slow, measured. Goliath could hear her heart pounding, could almost feel the adrenaline coursing through her. This was it. If Hilda didn't have answers, they were sunk.

Lily raised a hand to the doorbell, then hesitated. Goliath stared up at her, willing her to be strong. She had to do this. They had to know.

The doorbell chimed, its notes discordant and shrill. Lily flinched, then took a step back, wringing her hands. Goliath sat and curled his tail around his paws, the picture of feline calm. Inside, he was as anxious as she was.

The door opened a crack, then wider. Hilda stood in the entrance, a tall, angular woman with iron-gray hair and piercing blue eyes. She wore a Christmas apron over a plaid shirt, the kind a lumberjack might fancy. In one hand, she held a wooden spoon.

"Lily," Hilda said, her voice a tight coil of surprise. "And Goliath. What brings you here?"

Lily opened her mouth, closed it, then opened it again. "Hilda, we need to talk. It's about Maximus."

Hilda's eyes narrowed. The rest of her face remained a mask of polite curiosity, but Goliath could see the tension in her knuckles, the way they whitened around the spoon's handle.

"Oh?" Hilda said. "Has something happened to him?"

Lily took a deep breath. "He's missing. We thought you might know something."

The two women stared each other down, the silence stretching and straining like an old piece of taffy. Goliath's muscles tensed, ready to spring. He could almost taste the confrontation.

The Victorian loomed ahead, its pastel paintwork incongruous against the gray sky. Goliath paused at the gate, his fur bristling. Lily stopped beside him, biting her lip.

Lily wiped a trickle of sweat from her forehead. "We just want to make sure he's okay. You know how much Mrs. Kensington loves that dog."

Hilda's lips thinned, the corners tugging downward. "Mrs. Kensington loves herself. The dog is just an accessory."

Lily took a step back, eyes flicking to Goliath. He could see the wheels turning in her head, the calculations, the second-guessing. This was information, but was it useful? Was it true? He hoped she was smart enough to play along.

"Hilda," Lily said, her tone softer now, almost conciliatory. "We understand that there are... tensions. But taking Maximus won't solve anything."

Hilda barked a laugh, a single, sharp note. "You think I took him? Don't be ridiculous. I have no need for that mutt."

The three of them stood in a triangle of silence, each waiting for the other to make the next move. Goliath's eyes shifted from Hilda to Lily and back again. He could smell the conflict, the fear, the defiance. Humans were such volatile creatures.

"Perhaps," Lily said slowly, "but it would explain why his tracking chip led us here."

Goliath almost purred with pride. It was a lie, but a clever one. He hadn't known why Lily had dragged him to Hilda's, but now it made sense. She was betting on the old woman's guilt, on her cracking under pressure. It was a long shot, but it was all they had.

Hilda's shoulders tightened, then slumped. The change was subtle, but Goliath noticed. She was caving.

"The chip..." Hilda muttered, more to herself than to them. "Damn technology."

Lily waited, poised on the balls of her feet. Even Goliath held his breath.

"I was going to return him," Hilda said at last. "After the show."

Lily's eyes widened with triumph, then quickly tempered to caution. "Why, Hilda? Why take him in the first place?"

Hilda waved the wooden spoon in a dismissive arc. "To make a point. Mrs. Kensington needs to learn that she can't buy her way out of everything. That dog is her ticket to more sponsorships, more recognition. She doesn't care about the community, Lily. She doesn't care about us."

Goliath watched as Lily processed this new information. He could almost see the speech bubble forming above her head, the words stacking and unstacking themselves in different configurations. This was the moment. Whatever she said next would either defuse the situation or light the fuse.

"We get it now," Lily said, choosing her words with the care of a bomb technician. "But taking Maximus just puts him in the middle of something he doesn't understand. It's not fair to him, or to Mrs. Kensington, no matter how you feel about her."

Hilda's eyes softened, the blue fading to a washed-out gray. "Life isn't fair, Lily. You of all people should know that."

The two women stood down, their stances less combative, more resigned. Goliath saw his chance and took it. With the grace of a shadow, he slipped between Hilda's legs and into the house.

The interior was as he remembered: cluttered, yet homely. A fire crackled in the hearth, and the scent of baking filled the air. He moved quickly, silently, his paws absorbing the warmth of the wooden floor. Hilda's pack of small dogs was conspicuously absent; perhaps she'd banished them to the yard. Goliath was grateful for the reprieve.

He rounded a corner and came to a halt. A large kennel sat in the middle of the kitchen, a plaid blanket draped over its top. Goliath crept closer, ears pricked, whiskers twitching. He could hear breathing—slow, steady, and deep. With a tentative paw, he swatted at the blanket, pulling it back just enough to peek inside.

Maximus lay curled in the kennel, his golden fur dull in the low light. He looked up as Goliath's eyes met his, and a flicker of recognition sparked in the Retriever's tired gaze.

"Maximus," Goliath whispered, though he knew the dog couldn't understand him. "We're here to get you out."

The big dog stretched and yawned, then rose to his feet with the lethargy of an old man. Goliath inspected the kennel's door; it wasn't even locked. He nudged it with his nose, and it swung open with a creak.

"Come on," Goliath said, stepping back. "We don't have much time."

Maximus padded out of the kennel and shook himself, his fur fluffing up like a poorly made bed. He looked around the kitchen, then back to Goliath, as if unsure what to do next.

"Don't just stand there," Goliath hissed. "Follow me."

They moved toward the hallway, Maximus walking with the slow grace of a draft horse. Goliath's mind raced. How were they going to get the big oaf out without Hilda noticing? He hoped Lily could stall her long enough for them to make a plan.

As they reached the front of the house, Goliath peeked around the corner. Hilda and Lily were still on the porch, the door half-closed. He could hear Hilda's voice, softer now, almost pleading.

The Purr-fect Suspect

"I'm sorry, Lily. I just wanted her to understand."

Lily didn't respond. Goliath imagined her nodding, her mind already back at the dog show, at the next crisis. She was good at this, at managing people. He wasn't sure he could say the same about managing her.

Goliath signaled to Maximus with a flick of his tail. They crept to the door, staying low, every movement a calculated risk. If Hilda saw them now, it could all unravel.

"I'll let you finish your baking," Lily said, taking a step back from the door. "Thanks for being honest, Hilda."

Hilda sighed. "Take him, then. And good luck."

Lily turned as if to leave, then paused. "One more thing—"

Goliath's heart sank. They'd been so close. He braced himself for whatever bombshell Lily was about to drop.

"—do you have any spare ribbons? We've run out at the booth."

Hilda raised an eyebrow, then shrugged. "In the craft room. Take as many as you need."

With that, Hilda retreated into the house, leaving Lily standing alone on the porch. Goliath pushed the door open just as Lily reached for the handle. She looked down at him, then at Maximus, and her face lit with a mix of surprise and relief.

"Hurry," she whispered. "She'll be a minute."

Maximus squeezed through the doorway, his large frame awkward and ungainly. Goliath slipped out after him, and the three of them stood in the cold, unsure of their next move.

"Lily," came Hilda's voice from deeper in the house. "Don't forget your ribbons."

Lily bit her lip, then nodded to Goliath. "Go. I'll cover you."

Goliath didn't like the idea of splitting up, but he saw no other choice. He nudged Maximus, and the two dogs started down the porch steps.

"Be quick," Lily added, then opened the front door just enough to slip back inside.

Goliath led Maximus to the gate, his mind racing with possibilities. How were they going to get Maximus back to the show without a car and in this weather? And what if Hilda changed her mind and—

The front door opened, and Goliath's head snapped around. Hilda stood in the doorway, a bundle of ribbons in her hand. Lily was behind her, eyes locked on Goliath. He could see her willing him to run, to take Maximus and flee.

But he didn't move. He couldn't leave without her.

Hilda's gaze shifted to the porch, then to the yard, and finally to the sidewalk where Maximus stood, his golden coat now speckled with snow. An unreadable expression crossed her face, a mix of sadness and something else. Acceptance, perhaps.

"Lily," Hilda said, turning back to her. "You forgot these."

She handed the ribbons to Lily, then closed the door.

Lily rushed out, her movements hurried and tense. "Come on, we need to go now."

Goliath and Maximus followed her down the street, their pace quick despite the slippery conditions. Goliath kept looking back, half-expecting to see Hilda running after them, but the Victorian remained still, a pastel ghost in the snowy landscape.

They reached the corner, and Lily stopped. "We can't take him back yet. If Mrs. Kensington sees him and calls the police—"

Goliath interrupted with a low growl. He knew she was right, but the thought of delaying even longer was unbearable.

"—she'll find out we took him from Hilda without permission. We need her to believe that we just found him."

Maximus whined, and Goliath swatted him with a paw. "Quiet, you. We're trying to save your hide."

Lily looked around, her eyes searching for something. "We need a place to stash him, just for a little while. Somewhere safe."

Goliath thought hard. Most of the town's businesses were closed for the holidays, and the streets were too exposed. They needed a hideout, a temporary refuge where they could regroup and make a plan.

Then it came to him. The old library.

He darted ahead, barking once to get Lily's attention. She hesitated, then followed, calling after him. "Goliath, where are you—"

But he was already rounding the next corner, his paws slipping on the icy road. The library had been abandoned for years, ever since the new one opened on Main Street. It was a favorite haunt of Goliath's, a place where he could escape the noise of Lily's life. Few people ventured there, and it was perfect for their needs.

The Purr-fect Suspect

They arrived at the library's entrance, a grand set of stone steps now buried in snow. Lily was panting, Maximus lagging behind her.

"Here?" she asked, incredulous. "How do you even—"

Goliath didn't wait for her to finish. He bounded up the steps and squeezed through a broken window, landing softly on the other side. The interior was just as he remembered: rows of empty shelves, a thick layer of dust, and the faintest smell of mildew. He circled to the front door and stood on his hind legs, peering through the glass.

Lily's face appeared, her cheeks red from the cold. "Can you open it?"

Goliath dropped down and examined the door's lock. It was rusted and loose, more ornamental than functional. He stretched up, dug his claws into the metal, and twisted. With a groan, the lock gave way, and the door creaked open.

Lily and Maximus hurried inside, bringing a gust of cold air with them. Lily brushed snow from her hair and looked around. "I can't believe this place is still standing."

She removed Maximus's leash and set it in her purse. "Okay, this buys us some time. Now we just need to figure out how to get him back without—"

A loud bang interrupted her, echoing through the empty building. All three heads turned toward the source: the front door, now shut tight.

Lily ran to it and pulled on the handle. It didn't budge. She tugged harder, then looked through the glass. "Oh no."

Goliath joined her, standing on his hind legs to see outside. A large piece of debris, perhaps a chunk of ice or a fallen tree limb, lay against the door, barricading them in.

"We're trapped," Lily said, her voice sinking. "How are we going to—"

Goliath dropped to all fours and surveyed the room. The broken window he'd come through was too small for Maximus, and the rest of the building was solid stone and brick. They were stuck, at least until someone cleared the door.

Lily slumped against a shelf, sliding down to sit on the floor. "This is a disaster."

Maximus walked over to her and nuzzled her hand. She stroked his head, then looked at Goliath. "I'm sorry. I thought we could handle this."

Goliath trotted over to her and sat, his tail wrapping around his paws. He didn't blame her for any of it. They'd done their best with the limited time and information they had. But now, it seemed, their luck had run out.

Lily sighed and closed her eyes. "Maybe we just need to wait. The snowplow will come through eventually."

Silence settled over them, heavy and oppressive. Goliath's mind raced, trying to think of a way out, a Plan B, anything. He looked at Maximus, who had lain down beside Lily, his eyes half-closed in weary contentment. The big dog trusted them, believed they would save him. That kind of faith was alien to Goliath, but he understood its power.

He rose and walked to the door, peering through the glass again. The snow was falling harder now, driven by a rising wind. It swirled and eddied in the street, creating miniature tornadoes of white. He thought of the dog show, of the warm, chaotic crush of bodies. He even thought of the toddler and the Great Dane. As much as he hated that environment, it was preferable to this cold, empty stillness.

A sound caught his ear, faint but growing. He strained to listen, his heart quickening. It was a motor, accompanied by the crunch of snow.

He turned and ran to Lily, pawing at her leg. "Wake up! Someone's coming!"

Lily opened her eyes, dazed. "What?"

"The plow! It's here!"

She jumped to her feet and ran to the door, waving her arms. "Hey! Over here!"

Goliath joined her, standing on his hind legs again, his front paws tapping the glass. A large snowplow came into view, its yellow lights flashing, its blade sending arcs of snow onto sidewalks and yards. It approached slowly, the driver hunched over the wheel.

"Stop!" Lily shouted. "We're stuck!"

The plow came to a halt, and the driver looked down at them, confused. Lily pointed to the debris blocking the door. The driver nodded, then maneuvered the plow with deliberate care, angling the blade to push the obstruction aside.

The door rattled, and Goliath jumped back, landing on all fours. Lily tried the handle, and the door swung open, letting in a blast of frigid air. She turned to the driver and shouted her thanks, then looked down at Goliath.

"We're not out of the woods yet, but at least we have a chance now."

She stepped outside, and Goliath hesitated. The warmth of the old library called to him, but he knew they couldn't stay. Not if they wanted to save Maximus and themselves.

Lily held the door open, waiting. "Come on, Goliath. We need you."

With a reluctant flick of his tail, Goliath stepped into the cold. Lily closed the door behind them, and they started down the steps. Maximus followed, his movements slow and stiff from the unaccustomed rest.

The wind had picked up, driving snowflakes with the force of tiny needles. Goliath squinted against the blizzard, his thoughts a jumbled mess of hope and dread. They had a long way to go, and the clock was still ticking.

As they reached the bottom of the steps, Lily put a hand on Goliath's back. "Thank you," she said, her voice almost lost in the wind. "For everything."

He looked up at her, his green eyes meeting her brown. She was more than his partner. She was his family. And he would do whatever it took to protect her.

Even if it meant braving the storm.

"Goliath!" Lily's voice cut through the howling wind. "We need to move, now!"

Goliath turned to see Hilda standing in the doorway, her hands empty, her eyes burning with a desperate intensity. Lily held Maximus's leash, the big dog ready to bolt.

"You can't just take him!" Hilda shouted. "I'll tell them everything!"

Lily hesitated, and Goliath's heart sank. He sprinted back to her, snow spraying from his paws, and leaped up, swatting her hand with his. She looked down at him, conflicted, then back to Hilda.

"We'll take our chances," Lily said, her voice firm.

With that, she started to run, dragging Maximus behind her. Goliath kept pace, his muscles burning from the cold. He glanced back to see Hilda step onto the porch, then stop, her shoulders sagging. She wasn't going to chase them. Not in this weather.

They rounded a corner, and Lily slowed to a walk. "I can't believe we got out of there."

Goliath panted, his breath forming clouds of vapor. They weren't safe yet, but he shared her relief. For now.

The streets were nearly impassable, with snowdrifts forming in the wake of the plow. Goliath's paws were numb, and he could see Lily starting to shiver. Maximus, for his part, seemed to be gaining strength, his thick coat giving him an advantage over the humans.

"We need to think," Lily said, her teeth chattering. "If we take him back now, and Mrs. Kensington—"

Goliath growled. They didn't have time to think. The opening ceremony was in less than an hour, and if Maximus wasn't there...

Lily stopped and looked down at Goliath. "What do you think we should do?"

He stared up at her, incredulous. She was the human; she was supposed to have the answers. But in this moment, he realized she was as lost as he was. As lost as they all were.

"Fine," she said, interpreting his silence. "We'll take him back. But we need a story. Something believable."

They started walking again, slower this time. Goliath's mind raced, trying to concoct a tale that would satisfy Mrs. Kensington and keep them out of trouble. Nothing seemed plausible. Nothing seemed enough.

As they neared the town square, the sound of the dog show grew louder. The distant barks and human chatter mixed with the wind, creating a dissonant symphony. Goliath's ears perked; he could almost make out words.

Lily rubbed her hands together, then blew on them. "Maybe we say that we found him wandering. That we were bringing him back when the storm hit."

It was a weak story, but it had the ring of truth. Goliath nodded, or at least made a motion that could be interpreted as such.

They crossed onto Elm Street, the showgrounds now visible through a veil of snow. Large tents and booths created a makeshift village in the park, and a tall Christmas tree stood in the center, its ornaments sparkling like stolen jewels.

Lily stopped again. "Wait."

Goliath turned, his body protesting the pause. They were so close.

"If we just walk in with him," Lily said, thinking out loud, "it'll look suspicious. We need to make it seem like... like a big reveal."

Goliath's tail twitched. He understood what she was getting at. Perception was everything in this town. If they could stage Maximus's return in a way that deflected scrutiny...

Lily knelt down and unhooked Maximus's leash. "You got that, big guy? You need to make an entrance."

Maximus wagged his tail, the motion starting at his hips and working its way up his spine. He looked ready, even eager.

"Come on," Lily said, leading them toward the park. "We'll watch from the side."

They navigated through the crowd, which had grown thicker despite the weather. Goliath stayed close to Lily, his eyes scanning for familiar faces. He spotted Mrs. Kensington near a hot cocoa stand, her trademark red beret bobbing above the throng. She was alone, and Goliath wondered how she'd reacted when she found Maximus missing.

Lily stopped at the edge of the main lawn, where a small stage had been set up. A man with a microphone was making announcements, his voice crackling through speakers. Goliath looked up at Lily, and she down at him. This was it.

"Go, Maximus," Lily whispered.

The Golden Retriever trotted forward, his movements confident and regal. He weaved through the crowd with the ease of a true champion, his head held high. Goliath watched as people began to notice him, their eyes widening, their mouths forming O's of surprise.

"Is that—?" someone said.

"Maximus!" another voice called out.

The crowd's attention shifted and swirled, creating a vortex around the big dog. Goliath held his breath, waiting for the inevitable explosion of recognition.

"Maximus!" Mrs. Kensington shrieked, her voice piercing the air like a dog whistle. She ran toward him, her beret flying off in the rush. "Oh, my darling boy!"

The crowd parted for her, then closed in, forming a tight circle around Maximus and his owner. Goliath could see her through the crush of bodies, could see the tears streaking her makeup as she hugged the dog.

Lily put a hand to her mouth, and Goliath wondered if she was crying too. He hoped not. He didn't know how to comfort a crying human.

The man with the microphone spoke again. "Ladies and gentlemen, it looks like our champion has returned just in time!"

The crowd's gasps and murmurs formed a disbelieving chorus. Cameras flashed, and someone started to applaud. Goliath looked up at Lily, and for the first time, he allowed himself to believe that they might actually pull this off.

Chapter 15

Showdown at the Holiday Dog Show

The Holiday Dog Show's final day dawned crisp and bright, the morning sun glinting off fresh snow that blanketed Willow Creek. The town square had been transformed overnight into a winter wonderland, with red and green ribbons adorning every lamppost and a massive Christmas tree standing sentinel at the center. Banners announcing "Willow Creek's 25th Annual Holiday Dog Show" fluttered in the gentle breeze.

Lily stood at the edge of the square, watching as vendors set up their booths and contestants arrived with their precious cargo. The air hummed with excitement and anticipation—and underlying it all, a current of tension that only she, Goliath, and a handful of others could truly feel.

"There you are," said a voice behind her. Lily turned to see Evelyn Kensington approaching, Maximus trotting regally at her side. The Poodle's coat gleamed in the sunlight, a testament to Lily's grooming skills and his natural beauty.

"Evelyn," Lily greeted with a smile. "Maximus looks wonderful."

"Thanks to you," Evelyn said, adjusting her cashmere scarf. "Both for the grooming and... everything else."

The "everything else" hung between them—the rescue, the evidence gathering, the arrests. Tony Blackwood had been apprehended late yesterday trying to flee town. He and Sylvia Brightwell now sat in adjacent cells at the Willow Creek Police Department, each blaming the other for the plot to kidnap Maximus and sabotage his chances at the show.

"Has there been any word from the police?" Lily asked, keeping her voice low.

Evelyn's perfectly manicured hand stroked Maximus's head. "They're still building their case. Officer Reynolds says they're trying to connect the dots on some other suspicious incidents at past shows."

"Other incidents?" Lily asked, surprised.

"Apparently, several champions have suffered mysterious 'accidents' before competing against Sylvia or Tony over the years," Evelyn said with a frown. "Nothing as brazen as kidnapping, but enough to raise eyebrows in retrospect."

Goliath, who had been sitting silently at Lily's feet, looked up with interest. His tail twitched once, a sign that Lily had come to recognize as his "I told you so" gesture.

"I'm just glad it's over," Lily said. "And that you and Maximus can enjoy the show without looking over your shoulders."

Evelyn's lips curved into a smile that didn't quite reach her eyes. "I wouldn't be so sure it's over," she said quietly. "These types of people... they have friends."

Before Lily could respond, the show's announcer called for all participants to begin check-in. Evelyn gave Lily's arm a gentle squeeze. "We should get going. Maximus's category is first up after lunch."

"I'll be watching," Lily promised. "Good luck, though you hardly need it."

As Evelyn and Maximus made their way to the registration table, Lily felt a presence beside her. She looked down to see Mrs. Whiskers, bundled in a purple wool coat and matching hat, her eyes twinkling with mischief.

"The conquering heroes," Mrs. Whiskers said, her voice scratchy but warm. "Well done, you two."

Lily smiled at the elderly librarian. "We had a lot of help. You were the one who pointed us to Sylvia's old storage shed."

"Pish posh," Mrs. Whiskers waved a gloved hand dismissively. "I merely mentioned it in passing. You and that magnificent beast did all the heavy lifting." She nodded at Goliath, who blinked slowly in acknowledgment.

"Either way, we're grateful," Lily said. "Are you staying for the whole show?"

The Purr-fect Suspect

"Wouldn't miss it for the world," Mrs. Whiskers declared. "Not after all the excitement. Besides, I placed a rather sizable bet on our boy Maximus in the office pool."

Lily laughed, the sound carrying across the square and drawing a few curious glances. It felt good to laugh, to release some of the tension that had built up over the past week. With Maximus safely returned and the culprits in custody, she could finally relax and enjoy the event she'd been looking forward to all year.

Or so she thought.

As the morning progressed, Lily mingled with friends and clients, accepting their congratulations on her role in Maximus's safe return. Goliath stayed close, unusually attentive to the crowd around them. His green eyes scanned constantly, his ears swiveling to catch snippets of conversation.

Around eleven, as Lily was chatting with the owner of a spirited Corgi, Goliath suddenly stiffened. His tail puffed to twice its size, and a low growl rumbled in his chest.

"Goliath?" Lily looked down, alarmed. "What's wrong?"

The cat's gaze was fixed on a figure moving through the crowd—a tall woman in a camel coat and sunglasses, her blonde hair pulled back in a sleek ponytail. Lily didn't recognize her, but Goliath clearly did, and his reaction was troubling.

"Excuse me," Lily said to the Corgi owner, then followed Goliath as he began to weave through the crowd, tracking the mysterious woman.

They trailed her to the edge of the square, where she approached a man standing beside a van with "Bright Futures Pet Supplies" emblazoned on its side. The man—stocky, with a neatly trimmed beard—handed the woman a small paper bag. She slipped it into her coat pocket, nodded once, and turned to head back toward the show.

Goliath's growl deepened. Lily touched his back gently, trying to soothe him. "Who is she?" she whispered.

The cat looked up at her, frustration evident in his intelligent eyes. How could he tell her what he knew? That the woman was Margot Devereux, Sylvia's sister and business partner in ventures beyond the pet spa. That she had been present during planning sessions for Maximus's abduction, though she'd stayed carefully in the shadows. That whatever was in that paper bag spelled trouble for Maximus and Evelyn.

Lily straightened, decision made. "Let's follow her," she said softly.

They kept a careful distance as the woman in the camel coat—Margot, though Lily didn't know that yet—made her way through the crowd toward the competitors' area. She moved with purpose, her stride confident and unhurried.

Lily checked her watch. Almost noon. The champions would be gathering for final preparations before the afternoon competitions. Maximus would be there, with Evelyn and the other top dogs.

"We need to hurry," Lily said to Goliath, picking up her pace.

They reached the competitors' tent just as Margot slipped inside. Lily hesitated at the entrance, unsure of her next move. As a groomer, she had every right to be there, but following someone based solely on Goliath's suspicion seemed reckless.

Her moment of indecision ended when she heard a commotion from inside the tent—voices raised in alarm, the sound of something falling, a dog's startled yelp.

Lily rushed in, Goliath at her heels. The scene before her was one of controlled chaos. Several handlers were gathering around a water station, where paper cups and a large dispenser lay toppled on the ground. Water pooled on the floor, soaking the canvas.

"What happened?" Lily asked the nearest person, a man with a Dalmatian.

"Someone knocked over the water," he replied, shrugging. "Clumsy, if you ask me."

Lily scanned the tent for the woman in the camel coat but saw no sign of her. She had vanished as quickly as she had appeared.

"Has anyone seen Evelyn and Maximus?" Lily asked, a knot forming in her stomach.

"They were just here," the Dalmatian's owner said. "Probably stepped out for a last-minute touch-up."

Goliath meowed loudly, drawing Lily's attention. He was standing near the water dispenser, pawing at something on the ground. Lily moved closer and saw it—a small, empty glass vial, barely visible among the puddles.

She picked it up carefully, holding it by the edges. There was no label, but a faint, medicinal smell lingered around the rim.

"Oh no," she whispered.

Someone had tampered with the water—the water all the champion dogs would drink before their competition. Including Maximus.

Lily and Goliath burst from the tent, frantically searching the crowd for any sign of Evelyn or Maximus. The announcer's voice boomed over the loudspeakers, calling all championship contenders to the main ring in fifteen minutes.

"We need to find them," Lily said, her voice tight with urgency. "Before Maximus drinks anything."

They circled the main area, weaving through clusters of spectators and participants. Lily's height gave her an advantage, allowing her to see over many in the crowd, but there was no sign of Evelyn's distinctive silver chignon or Maximus's pure white coat.

Just as Lily was about to head toward the judging area, Goliath darted away, squeezing between legs and under chairs with surprising speed. Lily tried to follow but quickly lost sight of him in the dense crowd.

"Excuse me," she said repeatedly, pushing past people with as much politeness as panic allowed. "Sorry, coming through."

She emerged on the other side of the square, near the refreshment booths. There, seated at a small table, were Evelyn and Maximus. A paper cup sat on the table in front of them, and Evelyn was reaching for it.

"Evelyn, no!" Lily shouted, running toward them.

Evelyn looked up, startled, as Lily reached the table and knocked the cup away. Water splashed across the cobblestones.

"Lily! What on earth—"

"The water," Lily gasped, trying to catch her breath. "It's been tampered with. Someone put something in it."

Evelyn's face paled. "Are you certain?"

Lily nodded, pulling the empty vial from her pocket. "I found this by the water dispenser in the competitors' tent. And Goliath... he sensed something was wrong."

Goliath sat beside the table, his posture alert, eyes scanning the area.

"We need to tell the judges," Evelyn said, standing. "The show can't proceed if someone is sabotaging the competitors."

"First, we need to make sure you and Maximus are safe," Lily insisted. "Whoever did this might still be watching."

As if summoned by her words, the woman in the camel coat appeared at the edge of the refreshment area. She removed her sunglasses, and Lily was struck by the resemblance to Sylvia—the same sharp cheekbones, the same cold, calculating eyes.

"That's her," Lily whispered. "The woman Goliath and I followed. She was given a package just before the water was knocked over."

Evelyn followed Lily's gaze. "Margot Devereux," she said softly. "Sylvia's sister. I should have known she'd be involved."

"We need to call Officer Reynolds," Lily said, reaching for her phone.

"No need," came a voice from behind them. They turned to see Reynolds himself, in uniform, approaching with purposeful strides. "I've been keeping an eye on things, as promised."

"Officer," Lily said, relief flooding her voice. "Thank goodness. Someone's tampered with the water for the champion dogs. I believe it was that woman over there—Margot Devereux."

Reynolds followed her pointing finger, his expression hardening. "I know Ms. Devereux. She's been under unofficial surveillance since her sister's arrest." He took the empty vial from Lily. "I'll have this analyzed immediately. In the meantime, I'll have my officers secure all refreshments and water stations."

"What about the show?" Evelyn asked. "It's supposed to start in minutes."

"I'll speak with the organizers," Reynolds said. "We may need to delay the championship round while we investigate."

He moved away, speaking quietly into his radio as he approached Margot Devereux. Lily watched as Reynolds showed her his badge, and Margot's face cycled through shock, indignation, and finally, a resigned sort of defiance.

"It looks like they've got her," Lily said, turning back to Evelyn. "Are you alright?"

Evelyn nodded, though her hand trembled slightly as she stroked Maximus's head. "We're fine. Maximus didn't drink anything, thanks to you and Goliath."

The Poodle seemed blissfully unaware of how close he'd come to another sabotage attempt. He sat regally at Evelyn's feet, occasionally glancing at Goliath with what almost seemed like respect.

The Purr-fect Suspect

A hush fell over the crowd as the announcer's voice came over the loudspeakers once more. "Ladies and gentlemen, we regret to inform you that the championship round will be delayed by one hour due to unforeseen circumstances. We appreciate your patience and understanding."

Murmurs rippled through the gathered spectators, curiosity and concern evident on faces throughout the square.

"It seems your detective work has caused quite a stir," Evelyn said, a small smile playing at her lips.

"Our detective work," Lily corrected, looking down at Goliath. "I never would have suspected anything if not for him."

Goliath, typically immune to praise, seemed to stand a little taller at her words. His tail curled up in a rare display of satisfaction.

The next hour passed in a blur of police activity. Officer Reynolds coordinated with the show organizers, ensuring that all water sources were secured and tested. Margot Devereux was escorted from the premises in handcuffs, her expression a mask of cold fury. Several of her associates, including the man from the van, were also detained for questioning.

By the time the championship round was cleared to begin, the entire town of Willow Creek was buzzing with rumors and speculation. The story of Lily and Goliath's heroic intervention had spread like wildfire, and many in the crowd greeted them with smiles and thumbs-up as they made their way to the viewing area.

"You two are becoming quite the celebrities," Mrs. Whiskers said, making room for Lily on the bench beside her. Goliath jumped up between them, his tail flicking with impatience as the judges took their places.

The first competitor, a magnificent Golden Retriever, entered the ring to enthusiastic applause. The dog moved with grace and precision, its coat shimmering in the afternoon sun. Two more followed—a statuesque German Shepherd and an elegant Borzoi—each impressive in their own right.

Then it was Maximus's turn.

A hush fell over the crowd as Evelyn led the champion Poodle into the ring. Maximus walked with the confidence of a dog who knew his worth, his head held high, his steps measured and perfect. Despite everything he had endured—the kidnapping, the sedation, the attempted sabotage—he showed no sign of stress or fear.

"Would you look at that," Mrs. Whiskers whispered, her voice full of admiration. "Born to win, that one."

Lily couldn't help but agree. Maximus was simply magnificent. Her eyes filled with unexpected tears as she watched him complete his circuit of the ring, executing each command from Evelyn with flawless precision.

"He's going to win," she said softly.

"Of course he is," Mrs. Whiskers replied, patting Lily's hand. "Was there ever any doubt?"

The judges conferred, their heads bent together in serious discussion. Then the head judge stepped forward, microphone in hand, and the crowd leaned forward in anticipation.

"Ladies and gentlemen, it is my honor to announce the winner of the championship round of the 25th Annual Willow Creek Holiday Dog Show," he said, his voice echoing across the square. "This year's champion is... Maximus!"

The crowd erupted in cheers and applause. Evelyn beamed with pride as she accepted the trophy, a magnificent silver cup adorned with holly leaves. Maximus stood at her side, regal and composed, as if this was precisely the outcome he had expected all along.

Lily clapped until her hands hurt, her heart swelling with pride and relief. After everything they had been through, this victory felt especially sweet. Beside her, Goliath watched the proceedings with his usual air of detached interest, but Lily could have sworn she saw a flicker of satisfaction in his green eyes.

As the ceremony concluded and the crowd began to disperse, Evelyn made her way over to Lily, Maximus trotting beside her with a blue ribbon adorning his collar.

"We did it," Evelyn said, her usual composure cracking to reveal genuine emotion. "Or rather, you did it. Without you and Goliath, none of this would have been possible."

Lily shook her head. "We were just in the right place at the right time."

"It was more than that," Evelyn insisted. "It was intelligence, courage, and determination. Qualities I greatly admire." She glanced down at Goliath, who sat with his tail curled neatly around his paws. "In both of you."

Mrs. Whiskers cleared her throat. "Well, I for one think Willow Creek could use a proper pet detective agency. Seems we have more intrigue in this little town than we realized."

Evelyn's eyes lit up. "What an excellent idea. I'd be happy to provide initial funding for such a venture."

Lily looked between them, surprised. "A pet detective agency? Me and Goliath?"

"Why not?" Evelyn asked. "You've already proven your abilities. And it would provide a valuable service to the community."

Lily glanced down at Goliath, who was watching her with those inscrutable green eyes. "What do you think, partner? Should we make it official?"

Goliath stretched, arching his back in a leisurely motion, then sat up straighter and gave a slow, deliberate blink—his version of enthusiastic agreement.

Lily laughed. "I guess that's a yes."

As the winter sun began its descent, casting long shadows across the town square, Lily found herself surrounded by friends and well-wishers. The Holiday Dog Show had been saved, Maximus was safe and victorious, and the perpetrators would face justice for their actions.

But most importantly, she had discovered a new purpose—one that would allow her to use her skills and intuition to help the animals she loved so dearly. With Goliath by her side, there was no mystery they couldn't solve, no challenge they couldn't overcome.

The Detective Cat of Willow Creek was officially on the case.

Chapter 16

A Hero's Welcome

The townspeople gathered in the square, their excitement palpable as they prepared to celebrate Lily and Goliath. The buzz of conversation and the anticipation in the air was electric. Children ran around waving homemade banners, and several of Willow Creek's older residents had brought out chairs to sit and watch the proceedings. A large banner stretched across the front of the town hall, its bright letters proclaiming, "Thank You, Lily and Goliath!"

"Do you think they'll get here soon?" a young mother asked, bouncing her toddler on her hip.

"They have to!" exclaimed an older man with a bushy mustache. "Lily's the guest of honor!"

As if on cue, the crowd's murmur grew to a roar. Lily Green and Goliath appeared at the edge of the square. Lily waved, her warm smile lighting up her face. Goliath trailed behind, his large frame moving with a reluctant grace.

"Lily! Over here!" shouted a woman from the crowd. Lily made her way over, Goliath lagging with a flick of his tail.

"Thank you so much, Lily," the woman said, clutching Lily's hand. "You were so brave. We were all so worried about Maximus."

Lily squeezed the woman's hand gently. "It was a team effort. We're just glad he's safe."

The woman looked down at Goliath, who sat with a haughty air. "And you, Goliath. Such a hero!" She reached out to scratch his head, but he stood and moved just out of her reach, his green eyes narrowing.

Lily laughed softly. "He's not much for the spotlight."

The crowd parted as Lily and Goliath continued through the square. Various townspeople stopped them to express their thanks, and

The Purr-fect Suspect

Lily accepted each with genuine gratitude. Goliath, despite his grumpy demeanor, received his share of attention. His body language spoke volumes: a flick of the tail here, an ear twitch there, each movement a begrudging acknowledgment of the praise heaped upon him.

"Lily, darling!" The commanding voice of Evelyn Kensington cut through the din. The crowd hushed as Mrs. Kensington stepped forward, her silver hair gleaming in the afternoon sun. She held Maximus, her prized Poodle, in her arms. The dog looked as regal as ever, his white coat shimmering with an almost ethereal glow.

Mrs. Kensington approached Lily with a gracious smile. "I can't thank you enough for what you did. The safe return of Maximus means the world to me."

Lily's humility was evident as she responded. "We're just glad we could help, Evelyn. Maximus is like family to all of us."

The older woman nodded, her expression softening. "You have always been modest, Lily. That's one of the many reasons we love you." She paused, letting her words sink in. "I would like to make a donation to your grooming business, in honor of your bravery."

The crowd erupted in applause. Lily looked momentarily flustered, then deeply touched. "Thank you, Evelyn. That means so much."

Mrs. Kensington raised a hand, and the crowd quieted. "Please, everyone, join me in the town hall. We have much to discuss, and I know we're all eager to hear the full story of Maximus's rescue."

The townspeople filed into the hall, filling every seat and standing room in the back. Their curiosity and relief were evident in their animated expressions. Lily took a position at the front of the room, standing behind a wooden podium. Goliath sat nearby, his eyes scanning the room with a keen intellect.

Lily began to speak, her voice clear and warm. "As you all know, Maximus went missing just two days ago. We were all very worried, especially with the Holiday Dog Show coming up." The crowd murmured in agreement. "Goliath and I started by checking all the usual places: the park, the bakery, even the library."

A man in the back interrupted. "The library? Since when do dogs read?"

Laughter rippled through the room. Lily smiled. "Since they started offering story time for pets. Maximus is a regular." More laughter, then the room grew quiet again, eager for the next part of the story.

"When we didn't find him in any of those places, we started to get really worried. That's when Goliath had an idea."

All eyes turned to Goliath. The big Tom cat stretched languidly, his demeanor one of practiced indifference.

"He suggested we check the animal shelter. Sure enough, there was Maximus, safe and sound. Someone had thought he was a stray and brought him in."

The crowd let out a collective sigh of relief. Lily continued, "We were so happy to find him unharmed. The shelter staff were wonderful, and they took great care of him."

A child in the front row raised her hand. "Miss Lily, was Goliath scared?"

All heads turned to the little girl, then to Lily. She hesitated, choosing her words carefully. "Goliath is never scared. But he was very concerned."

The girl looked at Goliath with wide eyes. "He's so brave." Goliath's only response was a flick of his tail, which drew more chuckles from the crowd.

Lily went on, "We were just about to leave when a storm hit. The roads were closed, and we had to wait it out at the shelter. That's why it took so long to get Maximus home. We didn't want to risk his safety—or ours."

Mrs. Kensington stood, her authoritative presence commanding the room. "Lily, Goliath, we owe you a great debt. Your quick thinking and dedication saved the day. Thank you." She paused, surveying the crowd. "It's times like these that remind us how important community is. I'm committed to supporting not just Lily's business, but all of Willow Creek."

The meeting shifted to discussions about improving security for future events. Several townspeople offered suggestions: more frequent patrols, a neighborhood watch, better lighting in public areas. The sense of camaraderie and determination was strong. Lily listened attentively, occasionally offering her own thoughtful input.

As the meeting concluded, people lined up to personally thank Lily and Goliath. The atmosphere was one of relief and celebration, with a renewed sense of unity among the residents. Lily's genuine kindness and Goliath's reluctant heroism had endeared them even more to the community.

The Purr-fect Suspect

The evening air was cool and refreshing as Lily and Goliath walked home. Goliath, despite his grumpy exterior, moved with a subtle swagger, hinting at his quiet satisfaction with the day's events.

Their small house was cozy and inviting. Lily opened the door, and warm light spilled out onto the front porch. Goliath padded inside and made a beeline for his new bed, a plush arrangement that looked fit for a king. He circled twice, then flopped down, pretending not to care.

Lily hung up her coat and sat in her favorite chair, a well-worn recliner that had belonged to her grandmother. She looked over at Goliath, who was already half-asleep, his eyes mere slits of green.

"Not a bad day, huh?" she said softly. Goliath's only response was a slow, lazy flick of his tail.

Lily leaned back in her chair, closing her eyes and reflecting on the day's events. The gratitude of the townspeople, Mrs. Kensington's generosity, the laughter and the warmth of the community—it all filled her with a deep sense of contentment.

She was just beginning to drift off when a soft purring reached her ears. Opening her eyes, she saw Goliath in full stretch, his paws kneading the fabric of his bed. He looked, for once, completely content.

Lily smiled. "Sweet dreams, hero."

The big Tom cat settled back down, his purring growing fainter as he drifted into sleep. Lily watched him for a moment longer, then closed her eyes again, letting the cozy warmth of their home envelop her.

1 - 16

The townspeople of Willow Creek swarmed the town square, their excitement palpable as they prepared to celebrate Lily and Goliath. Banners flapped in the crisp winter air, proclaiming "Thank You, Lily!" and "Hurrah for Goliath!" The buzz of conversation and the clatter of mobile chairs created a cacophony of anticipation. Children darted between clusters of adults, their faces smeared with hot chocolate and joy.

"Can you believe it? Maximus, safe and sound!" one woman exclaimed, her hands waving in disbelief.

"They deserve a medal, those two," an elderly man replied, his voice cracking with emotion.

Lily Green and Goliath made their way through the crowd, Lily smiling warmly at every familiar face. Goliath, a massive Tom cat with a distinctive black and white coat, trailed behind with a reluctant air, his green eyes surveying the scene with a mix of annoyance and curiosity.

"Lily, over here!" A young mother waved, her toddler clutching a stuffed animal modeled after Goliath. Lily detoured, Goliath lagging further behind.

"Thank you so much, Lily," the mother said. "We were all so worried about Maximus."

Lily's smile was genuine. "I'm just glad he's back where he belongs. It was a team effort." She glanced down at Goliath, who flicked his tail dismissively.

As they continued, various townspeople stopped Lily to express their gratitude. She accepted their praise with humble grace, always quick to deflect the credit. Goliath, despite his grumpy demeanor, received his share of attention. Children reached out to stroke his fur, adults nodded in respect. His body language spoke volumes: a flick of the tail here, an ear twitch there, each movement a begrudging acceptance of the adoration.

"Lily, darling!" The commanding voice cut through the din. Evelyn Kensington stepped forward, her presence immediately drawing the crowd's attention. With perfectly coiffed silver hair and an air of unassailable sophistication, she was Willow Creek's de facto matriarch. In her arms, Maximus perched like a king on his throne, his white coat gleaming.

Evelyn approached Lily with a gracious smile. "We cannot thank you enough for what you did. Maximus is everything to me."

Lily's humility shone through. "I'm just glad we found him in time, Mrs. Kensington. He's a real trooper."

Evelyn's smile widened, though her eyes remained calculating. "You and that remarkable cat of yours are true heroes." She paused, letting the weight of her next words build. "To show our gratitude, I will be making a donation to your grooming business, Lily. We want to ensure it's around for many years to come."

Applause broke out, and Lily's eyes widened in surprise. "That's incredibly generous. Thank you."

With the announcement, the crowd's energy surged. People began to move toward the community center, where a makeshift stage awaited. Evelyn lingered a moment longer, her social radar always active.

"We'll talk details soon," she said, her tone as smooth as velvet. "Again, thank you."

The community center filled quickly, the warmth of bodies and the scent of pine decorations creating a festive atmosphere. Tension from the past week melted away as townspeople took their seats, eager to hear the full story of Maximus's rescue.

Lily stood before the crowd, a modest figure in a sea of adulation. "Thank you all for coming," she began, her voice steady but soft. "We know how much Maximus means to this community, and we're just happy he's home."

She recounted the events with clarity and warmth. How Maximus had gone missing during a grooming session, the sheer panic that had ensued, and the sleepless nights wondering if he would be found. Her storytelling was punctuated by moments of laughter and gasps from the audience, reflecting the emotional rollercoaster of the past week.

Goliath sat nearby, his eyes scanning the room with a keen intellect. He had been the one to discover the crucial clue: a tuft of white fur caught on a fence post near the park. Even as Lily maintained her composure, her recounting of their late-night search in the freezing temperatures had the crowd on the edge of their seats.

"And then," Lily said, "just when we thought we'd have to call it a night, Goliath heard something. A faint whine, coming from the old tool shed." The audience held their breath. "We opened the door, and there he was. Cold and scared, but unharmed."

Relief washed over the room. Lily let the silence settle for a moment before continuing. "We couldn't have done it without the community's support. Thank you for all the flyers, the phone calls, and the hot cocoa."

A child in the audience raised a hand timidly. "Miss Lily, does Goliath talk?"

The room tensed, then erupted in laughter. Lily chuckled, looking down at Goliath. "He doesn't need to. He's very good at making himself understood."

All eyes turned to Goliath, who regarded the crowd with a stony expression. After a long, dramatic pause, he flicked his tail. More laughter, and even a few "Aww"s. Despite himself, Goliath had become something of a local legend.

Lily continued, "We were lucky this time, but it's important we think about how to prevent something like this in the future."

Evelyn Kensington rose, her authoritative voice cutting through the murmurings. "Lily is right. We must take steps to ensure the safety of all our pets." The crowd fell silent. "I propose we form a committee to improve security and create a network for quicker communication."

The townspeople nodded in agreement, their curiosity shifting to a sense of civic duty. Suggestions began to flow: installing more pet-friendly fencing, creating a social media group, organizing regular patrols.

Lily listened attentively, occasionally offering thoughts of her own. Her nurturing nature shone as she encouraged even the quietest voices to speak up. The community's admiration for her grew with each passing minute.

As the meeting wound down, Evelyn took the floor once more. "Let us not forget why we are here tonight. To thank Lily and Goliath for their extraordinary efforts." She paused, the weight of her words settling on the room. "Your bravery and intelligence have inspired us all."

The crowd stood, their applause thunderous. Lily blushed, and even Goliath seemed momentarily taken aback, his ears perking up before he slouched back into his characteristic grumpiness.

The townspeople began to disperse, lingering in small groups to share their relief and make plans for the new committee. The atmosphere was one of unity and optimism, a community bound tighter by recent troubles and the hope of preventing future ones.

Lily and Goliath made their way to the exit, the cool night air a sharp contrast to the warmth inside. Goliath walked with a subtle swagger, his usual grumpiness tempered by a quiet satisfaction.

"You did good, buddy," Lily said, bending down to scratch behind his ears. He tolerated it, eyes half-closed in a rare moment of contentment.

They arrived at Lily's small cottage, the cozy warmth of the interior welcoming them home. Lily hung up her coat and put on a kettle for tea. Goliath sauntered over to his new bed, a plush affair that looked almost comically large for him. He sniffed it, circled twice, and flopped down, pretending not to care.

Lily sat at the kitchen table, cupping her hands around a steaming mug. She thought about the day, the outpouring of gratitude, and the unexpected donation from Evelyn. Her business would be in good shape now, and maybe she could even hire an assistant.

A contented smile spread across her face as she looked over at Goliath. He met her gaze briefly, then closed his eyes, his chest rising and falling in a slow, deep rhythm.

"Thank you," she whispered, knowing he understood.

The kettle whistled, the only sound in the tranquil night. Outside, snow began to fall, each flake a tiny, silent blessing on the town of Willow Creek.

Chapter 17

Reflections and Rewards

Lily stood in her grooming salon, surveying the bustling activity as she finished up with the last client of the day. The small space was filled with the sounds of barking dogs and meowing cats, the air thick with the scent of wet fur and shampoo. She wiped her hands on a towel, watching as a golden retriever shook itself dry, sending a spray of water across the tiled floor. The owner laughed and called the dog over, clipping a leash to its collar and waving to Lily as they made their way to the door.

"See you next week, Lily!" the owner called.

Lily smiled and waved, her mind already drifting to the recent events. Solving the mystery of Maximus's disappearance had been a whirlwind, and she still couldn't quite believe they had pulled it off. The thought of it filled her with a strange mix of pride and disbelief. Who would have guessed that she, a simple pet groomer, had the skills to play detective?

She turned to the counter and started putting away her tools, her movements slow and deliberate. The salon grew quiet, the absence of animal chatter almost eerie. Her thoughts wandered to the idea that had been nagging at her for the past few days. What if she expanded her business to include a pet detective agency? The more she thought about it, the more it seemed like a natural extension of what she already did. She loved animals, understood them in a way most people didn't. And after the whole Maximus ordeal, she had a newfound confidence in her ability to solve problems.

The Purr-fect Suspect

Lily's heart quickened with excitement as she imagined the possibilities. A new sign out front: "Lily's Grooming and Pet Detective Services." Business cards with a cute magnifying glass logo. She could help people find their lost pets, figure out why their animals were acting strange, maybe even solve more mysteries like Maximus's disappearance. It was a crazy idea, but the best ideas usually were.

On the windowsill, Goliath lounged in his usual spot, a king surveying his domain. The large Tom cat stretched, his black and white fur catching the last rays of the setting sun. Lily glanced over at him, wondering what he thought of all this. He had been the real hero in the Maximus case, his keen observations and stubborn persistence leading them to the poodle in the end. Not that he would ever admit to enjoying the detective work, but Lily had noticed a certain spark in his green eyes, a flicker of pride that suggested otherwise.

She walked over to the front desk and pulled a notebook from a drawer, flipping it open to a blank page. Her pen moved quickly as she jotted down ideas for the new venture, her enthusiasm growing with each bullet point. Potential services: Missing pets. Behavioral issues. Mystery injuries. Marketing ideas: Flyers at the vet's office. Social media posts. Word of mouth from satisfied grooming clients. The townspeople of Willow Creek were a tight-knit community; if anyone could make this work, it was them.

Lily paused, tapping the pen against her chin. Could she really do this? It would be a lot of extra work, and she was already busy enough with the salon. But the thought of helping more animals, of making a real difference, was too enticing to ignore. She looked at Goliath again, a smile creeping onto her face.

"You know, we make a pretty good team," she said to the cat. "I couldn't have done it without you."

Goliath flicked his tail, his eyes half-closed in an expression of bored indifference. But Lily thought she saw a flicker of something else in his gaze, a hint of pride perhaps. She liked to believe that he understood her, that he knew how much she appreciated him.

"I'm thinking of making it official," she continued. "A pet detective agency. What do you think?"

The cat stretched again, this time rolling onto his back for a brief moment before sitting up and licking a paw. Lily took his non-response as tacit approval.

"Don't worry, you'll still have plenty of time to nap," she said with a chuckle.

Lily put the notebook away and walked to the small kitchenette in the back of the salon. She opened a cupboard and pulled out a small plate, then reached into the fridge for a container of treats. These were Goliath's favorites, homemade by one of her clients who ran a pet bakery. She carefully arranged a few of the treats on the plate, then carried it to the front of the salon where Goliath waited on the windowsill.

"Here," she said, setting the plate down gently. "A thank you for all your hard work."

Goliath eyed the treats, then looked at Lily. For a moment, it seemed like he might turn up his nose and walk away, maintaining his facade of grumpy indifference. But the temptation was too great, and he lowered his head to take a tentative bite. His eyes closed in bliss as he chewed, his usual scowl replaced by a rare expression of contentment.

Lily watched him with a warm smile, her heart swelling with affection for the big lug. They had come a long way together, she and Goliath. He wasn't just a pet; he was her partner, her confidant. Their bond was something special, forged over years of living and working side by side.

She stood and started tidying up the salon, her mind buzzing with plans for the future. There was so much to do: create a business plan, design the new logo, update her website. The thought of it all should have been overwhelming, but instead, it energized her. This was something she could pour her passion into, a way to take her love for animals to the next level.

The bell above the door jingled, and Lily turned to see Mrs. Patterson, a regular client, stepping into the salon. She was an older woman with a kind face, holding the leash of her beagle, Baxter.

"Hi, Lily. Did you find Baxter's toy?" Mrs. Patterson asked.

Lily reached under the counter and pulled out a well-chewed rubber bone. "Here it is. He must have left it during his last bath."

Mrs. Patterson took the toy and handed it to Baxter, who wagged his tail furiously. "Thank you, dear. I don't know what we'd do without you."

Lily blushed at the compliment. "It's no trouble. How's Baxter doing with the new food?"

The Purr-fect Suspect

"Oh, he's loving it. And his coat is so much shinier now. You always have the best advice."

They exchanged a few more pleasantries before Mrs. Patterson and Baxter made their way out. Lily watched them go, her chest tight with emotion. The support of her clients meant the world to her, and she hoped they would be just as enthusiastic about her new venture.

The salon was quiet again, the only sound the soft crunch of Goliath finishing his treats. Lily walked to the window and looked out at the darkening street. Willow Creek was a small town, but it had a big heart. She felt lucky to be a part of it, to have built a life here surrounded by people—and animals—she cared about.

A nudge at her leg pulled her from her thoughts. Goliath stood at her feet, looking up at her with an intensity in his green eyes. She knelt down and scratched behind his ears, his fur soft and warm against her fingers.

"We're really going to do this, aren't we?" she said softly. "It's going to be a lot of work, but I think we can handle it."

Goliath's eyes met hers, and for a moment, it was as if he were giving her a silent promise. She liked to believe that he was as excited about this as she was, even if he would never show it.

"Just think of all the adventures we'll have," she continued. "All the mysteries we'll solve. It'll be like the Maximus case, but even better, because we'll know what we're doing this time."

She stood and Goliath followed, winding around her legs as they walked to the back of the salon. Lily grabbed her coat and shrugged it on, then picked up Goliath and held him close. He usually resisted such displays of affection, but tonight he let her have her moment.

"Come on, partner," she said, pushing the door open. "Let's go home and get some rest. We've got a big future ahead of us."

The cool evening air rushed in, and Lily stepped outside, holding Goliath in her arms. They stood for a moment, taking in the quiet of the town. She could almost see it: the new sign out front, the bustling activity of the salon mixed with the excitement of a growing detective agency. It was a daunting vision, but one that filled her with hope.

With Goliath still in her arms, Lily started the short walk to her house, their silhouettes long and lean in the streetlights. Whatever challenges lay ahead, she knew they would face them together, as they always had.

Goliath hopped from Lily's arms as they reached the front steps of her modest, two-story home. He trotted up the wooden stairs with the grace of a panther, pausing only to glance back at Lily, who fumbled with her keys in the cold. She opened the door, and Goliath slipped inside, making a beeline for the living room where his favorite perch awaited.

Lily hung her coat on the rack and kicked off her shoes, wiggling her toes to bring some warmth back into them. The house was cozy, filled with eclectic furnishings and a multitude of pet-related knickknacks. She made her way to the kitchen, where she put a kettle on the stove and pulled out a mug from the cabinet. The ceramic mug was chipped and worn, with a picture of a kitten and the words "World's Best Cat Mom" emblazoned on the side. It had been a gift from one of her first clients, and despite its state, it was her favorite.

As the kettle began to whistle, Lily's thoughts returned to the idea of the pet detective agency. Could she really balance it with the grooming business? She poured hot water over a tea bag and let it steep, the rising steam warming her face. Nothing worth doing was ever easy, she reminded herself. And the thought of giving it a shot filled her with a sense of adventure she hadn't felt in years.

She walked to the living room, cradling the mug in both hands. Goliath was already settled on his perch by the window, a tall cat tree that gave him a perfect view of the street outside. He looked out with his usual air of detachment, but Lily could tell he was alert, taking in every movement and sound.

"You really are a natural, you know," she said to him, sinking into the overstuffed couch. "Maybe in another life, you were a detective."

Goliath didn't turn, but his ears twitched at her words. Lily took a sip of her tea, the hot liquid soothing her throat and spreading warmth through her chest. She loved these quiet moments at home, where she could just sit and think, or not think, and let the day melt away.

Her mind wandered to the stack of mail on the coffee table. Among the usual bills and flyers was a thick envelope from the Small Business Development Center. She had requested information on starting a new venture, not really expecting to need it, but now the contents seemed invaluable. She reached for the envelope and tore it open, spilling a collection of brochures and worksheets onto the table. One of the brochures caught her eye: "Turning Your Passion Into Profit."

The Purr-fect Suspect

Lily picked it up and flipped through the pages, her excitement growing with each section. It talked about creating a business plan, setting realistic goals, finding your target market—all things she had some experience with from running the salon, but needed to revisit for this new endeavor. She made mental notes, her mind already crafting a rough outline of what the next few months would look like.

A loud thump drew her attention back to Goliath. He had jumped down from his perch and was now stretching on the floor, his claws digging into the carpet. He sauntered over to the couch and leaped up, settling next to Lily but just out of reach of her hands. She set the brochure down and leaned back, closing her eyes.

"I think we can really do this," she said, more to herself than to Goliath. "It's going to be hard, but I have a good feeling."

Her eyes opened, and she turned to look at the cat. He met her gaze, his green eyes unblinking and intense. For a moment, it was as if he were willing her to succeed, offering his silent support. Then he broke the stare and began to groom himself, licking his paw and rubbing it over his ear.

Lily stood and walked to the stairs, turning back to see Goliath already curled into a ball, his eyes heavy with sleep. "Goodnight, Goliath," she said softly, then made her way up to her bedroom.

The room was simple but inviting, with soft pastel walls and a quilted bedspread that her grandmother had made. She changed into pajamas and slid under the covers, reaching for the lamp on her nightstand. Next to the lamp was a framed photo of her and Goliath, taken the day she brought him home from the shelter. She picked it up and studied it, remembering how uncertain and afraid he had been at first. It had taken months for him to come out of his shell, but now she couldn't imagine life without him.

Setting the photo back down, Lily flicked off the lamp and closed her eyes. Her mind was a whirlwind of plans and dreams, but the physical exhaustion of the day soon took over, pulling her into a deep, restful sleep.

Morning came too quickly, the winter sun casting a pale light through her bedroom window. Lily stretched and yawned, her body reluctant to leave the warmth of her bed. Today was her day off, a rare and precious thing, but she knew she wouldn't be able to relax with so much on her mind.

She made her way downstairs, where Goliath was already waiting by his empty food bowl. He let out a plaintive meow, more of a demand than a request.

"Alright, alright," Lily said, rubbing the sleep from her eyes. She opened a cabinet and scooped some kibble into the bowl, Goliath diving in with gusto. "Don't forget to chew," she added, knowing full well he wouldn't.

Lily brewed a pot of coffee and poured herself a tall cup, the dark, bitter aroma waking her senses. She sipped it slowly, savoring each taste as she walked to the living room. The materials from the Small Business Development Center were still scattered on the coffee table, and she picked up one of the worksheets, skimming over its contents.

Creating a business plan was the first step. It needed to be detailed and realistic, something she could follow like a roadmap. She set the worksheet down and retrieved her notebook from her purse, flipping to the page where she had scribbled her initial ideas. With a pen in hand, she started to write more deliberately, crafting a vision for the pet detective agency that was both ambitious and attainable.

An hour passed in a blur of writing and brainstorming. Lily's notebook was filled with pages of notes, her hand cramping from the effort. She leaned back and stretched, feeling a sense of accomplishment wash over her. This was really happening. She was doing it.

The sound of the mail slot clattering drew her attention to the front door. She got up and retrieved the small stack of letters, flipping through them as she walked back to the living room. One of the envelopes made her stop in her tracks. It was from the Willow Creek Chamber of Commerce, addressed to "Lily Green and Goliath."

She opened it carefully, her heart pounding with anticipation. Inside was a formal letter and a certificate, along with a small pin in the shape of a paw print. The letter read:

Dear Lily and Goliath,

Congratulations on your outstanding efforts in solving the Maximus case! The Willow Creek Chamber of Commerce is pleased to recognize your dedication and teamwork with the title of "Honorary Pet Detectives." We are proud to have community members like you who go above and beyond to help our furry friends.

Warmest regards,
Willow Creek Chamber of Commerce

Lily's eyes widened as she looked at the certificate. It had her name and Goliath's, along with a bold header that read "Honorary Pet Detectives." A huge smile spread across her face, and she let out a small, disbelieving laugh.

"Goliath, look at this!" she exclaimed, holding up the certificate for the cat to see. He was lounging on the couch, and he lifted his head briefly before returning to his nap. "We're officially official!"

She couldn't contain her excitement. This was the validation she hadn't even realized she needed. The community believed in them, and that belief gave her the confidence to move forward. They weren't just playing at being detectives; they had proven themselves, and now they had recognition to show for it.

Lily set the certificate down gently and picked up the pin, running her fingers over its smooth surface. She thought about where she would put it—maybe frame it with the certificate and hang it in the salon. It would be a great conversation starter and could help build credibility for the new business.

Her phone buzzed in her pocket, snapping her out of her thoughts. She pulled it out and saw a text from Emily, her best friend since high school.

"Coffee?" the text read.

Lily hesitated. She had so much she wanted to work on, but she also knew she needed to tell Emily about her plans. Emily had always been her sounding board, the one person she could count on for honest advice.

"Sure," Lily typed back. "Meet you at Bean's in 20."

She put the phone away and rushed upstairs to change. As she pulled on a sweater and jeans, her mind raced with how she would present the idea to Emily. Would she think it was crazy? Brilliant? Only one way to find out.

Back downstairs, she grabbed the certificate and stuffed it carefully into her purse. She looked at Goliath, who was now stretching and yawning on the couch.

"Don't wait up," she said with a wink, then headed out the door.

Bean's was a small, independently-owned coffee shop in the heart of Willow Creek. Its rustic interior and eclectic mix of furniture gave it a warm, inviting atmosphere. Lily loved coming here, not just for the coffee, but for the sense of community it provided. She walked in and was greeted by the familiar sounds of clinking mugs and quiet conversation.

Emily was already seated in a corner booth, her auburn hair pulled back in a messy bun. She waved enthusiastically when she saw Lily, and Lily's heart lifted. No matter how long it had been since they last hung out, Emily's infectious energy always made her feel instantly at ease.

"Lil!" Emily said, standing to give her a hug. "It's so good to see you. How've you been?"

"Busy," Lily admitted, taking a seat. "But good. How's work?"

Emily shrugged. "Same old. You know how corporate life is. I'm more interested in hearing about you. I saw the news about Maximus! You guys are heroes."

Lily blushed. "It was a team effort. Goliath did most of the work."

They placed their orders—a lavender latte for Emily and a black coffee for Lily—then settled back into the booth. Lily took a deep breath, ready to dive into her pitch, but Emily spoke first.

"So, tell me everything. How did you figure it out? Was it really Mrs. Kline who took him?"

Lily recounted the story, explaining how Goliath had noticed the poodle fur on Mrs. Kline's coat and how they had followed her to the next town over. She left out the more mundane parts, like the hours of searching and the dead ends they had encountered. By the time she finished, their drinks had arrived, and Emily was leaning forward with rapt attention.

"That's amazing," Emily said, sitting back and taking a sip of her latte. "You should write a book or something."

Lily laughed. "Funny you should say that. I have an idea, and I want to get your opinion."

Emily raised an eyebrow, her expression turning serious. "Oh? Do tell."

Lily explained her thoughts about starting a pet detective agency, laying out the details as she had envisioned them. She told Emily about the certificate from the Chamber of Commerce and how it had given her the push she needed to take the idea seriously. Throughout, Emily listened intently, her face a mix of curiosity and contemplation.

When Lily finished, she held her breath, waiting for Emily's verdict.

"I think it's brilliant," Emily said, and Lily exhaled in relief. "But..."

Lily's heart sank. There was always a but.

"...you need a solid plan. This isn't like starting from scratch; you already have a successful business. You need to make sure the new venture complements what you're doing and doesn't take away from it."

Lily nodded. "I know. I was hoping you could help me with the planning. You have way more business experience than I do."

Emily smiled. "Of course I'll help. But you need to be realistic about the time and effort it's going to take. You're already working crazy hours with the salon. How are you going to balance both?"

Lily thought for a moment. "Maybe I could hire an assistant for the grooming side, someone to take on the more routine tasks. That would free me up to focus on the detective work."

Emily nodded slowly. "That could work. Or you could bring someone in as a partner, someone who has experience with pet investigations. You don't have to do it all alone, you know."

The idea of a partner was intriguing, but Lily wasn't sure she could trust anyone else with her vision. Still, it was something to consider.

"I'll think about it," Lily said. "Thanks, Em. I knew you'd have good advice."

Emily waved her hand dismissively. "You know I'm just looking out for you. I think it's an awesome idea, Lil. Really. And who knows? Maybe one day you'll be able to quit grooming and just focus on solving mysteries."

Lily wasn't sure she could ever give up grooming. It was her first love, and she couldn't imagine not working with the animals in that way. But the thought of having the option was exciting.

"One step at a time," Lily said, raising her mug. "To new adventures."

Emily clinked her latte glass against Lily's mug. "To new adventures."

Lily walked home, the cold air biting at her cheeks and nose. Her head was buzzing with all the possibilities and challenges that Emily had pointed out. She felt a mix of excitement and trepidation, knowing that this was going to be a much bigger undertaking than she had initially thought.

When she arrived home, she found Goliath sitting by the door, his posture rigid and impatient. He let out a yowl as she opened the door, and she scooped him up, scratching his chin.

"I'm back, I'm back," she said. "Guess what? Emily thinks it's a good idea. We've got some planning to do, but I think we can make it work."

She set Goliath down, and he trotted off to the kitchen. Lily followed, her stomach growling from the scent of something delicious. She peeked into the oven and saw a casserole baking; her mother must have stopped by while she was out. They lived just a few blocks apart, and her mom had a key for emergencies—or impromptu cooking sessions.

A note on the fridge read, "Made your favorite. Call me later. Love, Mom."

Lily smiled and took a deep breath, the warmth of the kitchen seeping into her bones. She loved her mom, but sometimes she wished they had more balance in their relationship. Her mother had a tendency to overstep, though always with the best of intentions.

She took the casserole out of the oven and let it cool on the stovetop. Goliath sat expectantly by his food bowl, hoping for a scrap.

"You'll get a taste," Lily promised. "But first, I have something to show you."

She walked to the living room and retrieved the certificate from her purse, then went to a cabinet in the dining room where she kept various picture frames. After a bit of digging, she found an empty frame that was just the right size. She carefully placed the certificate in the frame, making sure it was centered and wrinkle-free.

Holding it up, she admired the way it looked behind the glass. This was a tangible piece of their accomplishment, something she could point to with pride.

Lily walked to the wall near the front door, where a collage of pet photos hung. She found an empty space and held the framed certificate against the wall, envisioning how it would look among the pictures. It fit perfectly, like it was meant to be there.

With a nail and hammer, she gently tapped the nail into the wall, then hung the frame on it, stepping back to admire her work. A sense of fulfillment washed over her. This was just the beginning, but it already felt so real.

Goliath wandered over and sat at her feet, looking up at the certificate. Lily bent down and picked him up, holding him close.

"We did good," she said. "And we're going to do even better."

She carried Goliath to the kitchen and set him on the counter, then dished out a small portion of the casserole onto a plate. The smell of melted cheese and savory vegetables made her mouth water. She took a fork and divided the portion in half, then set the plate in front of Goliath. He sniffed it cautiously before diving in, his whiskers twitching with every bite.

Lily took a forkful and savored it, the flavors bursting in her mouth. It was exactly what she needed, a comfort food that made her feel instantly at home.

As Goliath finished his portion, Lily stroked his back, feeling the warmth of his body through his fur. Their partnership had come a long way, and she knew that whatever the future held, they would face it together.

Lily looked toward the front hall, where the certificate now hung proudly on the wall. The words "Honorary Pet Detectives" seemed to glow with a special significance. This was a new chapter for them, one filled with unknowns but also with endless possibilities.

"We're ready for it," she said, more to herself than to Goliath. "We're ready for whatever comes next."

Goliath let out a small, contented purr, and Lily took it as a sign of agreement. Their journey was just beginning, and she couldn't wait to see where it would take them.

Chapter 18

Tying Up Loose Ends

Lily paused at the threshold of her grooming salon, the crisp autumn air biting at her cheeks. She glanced back at the cozy interior where Goliath lounged imperiously on the counter, his green eyes tracking her every move. With a final, determined breath, she pushed the door open and stepped into the street.

Willow Creek's main drag bustled with midday activity. Shops decorated in harvest themes, their displays overflowing with pumpkins and cornstalks, beckoned the townspeople preparing for the seasonal change. Lily navigated the crowd with purpose, her thoughts fixed on the conversation ahead.

Sylvia's shop came into view, its vibrant purple facade standing out like a peacock among sparrows. Once, Lily had admired the color. Now, it elicited a pang of something she didn't care to name. She halted in front of the large bay window, peering inside. The scene was familiar: Sylvia, every bit the consummate professional, wielded a pair of clippers with the precision of a maestro conducting an orchestra. Her current subject, a spirited spaniel, wiggled with an excitement that bordered on manic.

Lily hesitated, her hand hovering over the door handle. The bell above the door jingled as she pushed it open, and a warm, aromatic rush of pet shampoo and coffee beans enveloped her. Sylvia glanced up from her work, her eyes widening with a mixture of surprise and something that might have been relief.

"Lily," Sylvia said, setting the clippers down and patting the spaniel on the head. "I didn't expect to see you here."

"Hi, Sylvia." Lily shifted her weight from one foot to the other. "I wanted to talk about the animals. The ones we rescued."

Sylvia wiped her hands on her apron, which was covered in a fine layer of dog hair. "They're all doing well. I've been checking in on them regularly."

The spaniel's owner, an older man with a bushy mustache, handed Sylvia some cash and took the dog in his arms. Sylvia waved as he left, then turned her full attention to Lily.

"I'm glad you're keeping tabs," Lily said. "I was worried when I didn't hear from you."

Sylvia shrugged, a gesture that seemed to carry the weight of more than just the past few weeks. "I thought you might not want to hear from me."

Lily studied Sylvia's face. The other woman looked tired, but there was a softness in her eyes that Lily hadn't seen before. "We both want what's best for the animals," Lily said. "That's all that matters."

"Is it?" Sylvia asked, but there was no challenge in her voice, only curiosity.

Lily took a deep breath. "I hope so. Look, Sylvia, I know we've had our differences. But I think we can work together. For the animals."

Sylvia's lips curved into a small, tentative smile. "I'd like that. Really. I'm sorry for... everything. I let my ambition get in the way of what's important."

Lily nodded, feeling some of the tension in her shoulders release. "We all make mistakes."

The two women stood in a moment of silent understanding. They had a long way to go, but this was a start.

Lily pulled into the circular driveway of Margot Devereux's stately home. The tall, white columns of the front porch gave the house an air of old Southern elegance, a stark contrast to the more modest homes in Willow Creek. She killed the engine and sat for a moment, collecting her thoughts. The meeting with Sylvia had gone better than she'd expected, but this—facing Margot—felt like a different beast altogether.

With a sigh, she opened the car door and walked up the stone path to the front entrance. Before she could ring the bell, the door swung open, and Margot stood before her, every bit the picture of refined grace. Her blonde hair was swept up in a chignon, and she wore a silk blouse that shimmered in the afternoon light.

"Lily," Margot said, her voice warm. "Thank you for coming."

Lily forced a smile. "Thank you for inviting me."

Margot stepped aside, motioning for Lily to enter. The foyer was as grand as the exterior, with a sweeping staircase and crystal chandelier that sparkled like a cluster of stars. Lily had been here once before, years ago, for a charity event. It was the kind of house that left an impression.

"Please, have a seat in the parlor," Margot said, indicating a room to the left of the foyer. "I'll bring the tea."

Lily walked into the parlor, which was furnished with antique settees and a mahogany coffee table. Framed photographs lined the walls, most of them featuring Margot with various dignitaries and celebrities, all smiling for the camera. One photo caught Lily's eye: Margot as a young woman, holding a trophy and beaming with pride, a schnauzer perched on her lap. It was the only picture in the room that looked remotely candid.

Margot returned with a silver tray, complete with a porcelain tea set and a tiered stand of finger sandwiches. She set the tray on the coffee table and took a seat opposite Lily.

"I hope you like Earl Grey," Margot said, pouring two cups.

"It's perfect," Lily said, taking hers with a polite nod. The aroma of bergamot filled the room, cutting through the otherwise stuffy atmosphere.

Margot took a sip of her tea, then set it down gently in its saucer. "I wanted to clear the air between us," she said. "We've been at odds for too long."

Lily raised an eyebrow. This directness was new. "I appreciate that, Margot. I think we all want the same thing—to make Willow Creek a better place for our furry friends."

"Indeed," Margot said, her lips curving into a smile. "Which is why I wanted to talk about the Holiday Dog Show."

Here it comes, Lily thought. She braced herself for the pitch, the plea, the demand.

"You know how much that show means to me," Margot continued. "It's been a tradition for twenty years. This year, with everything that's happened, I was worried it might not go on."

Lily stayed silent, waiting.

"But," Margot said, leaning back in her seat, "I've come to realize that the show is more than just a competition. It's a way to bring the community together. To celebrate our love for dogs."

Lily studied Margot's face, looking for the angle, the ulterior motive. What she saw was something closer to sincerity than she'd expected.

"We've always been competitive," Margot said, "but I hope you know that I respect what you do, Lily. Your dedication to the animals is admirable."

"Thank you," Lily said, cautiously. "We've worked hard to build something lasting."

Margot nodded. "I suppose what I'm trying to say is that I'd like us to find a way to support each other. The community needs us both."

Lily took a slow sip of her tea, letting Margot's words sink in. Could it really be this simple? She wanted to believe it, but years of rivalry weren't so easily forgotten.

"So," Lily said, setting her cup down, "you're proposing a truce?"

Margot's smile widened. "I'm proposing a partnership. For the good of Willow Creek."

Lily considered this. A partnership with Margot would be tricky, but it could also be incredibly beneficial. If Margot was truly willing to put the community first, it might even be worth the risk.

"I'll think about it," Lily said.

"That's all I ask," Margot replied, her tone gracious.

Lily left Margot's home with a lot to think about. Perhaps true reconciliation was possible.

Lily knocked on the front door of the quaint cottage, a small bouquet of autumn flowers in hand. The door opened to reveal Mrs. Hargrove, a spry woman in her seventies, with a tiny Chihuahua perched on her shoulder like a parrot.

"Lily! Come in, come in," Mrs. Hargrove said, her eyes sparkling.

Lily stepped inside and handed Mrs. Hargrove the flowers. "How's Peanut?"

Mrs. Hargrove kissed the Chihuahua on its nose. "He's an absolute angel. We're inseparable."

Lily watched as Peanut licked Mrs. Hargrove's cheek with fervent affection. "I'm so glad. He looks right at home."

After a few more minutes of cheerful conversation, Lily made her way back to her car. She checked her list and smiled. One more stop.

The door to the Andersons' suburban home swung open before Lily could even ring the bell. A chorus of children's voices shouted her name, and she was quickly pulled inside by eager hands. In the living room, the once-sedate Basset Hound, now renamed Buster, wagged his tail with the enthusiasm of a puppy.

"Look, Miss Lily!" one of the children exclaimed, holding up a craft project. It was a picture frame made of popsicle sticks, with a photo of Buster and the kids nestled inside.

"That's beautiful," Lily said. "Buster looks so happy."

The children took turns telling Lily about Buster's latest antics: stealing socks, howling along to the piano, snuggling during movie nights. Lily's heart swelled with each story.

Back in her car, Lily took a moment to savor the happiness she'd seen. The animals were thriving, and it gave her a deep sense of satisfaction. She started the engine and headed for home, her mind replaying the joyful scenes like a favorite movie.

She drove home with a light heart, grateful for the small victories.

Lily unlocked the door to her grooming salon and stepped inside. The warmth was a welcome relief from the brisk autumn air. Goliath, her enormous Maine Coon, stretched languidly on the counter and gave a nonchalant yawn. His green eyes followed Lily as she hung up her coat and checked the day's mail.

"Don't look at me like that," Lily said. "It's been a productive day."

Goliath flicked his tail, as if to say, "I know."

Lily was about to pour herself a cup of herbal tea when the door burst open with a jingle of bells. She turned to see Mrs. Whiskers, an eccentric elderly woman known around town for her collection of vintage hats and her unerring eye for gossip. Today, she wore a purple cloche hat adorned with a large, feathery plume.

The Purr-fect Suspect

"Lily, darling!" Mrs. Whiskers exclaimed, her eyes twinkling with mischief. She closed the door and shuffled toward the counter where Goliath lay. "And how is our little Sherlock?"

Lily raised an eyebrow. "Sherlock?"

Mrs. Whiskers waved a dismissive hand. "Oh, you know what I mean. Goliath here is the talk of the town, you know. Solving mysteries left and right."

Lily walked over to Mrs. Whiskers, curious. "Is he now?"

Mrs. Whiskers leaned in, conspiratorially. "I always knew he was a clever one. The way he watches everything, the way he moves. A born detective."

Lily couldn't help but smile. "He does have a knack for getting into things."

Mrs. Whiskers straightened up and pointed a finger at Lily. "You mustn't downplay it, dear. The two of you have done a great service for the community. Saving those animals, uncovering the truth. We're all very grateful."

Lily's smile faded as she took in Mrs. Whiskers' earnest expression. "We just did what anyone would have done."

"Nonsense," Mrs. Whiskers said. "You did what needed to be done, and not everyone has the courage for that." She turned her attention back to Goliath, stroking his massive head. "Don't let her modesty fool you, Goliath. I know you two make a formidable team."

Lily watched as Goliath accepted the affection with regal indifference. "We're not exactly a team of detectives, Mrs. Whiskers."

"Not yet," Mrs. Whiskers said, her eyes once again sparkling with that familiar mischief. "But who knows what the future holds?"

Lily considered this. The past few weeks had been intense, but also invigorating. She'd almost forgotten the rush of solving a mystery, the satisfaction of setting things right.

"Thank you," Lily said. "It means a lot, coming from you."

Mrs. Whiskers smiled, a genuine, warm curve of her lips. "Just remember, the community needs people like you. Don't stop now."

With that, Mrs. Whiskers began to make her way to the door. Lily followed, opening it for her. "Take care, Mrs. Whiskers."

"Oh, I will," the older woman said. "And you take care of that brilliant cat." She paused, then added, "And yourself, Lily."

As Mrs. Whiskers walked down the street, Lily closed the door and leaned against it, thinking about all that had happened today. Sylvia, Margot, the animals—they were all part of a larger picture, one that she was starting to see more clearly.

She looked at Goliath, who had resumed his lounging on the counter. "What do you think?" she asked him. "Could we really keep this up?"

G Goliath stretched again, his muscles rippling under his thick fur, and regarded Lily with an unreadable expression. Then, almost imperceptibly, he gave a slow, deliberate nod.

Lily laughed softly. "Alright, partner."

She walked to the back of the salon, where a small kitchenette held an assortment of teas and a vintage kettle. The walls were lined with photos of her and various pets she'd groomed over the years, a visual timeline of her career and her life in Willow Creek. Each picture told a story, and as she looked at them, she felt a deep well of gratitude for the community that had supported her.

The kettle whistled, and Lily poured the hot water over a sachet of chamomile. The steam rose in delicate tendrils, and she breathed in the calming scent. With tea in hand, she returned to the front of the salon and took a seat in one of the plush waiting chairs.

Her mind drifted to the Holiday Dog Show. Could she and Margot really put aside their differences? Could Sylvia and she work together without reopening old wounds? The thought of genuine collaboration, of all of them united for the sake of the animals, was both daunting and hopeful.

She sipped her tea, letting the warmth seep into her bones. The salon was quiet, a stark contrast to the bustling streets outside. This was her sanctuary, the place where she felt most at home. But lately, she realized, home had extended beyond these walls. It included the rescued animals, the clients who had become friends, and even the rivalries that had pushed her to be better.

Lily finished her tea and stood, stretching out the kinks in her back. She walked to the counter where Goliath lay and scratched him behind the ears. "Time to clean up."

She moved with practiced ease, putting away grooming tools, wiping down surfaces, and straightening the small retail section that offered pet toys and treats. Goliath watched her, his eyes half-closed but alert.

When everything was in its place, Lily turned off the lights, leaving only the soft glow of a lamp near the reception desk. She loved the way the salon looked in this light—warm, inviting, like a scene from a nostalgic memory.

Goliath hopped down from the counter and padded over to a new bed Lily had set up for him in the corner. It was oversized and plush, fitting for a cat of his stature. He circled it once, then twice, before settling in. A contented purr filled the room.

Lily stood for a moment, taking in the serene scene. "Goodnight, Goliath."

She started to walk toward the door, then paused and looked back. Goliath's eyes met hers, and in them, she saw the unspoken bond they shared. He was more than just a pet; he was her confidant, her silent partner, her friend.

Lily looked at Goliath, who gave a subtle nod, signaling his agreement. She tidied up the salon, ensuring everything was in order for the next day. Goliath settled into his cozy new bed, a contented purr rumbling in his chest.

The scene faded to a peaceful close as Lily locked the door and stepped into the night, ready for whatever tomorrow would bring.

Chapter 19

A New Case Emerges

The final day of the Holiday Dog Show dawned bright and cold, the air filled with the scent of pine, peppermint, and wet fur. Willow Creek's town square was transformed into a bustling winter wonderland, with booths lining the sidewalks, a brass band warming up near the gazebo, and dogs of every size and color trotting proudly on leash.

Lily stood just outside the show tent, watching Maximus with a cautious eye as he sat beside Evelyn, both of them regal and composed. It had been days since his return, and though Evelyn insisted he was fine, Lily noticed the way he flinched at loud noises and stuck close to Evelyn's heels, as though any moment might snatch him away again.

She glanced toward the grooming tent, where Sylvia Brightwell's Pomeranians were being fluffed and sprayed to perfection. Sylvia caught her eye and offered a smile—tight-lipped and too sweet.

Goliath sat on a hay bale behind her, tail flicking, his eyes trained not on the dogs, but on the people.

"You're not even pretending to be interested in the show, huh?" Lily murmured.

He blinked slowly, unimpressed.

"Fair enough."

Just then, Mrs. Whiskers approached, bundled in a plaid scarf and holding two hot cocoas. She handed one to Lily. "You're wound tighter than a holiday bow."

"I can't help it," Lily said. "Something feels… unfinished."

Mrs. Whiskers sipped her cocoa. "Because it is. Whoever took Maximus hasn't been caught. And people around here don't do well with unresolved tension."

"I've been thinking the same thing," Lily replied. "We got him back, but the truth? That's still missing."

Mrs. Whiskers nodded toward the judges assembling by the main platform. "Then you'd best pay attention. Truth tends to trip over itself when it's forced into the spotlight."

As if on cue, Sylvia marched up to the judging table and began speaking in a voice loud enough to carry over the crowd. "I just want to thank everyone for their support—especially after such a disruptive week."

Lily's ears perked up. "Disruptive?"

"Some of us," Sylvia continued, "have had to carry on despite the chaos caused by… certain lapses in professionalism."

Mrs. Whiskers muttered, "Well, well. The claws are out."

Evelyn's head snapped around. She gave Sylvia a glare sharp enough to slice ribbon. Maximus gave a low growl.

The crowd shifted with murmurs as Sylvia returned to her corner.

"Showboating," Lily said under her breath.

"And not subtle," Mrs. Whiskers added. "Which tells me she's nervous."

Just then, Officer Deeks appeared, threading through the crowd until he reached Lily.

"Green," he said, nodding. "Mind if I steal a moment?"

She followed him to the edge of the square where the noise thinned out.

"What's going on?"

"We got results back from the tire treads near the shed," he said. "They match a van registered to a contractor who did plumbing work for both Sylvia Brightwell *and* Tony Blackwood."

Lily's brow furrowed. "And?"

"The van was reported stolen—two days before Maximus went missing. Then 'found' again yesterday, mysteriously returned, no damage."

"You think they used it to move Maximus?"

Deeks shrugged. "It's circumstantial. But enough to start asking questions."

Lily's mind spun. Sylvia and Tony—still working together? Or was one setting up the other?

She returned to the grooming tent where Evelyn was brushing Maximus's coat with tender precision.

"I need to ask you something," Lily said quietly.

Evelyn didn't look up. "Go on."

"When you and Tony were partners—before everything went wrong—did you ever suspect he might… sabotage you?"

Evelyn's hand paused mid-brush. "Sabotage? No. Betray me? Yes."

Lily blinked. "That's strong."

Evelyn straightened. "He used my money, my contacts, my reputation. Then turned the business into his name. He knew how to charm everyone but had no loyalty."

"So it's possible he'd help Sylvia?"

Evelyn's jaw tightened. "Not for free."

Across the lawn, Tony stood by the refreshment booth, sipping from a Styrofoam cup and chatting with a vendor.

"I'll handle him," Evelyn said.

"No," Lily said firmly. "Let me."

She crossed the square, Goliath shadowing her like a sleek bodyguard. She reached Tony just as he tossed his cup in a bin.

"Tony."

He turned, eyebrows raised. "Lily. How's Maximus? Heard he had quite the adventure."

"You know more than you're letting on."

His smile faltered. "Do I?"

"The van. The shed. The plumbing connection. If you were trying to tank Evelyn's chances, you went too far."

Tony's face darkened. "Careful, Lily. Accusations like that can turn ugly."

"So can secrets."

He stepped in closer. "Whatever you think you know, keep it to yourself. This town forgets fast, but it *never* forgives."

Lily held her ground. "Then maybe it's time someone remembered."

Tony glanced down at Goliath, who stared up with unblinking contempt. Then he turned and walked away.

The Purr-fect Suspect

Lily returned to Mrs. Whiskers, who handed her a gingerbread cookie. "That went well?"

"Like stepping on a rake."

On stage, the judges called for final presentation. Dogs began parading across the platform, tails wagging, handlers smiling tight.

Sylvia's Pomeranian went first, twirling on cue. Then a regal schnauzer. A bulldog in a sequined vest. And then—

"Maximus Kensington," the emcee announced.

Evelyn walked Maximus onto the stage. The crowd hushed.

He held his head high. His gait was smooth. But his eyes—Lily saw it—darted to the crowd, seeking.

He spotted Sylvia and stopped.

For a breathless second, Maximus froze.

Then Evelyn whispered something, and he moved again, finishing the walk with grace.

After the applause, the judges gathered to deliberate.

Lily joined Evelyn backstage.

"He paused when he saw her," Lily whispered.

"I saw it," Evelyn replied. "She trained with him once. Years ago."

"Enough to earn his trust?"

"Enough to lure him."

A hush fell as the emcee returned.

"In third place... Clover Brightwell!"

Polite applause.

"In second... Duke Blackwood!"

More clapping.

"And the winner of this year's Holiday Dog Show..."

A long pause.

"...Maximus Kensington!"

The crowd erupted.

Evelyn's face remained calm, but her eyes gleamed.

As Maximus received his ribbon, a camera flash lit up the square—and in that moment, Lily saw Sylvia turn away, her mouth a tight line, her posture rigid.

Goliath jumped onto a nearby bench, surveying everything.

Later, as the crowd dispersed, Mrs. Whiskers appeared with a small envelope.

"Found this near Sylvia's booth. No name, but I peeked."

She handed it to Lily.

Inside: a photograph of Maximus and Sylvia, dated two years ago. Her hand on his collar. A training session.

Proof.

Lily exhaled. "This isn't over."

"No," Mrs. Whiskers agreed. "It's just beginning."

Epilogue

Willow Creek's Finest

Spring had come to Willow Creek, painting the town in a palette of soft greens and delicate pinks. Cherry blossoms drifted like snow along Main Street, and window boxes overflowed with pansies and primroses. The harsh winter that had witnessed Maximus's kidnapping and triumphant return seemed a distant memory now, relegated to newspaper clippings and fading gossip.

The sign above Lily's grooming salon had changed. It now read "The Whisker's Edge: Pet Grooming & Detective Agency," with a clever logo featuring a silhouette of Goliath in profile, his tail curled into a question mark. The addition had raised eyebrows at first, but after three successful missing pet cases and one notable recovery of a rare parrot that had been smuggled across state lines, no one questioned Lily's unusual career expansion anymore.

Inside the shop, Lily was putting the finishing touches on a Yorkshire Terrier's topknot, her hands steady and gentle. The dog's owner, Mrs. Patterson, chatted amiably while Goliath observed from his perch on a custom-built shelf that ran the perimeter of the room, giving him a complete view of all activities.

"I still can't believe Tony Blackwood got five years," Mrs. Patterson was saying, picking up the thread of a conversation that had circulated through town for months. "Such a shame. He had such potential."

"The judge took the prior incidents into account," Lily reminded her, securing the topknot with a tiny blue bow. "It wasn't just Maximus. They found evidence linking him to at least seven other cases of show dog sabotage."

"And that Brightwell woman? Sylvia? What happened to her?"

"Three years, plus restitution," Lily said, lifting the Yorkie to admire her handiwork. "Her sister Margot took a plea deal for eighteen months, in exchange for testimony about their larger plans."

"The pet food monopoly," Mrs. Patterson nodded sagely. "My Harold says it was brilliant, in a devious sort of way. Buy up all the local pet businesses, control the show circuit, and then launch their own premium brand with Maximus's competitor as the face of it."

"Brilliant but illegal," Lily agreed, setting the Yorkie down and brushing a few stray hairs from her smock. "Antitrust violations, corporate espionage, and that's before we get to the kidnapping and drugging."

Mrs. Patterson shook her head, clicking her tongue in disapproval. "Such lengths to go to for a dog show. I'll never understand it."

Goliath, who had been watching the conversation with his usual inscrutable expression, made a soft sound that might have been agreement or derision. It was often hard to tell with him.

"Well," Mrs. Patterson said, accepting her freshly groomed pet and reaching for her purse, "Trixie and I had better be going. Book club starts in half an hour, and you know how Hilda gets when someone's late."

Lily smiled at the mention of Mrs. Whiskers, who had finally convinced everyone to use her first name after decades of formality. "Tell her I'll stop by later. We have that... consultation to discuss."

Mrs. Patterson's eyes lit up with interest, but she didn't pry—a remarkable show of restraint in a town where curiosity was practically a competitive sport. "I'll let her know. Good luck!"

After Mrs. Patterson left, Lily cleaned up her workstation, her movements efficient after years of practice. The salon was quiet now, the afternoon lull giving her time to prepare for her next appointment—a very different kind of client.

She glanced at the wall where she had hung framed news clippings about their more notable cases. The centerpiece was the Willow Creek Gazette's front-page story about Maximus's return: "CHAMPION POODLE RESCUED! Local Groomer and Her Remarkable Cat Crack the Case." The accompanying photo showed Maximus at the Holiday Dog Show, resplendent in his blue ribbon, with Lily and Goliath standing proudly beside Evelyn Kensington.

The Purr-fect Suspect

That day had changed everything. What began as a desperate search for a missing dog had evolved into a calling neither Lily nor Goliath had anticipated.

The transformation of the salon had been gradual but deliberate. A section of the waiting area had been converted into a small reception space for detective clients, with a separate entrance for those who preferred discretion. Filing cabinets lined one wall, organized by case type and date. A television mounted in the corner played a rotation of educational programs about pet care, interrupted occasionally by the local news.

The biggest change, however, was the addition at the back of the salon—a proper office with a desk for Lily, comfortable seating for clients, and, most notably, custom feline furniture for Goliath that allowed him to observe and participate in consultations without being underfoot.

Just as Lily was putting away the last of her grooming tools when the bell above the door chimed, heralding Evelyn Kensington's arrival. The older woman was as elegant as ever in a spring suit of pale blue, her silver hair styled in its usual perfect chignon. Maximus walked beside her, his white coat pristine, his gait confident and proud.

"Right on time," Lily greeted them warmly. "Come in, come in."

Evelyn removed her sunglasses, surveying the salon with approval. "The new sign looks wonderful, Lily. Business good?"

"Better than expected," Lily admitted, leading them to her office at the back of the salon—a recent addition, funded in part by Evelyn's investment in the detective side of the business. "The grooming keeps the lights on, but the investigations are what's really taking off."

The office was small but well-appointed, with comfortable chairs for clients and a wall of filing cabinets for case records. Most striking was the large map of Willow Creek and surrounding counties that dominated one wall, with colored pins marking the locations of various cases—solved and still pending.

Goliath followed them in, jumping onto Lily's desk and settling in what had become his unofficial position as co-investigator. Maximus, familiar with the routine now, took a seat by Evelyn's chair, his posture as regal as his owner's.

"So," Evelyn said, getting straight to business as was her way, "what have you found?"

Lily pulled a folder from her desk drawer. "The anonymous letters you've been receiving—I think I know who's sending them."

Evelyn's expression remained composed, but her fingers tightened slightly on her purse. "Go on."

"The handwriting analysis was inconclusive," Lily explained, opening the folder to show several pieces of paper covered in different scripts. "But the paper itself is quite distinctive—a watermarked stationery that's only sold at Hendrick's in the city."

"That hardly narrows it down," Evelyn observed. "Anyone could shop there."

"True," Lily acknowledged. "But the ink is another matter. It's a custom blend, made specifically for fountain pens, and only three people in Willow Creek use it." She tapped a photograph in the folder. "One of them is Judge Harmon."

Evelyn's eyebrows rose slightly. "Richard? Why on earth would he be sending me anonymous warnings about the summer dog show circuit?"

"That's where it gets interesting," Lily said, warming to her subject. She flipped to another page in the folder. "Judge Harmon's son works for Canine Elite."

"The pet food company?" Evelyn's interest was clearly piqued now.

"The very same," Lily confirmed. "And according to my source at their corporate office, they're planning a major campaign centered around the National Championship next year. They want Maximus as their spokesdog, if you will."

"They could have simply approached me directly," Evelyn pointed out.

"Except they're worried about your existing contract with Natural Pet," Lily countered. "The warnings are meant to scare you away from certain competitions where Natural Pet has exclusive sponsorship deals."

Evelyn leaned back in her chair, absorbing this information with the careful consideration she brought to all business matters. "Manipulative," she said finally. "But clever. If I avoided those shows, it would create a loophole in my Natural Pet contract."

"Exactly," Lily agreed. "And Canine Elite would swoop in with an offer that, I'm guessing, would be substantially better than your current arrangement."

"How substantially are we talking?"

The Purr-fect Suspect

Lily smiled. "Let's just say you might need to build Maximus his own wing of the house to store all his gourmet treats."

Evelyn laughed, a rare and delightful sound. "Well done, Lily. This is precisely why I invested in your detective agency."

"It's what we do," Lily said modestly.

Goliath made a noise that sounded suspiciously like a snort, and both women turned to look at him.

"Yes, yes, it's what *we* do," Lily corrected, scratching him behind the ears. "Goliath deserves at least fifty percent of the credit. He was the one who found the ink sample in Judge Harmon's trash."

"Remarkable animal," Evelyn said, studying the cat with genuine admiration. "I've never seen anything like him."

"He's one of a kind," Lily agreed.

The relationship between Lily and Goliath had evolved since the Maximus case. What had once been a comfortable coexistence had deepened into something richer—a partnership built on mutual respect and understanding. Lily had always known Goliath was intelligent, but the investigation had revealed depths to his cognitive abilities that still astonished her daily.

Evelyn, who had witnessed this evolution firsthand, often marveled at their unspoken communication. "Sometimes," she'd once observed, "it's as if you're having an entire conversation without saying a word."

And Lily had smiled, because it was true. More and more, she found herself understanding Goliath's subtle signals—the particular twitch of his whiskers that indicated skepticism, the slow blink that conveyed approval, the distinctive chirp that meant he'd found something important. In return, he seemed increasingly attuned to her thoughts and emotions, anticipating her needs with uncanny accuracy.

After discussing a few more details of the case and agreeing on next steps, Evelyn prepared to leave. As she stood, she paused, her expression turning more serious.

"Have you heard the news about Margot Devereux?"

Lily looked up, surprised. "No, what's happened?"

"She's being released next month. Good behavior, apparently." Evelyn's tone was neutral, but her eyes conveyed concern. "The parole board approved it yesterday."

Lily absorbed this information, her mind already running through the implications. "Do you think she'll come back to Willow Creek?"

"I think we should be prepared for that possibility," Evelyn said. "She still owns property here, and while Sylvia's business was liquidated to pay restitution, Margot's personal assets were untouched."

"I'll keep an ear to the ground," Lily promised. "And an eye on any unusual activity."

Evelyn nodded, satisfied. "I know you will." She turned to leave, then stopped at the door. "Oh, I nearly forgot. The National Championship committee called. They've asked me to serve as a judge this year."

"Evelyn, that's wonderful!" Lily exclaimed. "Will you accept?"

"I'm considering it," Evelyn said, a small smile playing at her lips. "It would mean Maximus couldn't compete, of course, but after six consecutive titles, perhaps it's time to pass the torch."

"He's already a legend," Lily agreed, looking at the Poodle with fondness. "No one will forget his comeback at the Holiday Dog Show. It was the perfect ending to a remarkable career."

"Indeed," Evelyn said softly. "Thank you, Lily. For everything."

The Maximus case had transformed Lily's relationship with Evelyn as well. What had started as a professional connection—groomer and client—had deepened into friendship and mutual respect. The shared experience of searching for Maximus, the tense hours of waiting, the triumph of his return and subsequent victory at the show—all had forged a bond that surprised them both.

This was true of many relationships in Lily's life now. The crisis had revealed the true nature of the people around her—their strengths, their weaknesses, their capacity for goodness or its opposite. Some, like Mrs. Whiskers, had emerged as steadfast allies. Others, like Tony and Sylvia, had shown their true colors in ways that still shocked the community.

Most significant, though, was the change in Lily herself. The timid groomer who once avoided confrontation had discovered a core of steel within herself—a determination and resourcefulness she hadn't known she possessed. The detective agency wasn't just a business expansion; it was an expression of her newfound confidence and purpose.

After Evelyn and Maximus departed, Lily returned to her desk, flipping through her calendar to check the rest of the day's appointments.

Goliath watched her with his usual attentive gaze, occasionally reaching out a paw to tap at a particular entry.

"Yes, I see it," Lily told him, pausing at an appointment marked simply "M.W. - Consultation" in the late afternoon slot. "Mrs. Whiskers is bringing us a new case. Something about missing library books with secret codes in the margins."

Goliath's ears perked up with interest, and Lily couldn't help but laugh. "You're right, it does sound intriguing. And after the Maximus case, I think we've proven we can handle just about anything."

The cat stretched, his massive frame extending to its full impressive length, then settled back with a contented purr—a sound Lily was hearing more frequently these days. It seemed Goliath had found his calling, just as she had found hers.

A soft knock at the door interrupted their moment of companionship. Lily looked up to see Mrs. Whiskers standing in the doorway, a leather satchel under one arm, a knowing smile on her lined face.

"I hope I'm not too early," the librarian said, her eyes twinkling behind her glasses.

"Not at all," Lily assured her, gesturing to the chair Evelyn had recently vacated. "Goliath and I were just discussing how much we enjoy our new line of work."

"It suits you both," Mrs. Whiskers observed, setting her satchel on the desk with a gentle thud. "Lily, because you've always had a knack for understanding others, and Goliath, because he sees what most people miss."

The cat in question blinked slowly at Mrs. Whiskers, a gesture of approval that made the elderly woman smile wider.

"Now then," she said, opening her satchel and withdrawing a stack of books tied together with twine. "These were all checked out and returned within the past month by the same patron—a man who calls himself John Smith."

"An obvious pseudonym," Lily noted.

"Obviously," Mrs. Whiskers agreed. "But it's what I found inside the books that concerns me." She untied the twine and opened the top book to a page marked with a slip of paper. "See here, in the margin? And here, and here."

201

Lily leaned forward, examining the tiny notations. They appeared to be random numbers and letters, scribbled in pencil so faintly they were easy to miss.

"They're in all seven books," Mrs. Whiskers continued. "Different pages, different sections, but the same handwriting. And when I tried to cross-reference the notations with the Dewey Decimal System, I found something... disturbing."

She pulled out a sheet of paper with her own neat handwriting, showing how the notations, when arranged in a certain order, formed what appeared to be GPS coordinates.

"Coordinates to what?" Lily asked, intrigued despite herself.

"That," Mrs. Whiskers said, tapping the paper with one gnarled finger, "is what I'm hoping you and Goliath can find out."

Goliath, who had been examining the books with careful attention, looked up and gave a definitive meow.

"I believe," Lily translated with a smile, "that means we're on the case."

As Mrs. Whiskers began explaining the details of her discovery, Lily felt a familiar thrill of excitement. This was her life now—solving mysteries, helping her community, working alongside the most intelligent cat in Willow Creek. It wasn't what she had expected when she opened her grooming salon all those years ago, but it was exactly where she was meant to be.

And as for Goliath? Well, The Detective Cat of Willow Creek was just getting started.

The investigation into the mysterious library books consumed the next several days. Lily and Goliath worked methodically, first examining each book for additional clues, then researching the GPS coordinates that Mrs. Whiskers had uncovered. The location turned out to be an abandoned quarry just outside town limits—a place with a history as murky as its stagnant waters.

"There has to be more to this," Lily told Goliath as they sat in their office, surrounded by maps and printouts. "Why would someone go to such lengths to hide these coordinates in library books? And why these particular books?"

Goliath, perched on the edge of the desk, pawed at one of the volumes—a history of local mining operations. The action seemed deliberate, and Lily had learned to trust these gestures.

"The quarry," she mused, picking up the book. "It was operational until the late 1990s, when it was shut down due to environmental concerns. According to this, the company that owned it went bankrupt shortly after."

She flipped through the pages, searching for additional information, when a small newspaper clipping fell out. It had been pressed between two pages so perfectly that she had missed it during her initial examination.

"Goliath, look at this," she said, smoothing the clipping on the desk. It was a brief article about the quarry's closure, mentioning protests by local environmental groups and allegations of illegal dumping. One name jumped out: Harrison Blackwood, identified as the quarry's final manager.

"Blackwood," Lily repeated. "Any relation to Tony, I wonder?"

Goliath made a soft chirping sound, which Lily had come to recognize as his way of indicating a connection.

"You think they're related," she said, reaching for her phone. "Let me call Mrs. Whiskers. She'll know."

The librarian answered on the second ring. "I was just about to call you," she said, bypassing hello. "I found something in our archives that might interest you. Harrison Blackwood was Tony's uncle. He died about five years ago, but not before transferring ownership of several properties in Willow Creek to his nephew."

"Including the quarry?" Lily asked.

"That's the curious thing," Mrs. Whiskers replied. "The quarry wasn't among the properties listed in the will. In fact, there's no record of who currently owns it. It's as if it simply fell off the map after the company went bankrupt."

Lily's mind raced. "So the quarry is essentially abandoned. No owner, no oversight. The perfect place to hide something."

"Or retrieve something that was hidden long ago," Mrs. Whiskers suggested.

After ending the call, Lily turned to find Goliath already waiting by the door, his tail twitching with anticipation.

"You want to go there now, don't you?" she asked, though she already knew the answer. "Okay, let me just grab my coat. And maybe a flashlight. And definitely my phone."

The drive to the quarry took them along winding back roads rarely used by the townsfolk of Willow Creek. Spring greenery softened the landscape, but the beauty faded as they approached their destination. The quarry itself was a massive gash in the earth, its steep sides descending to a pool of unnaturally blue-green water far below.

Lily parked at what remained of an access road, the entrance partially blocked by a rusted chain-link fence with a prominently displayed "No Trespassing" sign. The fence had been cut at some point, creating a gap just wide enough for a person to slip through.

"Someone's been here recently," Lily observed, examining the clean edges of the cut metal. She hesitated, her law-abiding nature conflicting with her investigative instincts. "We're not technically breaking in if the fence is already open, right?"

Goliath's expression was the feline equivalent of an eye roll as he squeezed through the gap. Lily sighed and followed suit, her conscience assuaged, if not entirely comfortable.

The quarry grounds were eerie in their abandonment. Nature had begun reclaiming parts of it—weeds pushing through cracks in the concrete pad where machinery had once stood, vines crawling up the walls of a decrepit office building. But signs of recent human activity were also apparent: fresh tire tracks in the dirt, cigarette butts that hadn't had time to weather, a crushed water bottle that still held its shape.

Goliath led the way, following a path that only he could see. His confidence was striking, as if he had some internal compass guiding him. They circled the perimeter of the quarry until they reached a small equipment shed partially hidden by overgrown bushes.

The shed's door hung askew, one hinge broken. Inside was darkness, thick and impenetrable. Lily hesitated, flicking on her flashlight.

"Hello?" she called, immediately regretting the sound of her voice echoing in the stillness. "Is anyone here?"

No response came, but Goliath had already slipped inside. Lily followed, the beam of her flashlight sweeping across the interior. The shed was mostly empty, save for rusted tools and debris. But the floor showed signs of recent disturbance—the dust had been disturbed in a pattern that suggested boxes or crates had recently occupied the space.

"Someone's been using this place for storage," Lily murmured. "But what were they storing?"

The Purr-fect Suspect

Goliath pawed at a spot in the far corner, and Lily directed her flashlight there. A section of the concrete floor looked different—newer, less weathered than the rest.

"It's been patched," she realized. "Something was buried here, and then covered up again. Recently."

She was about to examine it more closely when the sound of an approaching vehicle sent her heart racing. Without thinking, she turned off the flashlight and crouched behind a pile of debris, Goliath pressing against her side.

Through a gap in the shed's warped boards, she could see a black SUV with tinted windows pulling up to the quarry's edge. Two men got out—one tall and lean, the other shorter but solidly built. Both moved with the cautious deliberation of those who didn't want to be observed.

The taller man gestured toward the shed, saying something Lily couldn't hear. The shorter man nodded and reached into the SUV, retrieving what looked like a crowbar. They began walking in her direction.

Panic fluttered in Lily's chest. There was no way out except past the approaching men, and nowhere to hide except among the meager debris. She pressed back against the wall, hoping the shadows would conceal her, and felt Goliath tense beside her, his body coiled and ready.

Just as the men were about to reach the shed, the distinctive wail of a police siren cut through the air. Blue and red lights flashed at the quarry entrance, and Officer Reynolds's voice boomed through a loudspeaker.

"This is the police! Stop where you are and put your hands up!"

The men froze, then scrambled back to their SUV. The engine roared to life, and the vehicle shot forward, ignoring the approaching police car. For a moment, Lily thought they would collide, but the SUV swerved at the last second, careening onto a dirt path that led away from the quarry.

Reynolds's cruiser gave chase, sirens blaring. The sounds receded into the distance, leaving Lily and Goliath alone once more in the settling dust.

"That was close," Lily breathed, her heart still racing. "How did Reynolds know we were here?"

Her phone buzzed in her pocket. A text from Mrs. Whiskers: "Are you safe? I called Reynolds when I realized where you were headed. The quarry has been under surveillance for weeks. Suspected smuggling operation."

Lily texted back a quick assurance, then turned to Goliath. "Smuggling? That would explain the fresh patch in the floor. They were hiding something here, something they've now moved elsewhere."

Goliath meowed, the sound echoing in the empty shed.

"You're right," Lily agreed, as if they were having a normal conversation. "Whatever it was, it's connected to our mysterious library patron. And possibly to Tony Blackwood, through his uncle."

The link was tenuous, but Lily's instincts told her they were onto something significant. If Tony was involved in illegal activities beyond dog show sabotage, it could explain his desperate need to win at all costs. Prestige and sponsorship money were powerful motivators, but perhaps he had other debts to pay, other masters to please.

She looked around the shed once more, committing details to memory, then gestured to Goliath. "We should go. Reynolds will want to know what we found."

As they made their way back to her car, Lily's mind was already piecing together the broader picture. The Maximus case, which had seemed so straightforward at its resolution, was now revealing deeper layers—connections to other crimes, other players. And at the center of it all was Tony Blackwood, whose imprisonment might have disrupted operations without shutting them down completely.

"Margot Devereux's early release takes on a new significance," she told Goliath as they reached the car. "If she was part of this larger scheme, her return to Willow Creek could signal the revival of whatever they were planning."

Goliath jumped into the passenger seat, arranging himself with dignity. He gave a soft meow that Lily interpreted as agreement.

"We need to be ready," she said, starting the engine. "All of us."

The following morning, Lily met with Reynolds at the police station, recounting her discovery at the quarry and her suspicions about a connection to Tony Blackwood.

"We've been watching that quarry for weeks," Reynolds admitted, leaning back in his chair. "Anonymous tip came in about unusual activity, vehicles coming and going at odd hours. We suspected drugs at first, but now we're leaning toward illegal wildlife trafficking."

"Wildlife?" Lily echoed, surprised.

The Purr-fect Suspect

"Exotic animals, rare breeds. There's a black market for that sort of thing, especially among certain collectors. The theory is that they're moving the animals through here to larger cities."

Lily thought of the animal welfare issues involved and felt a surge of anger. "And you think Tony was involved in this? Beyond the dog show sabotage?"

Reynolds shrugged. "We're still connecting the dots. But his uncle's history with the quarry, coupled with Sylvia's access to pet transportation methods and Margot's business connections? It's a plausible setup for moving contraband."

The implications were staggering. What had begun as an investigation into a single missing dog was expanding into something much larger—a criminal enterprise with tentacles reaching far beyond Willow Creek.

"What happens now?" Lily asked.

"Now we wait," Reynolds said grimly. "The men who escaped yesterday won't be back to that location, but they'll have others. And with Margot coming back to town next month, we might see a shift in their operations."

"You're going to let her come back? Even with these suspicions?"

Reynolds spread his hands in a gesture of resignation. "We don't have enough to hold her beyond her original sentence. But we'll be watching. And I hope you and Goliath will keep your eyes open too."

"We will," Lily promised, though the responsibility settled heavily on her shoulders.

Back at The Whisker's Edge, Lily briefed Mrs. Whiskers on the morning's revelations. The librarian listened without interruption, her sharp eyes calculating behind her glasses.

"So we were right about the coordinates," she said when Lily finished. "But wrong about what they indicated."

"Not entirely wrong," Lily pointed out. "The quarry is significant. It's just not the entire story."

Mrs. Whiskers tapped her fingers on the desk, thinking. "The books themselves might still hold clues. John Smith—whoever he is—chose those specific volumes for a reason. The coordinates were just part of the message."

Together, they spread the books across Lily's desk, examining them with fresh eyes. Goliath prowled around the perimeter, occasionally pausing to scrutinize a particular page.

"Local history, geology, wildlife, business law," Mrs. Whiskers cataloged, sorting the books by subject. "A diverse selection, but with a clear theme: resources and commerce."

"The quarry was a resource," Lily mused, "now being used for commerce of a dubious nature."

"Precisely," Mrs. Whiskers agreed. "But there's more. Look at the publication dates."

Lily flipped to the front of each book. All had been published within months of each other, twenty years ago.

"That can't be coincidence," she said.

"No," Mrs. Whiskers confirmed. "And that year was significant for Willow Creek. It was when several major industries in the area went bankrupt or relocated. The quarry, the factory on the north side, the old mill. An economic downturn that affected dozens of families."

"Including the Blackwoods," Lily realized. "Harrison lost his job at the quarry, and eventually, his home. That's when he moved in with Tony's family, according to town gossip."

Mrs. Whiskers nodded. "A setback that fostered resentment. Perhaps a desire for revenge against those who came through the downturn unscathed. Families like the Kensingtons."

The pieces were falling into place. Tony's grudge against Evelyn wasn't just about their business partnership gone sour—it was rooted in a deeper, more personal history of perceived injustice.

"We need to warn Evelyn," Lily said. "If this is about more than just dog show rivalry, she could still be a target. Especially with Margot coming back to town."

"Agreed," Mrs. Whiskers said. "And perhaps it's time to involve other authorities beyond our local police. If we're dealing with wildlife trafficking across state lines, that's federal jurisdiction."

The prospect of expanding their investigation to include federal agencies was both daunting and exhilarating. Lily's small detective agency had stumbled onto something far larger than missing pets and dog show sabotage.

Yet even as the scope of the case grew, her focus remained clear: protect the animals, both those at risk from traffickers and those, like

Maximus, who might be targeted again by individuals with long-standing grudges.

As Mrs. Whiskers gathered the books to return to the library, Lily's phone rang. The screen showed Evelyn's name, and a chill ran down Lily's spine.

"Evelyn?" she answered, trying to keep her voice steady. "Is everything okay?"

"Not exactly," Evelyn replied, her own voice unusually tense. "I've just received a letter. No return address, no signature. Just a photograph of Maximus and a line of text: 'History repeats itself.'"

"Where are you?" Lily asked, already reaching for her coat.

"At home. Maximus is with me."

"Stay there. Lock the doors. I'm on my way." Lily ended the call and turned to Mrs. Whiskers. "We need to go. Now."

The librarian nodded, her expression grim. "I'll call Reynolds. You go ahead."

As Lily and Goliath hurried to her car, the weight of their responsibility settled firmly on her shoulders. The threats were no longer theoretical, the danger no longer past. Whatever resolution they had thought they'd achieved with the Maximus case had been merely a pause, a catching of breath before the next challenge.

But they were ready. The Detective Cat of Willow Creek and his human partner had faced danger before and emerged victorious. Together, they would do so again.

The sign above the shop door swung gently in the spring breeze, its new name a declaration and a promise: The Whisker's Edge—where mysteries meet their match.

And as Lily's car pulled away from the curb, headed toward Evelyn's house with Goliath alert in the passenger seat, that promise had never felt more real.

The adventure was just beginning.

Patti Petrone Miller

The Purr-fect Suspect

Meet Patti, the creative force behind "Where the Magic Happens." More than just an author, Patti brings stories to life as the Executive Producer of an animated TV series based on her heartwarming tale "ELLIOT FINDS A HOME"—the story of a special dog with thumbs and his silent friend who prove that sometimes, actions speak louder than words.

Patti's writing journey has been nothing short of remarkable. A cherished author at Polygon Entertainment, she's danced her way onto the USA TODAY bestseller list and claimed Amazon's #1 spot multiple times. With 7 dozen books spanning from Urban Fantasy to Horror, Patti weaves tales that transport readers to worlds limited only by imagination.

Her life reads like an adventure novel filled with fascinating chapters:

At just 4 years old, she charmed audiences on "Romper Room" She shared memorable moments with Captain Kangaroo and Mr. Green Jeans She once enjoyed a train ride and sandwich with Sidney Poitier She high-fived President Nixon during a circus visit She attended school alongside magician David Copperfield She roller-skated with John Travolta before his rise to fame She warmed her hands and heart sharing cocoa with Abe Vigoda

When she's not crafting bestsellers, Patti embraces life as a teacher, grandmother, and devoted pet parent. Known affectionately as the "Queen of Halloween," this Wiccan High Priestess infuses her spooky stories with authentic magic that keeps readers spellbound.

Patti's books fly off shelves as quickly as they're stocked, so follow her social media to stay connected with this one-of-a-kind storyteller whose magical worlds welcome all who dare to dream.

www.ingramcontent.com/pod-product-compliance
Lightning Source LLC
LaVergne TN
LVHW041806060526
838201LV00046B/1151